TANYA HUFF

BLOOD BANK

DAW BOOKS, INC.

DONALD A. WOLLHEIM, FOUNDER

375 Hudson Street, New York, NY 10014

ELIZABETH R. WOLLHEIM
SHEILA E. GILBERT
PUBLISHERS

www.dawbooks.com

Raves for Tanya Huff:

ACKNOWLEDGMENTS

"This Town Ain't Big Enough" originally published in *Vampire Detectives*, edited by Martin H. Greenberg (DAW Books, 1995).

"What Manner of Man" originally published in *Time of the Vampires*, edited by P. N. Elrod and Martin H. Greenberg (DAW Books, 1996).

"The Cards Also Say" originally published in *The Fortune Teller*, edited by Lawrence Schimmel and Martin H. Greenberg (DAW Books, 1997).

"The Vengeful Spirit of Lake Nepeaka" originally published in *What Ho, Magic!*, by Tanya Huff (Meisha Merlin Publishing, Inc., 1999).

"Someone to Share the Night" originally published in *Single White Vampire Seeks Same*, edited by Martin H. Greenberg and Brittany A. Koren (DAW Books, 2001).

"Another Fine Nest" originally published in *The Bakka Anthology*, edited by Kristen Pederson Chew (Bakka Books, 2002).

"Scleratus" originally published in *The Repentant*, edited by Brian M. Thomsen and Martin H. Greenberg (DAW Books, 2003).

"Critical Analysis" originally published in *Slipstreams*, edited by Martin H. Greenberg and John Helfers (DAW Books, 2006).

"So This Is Christmas" originally published in *The Blood Books, Volume Three* (*Blood Bank*) (DAW Books; Copyright © 2006 by Tanya Huff).

For Heather,
who gave me a Henry I can cuddle.

Contents

Introduction

Because the Blood books were as much about the relationship between the three protagonists as they were about the metaphysical or the mystery, and because in *Blood Debt* I had wrapped those relationships up definitely, there will be no more Vicki Nelson books. I have now said everything I have to say about these people. This is it. The end.

Well, except for the collected short stories, which we are calling *Blood Bank*.

"This Town Ain't Big Enough" is a direct sequel to *Blood Pact* and is referred to in *Blood Debt*. Given what Vicki has become, the title pretty much explains the entire plot.

"The Cards Also Say" also takes place between *Blood Pact* and *Blood Debt*. In a way, *Debt* couldn't have happened like it did without this story since the blue van Vicki is driving in *Debt* makes its first appearance here.

"What Manner of Man" is a look at Henry's past. I'm a huge fan of Georgette Heyer's Regency novels and was thrilled to be able to dip into the time period. The names of those who aren't actual historical characters were taken from classic vampire stories.

"The Vengeful Spirit of Lake Nepeakea" was inspired partly by a sales pitch I endured at a Florida timeshare and Michael Bradley's fascinating book *More Than a Myth: The Search for the Monster of Muskrat Lake.* Bradley not only killed any romance surrounding the Loch Ness Monster but convinced me to stay out of deep water lakes.

"Someone to Share the Night" was written for a theme anthology called *Single White Vampire Seeks Same.* No, really, it was. I swear to you, I wouldn't make up a title like that. I adore the last line of this story.

"Scleratus" is another story about Henry's past. This one, however, is a little darker than most of the others. The story spring-boarded off one of Henry's flashbacks in *Blood Price.*

"Another Fine Nest" involves Vicki and Mike with giant intelligent blood-sucking bugs in the Toronto subway. And once you know that much, everything else just kind of drops into place. . . .

"Critical Analysis" is essentially a locked door murder mystery. Well, not a traditional locked door murder mystery perhaps but then the person solving the mystery is a vampire so that kind of goes without saying.

"So This Is Christmas" is the story original to this book and is a direct result of my having to write a story at Christmastime. Originally, the part of Scrooge was to have been played by Mike Celluci but a page in I realized that just didn't work so Vicki, definitely the more cynical of the two, stepped into the breach. You can thank me later for deciding against Tiny Tony.

Also in this volume is the shooting script for "Stone Cold," episode nine of *Blood Ties.* It was weird but wonderful working with a second generation Vicki, Henry, and Mike, and I hope I managed to maintain the excellent writing that's been a hallmark of the show. You may notice some small changes remain between this script and what actually went out on the air—television is a shining example of that old saying, "change is constant."

Athough I attempted to remain cool, I was thrilled beyond measure that Peter Mohan, our brilliant show runner/executive producer, asked me to write a script. Writing for television is very, very different than writing for print and he took a chance in assuming that I'd be able to adapt. Just before the episode aired on Lifetime back in the spring of 2007, I wrote about the experience in my LiveJournal. We've cleaned that bit of blogging up a tad, added a couple of current observations, and included that as well.

As it stands right now, you're all caught up.

This Town Ain't Big Enough

"Ow! Vicki, be careful!"

"Sorry. Sometimes I forget how sharp they are."

"Terrific." He wove his fingers through her hair and pulled just hard enough to make his point. "Don't."

"Don't what?" She grinned up at him, teeth gleaming ivory in the moonlight spilling across the bed. "Don't forget or don't . . ."

The sudden demand of the telephone for attention buried the last of her question.

Detective-Sergeant Michael Celluci sighed. "Hold that thought," he said, rolled over, and reached for the phone. "Celluci."

"Fifty-two division just called. They've found a body down at Richmond and Peter they think we might want to have a look at."

"Dave, it's . . ." He squinted at the clock. ". . . one twenty-nine in the A.M. and I'm off duty."

On the other end of the line, his partner, theoretically off duty as well, refused to take the hint. "Ask me who the stiff is."

Celluci sighed again. "Who's the stiff?"

"Mac Eisler."

"Shit."

"Funny, that's exactly what I said." Nothing in Dave Graham's voice indicated he appreciated the joke. "I'll be there in ten."

"Make it fifteen."

"You in the middle of something?"

1

Celluci watched as Vicki sat up and glared at him.
"I was."

"Welcome to the wonderful world of law enforcement."

Vicki's hand shot out and caught Celluci's wrist before he could heave the phone across the room. "Who's Mac Eisler?" she asked as, scowling, he dropped the receiver back in its cradle and swung his legs off the bed.

"You heard that?"

"I can hear the beating of your heart, the movement of your blood, the song of your life." She scratched the back of her leg with one bare foot. "I should think I can overhear a lousy phone conversation."

"Eisler's a pimp." Celluci reached for the light switch, changed his mind, and began pulling on his clothes. Given the full moon riding just outside the window, it wasn't exactly dark, and given Vicki's sensitivity to bright light, not to mention her temper, he figured it was safer to cope. "We're pretty sure he offed one of his girls a couple of weeks ago."

Vicki scooped her shirt up off the floor. "Irene MacDonald?"

"What? You overheard that, too?"

"I get around. How sure's pretty sure?"

"Personally positive. But we had nothing solid to hold him on."

"And now he's dead." Skimming her jeans up over her hips, she dipped her brows in a parody of deep thought. "Golly, I wonder if there's a connection."

"Golly yourself," Celluci snarled. "You're not coming with me."

"Did I ask?"

"I recognized the tone of voice. I know you, Vicki. I knew you when you were a cop, I knew you when you were a P.I. and I don't care how much you've changed physically, I know you now you're a . . . a . . ."

"Vampire." Her pale eyes seemed more silver than gray. "You can say it, Mike. It won't hurt my feelings. Bloodsucker. Nightwalker. Creature of Darkness."

"Pain in the butt." Carefully avoiding her gaze, he shrugged into his shoulder holster and slipped a jacket on over it. "This is police business, Vicki. Stay out of it. Please." He didn't wait for a response but crossed the shadows to the bedroom door. Then he paused, one foot over the threshold. "I doubt I'll back by dawn. Don't wait up."

Vicki Nelson, ex of the Metropolitan Toronto Police Force, ex-private investigator, recent vampire, decided to let him go. If he could joke about the change, he accepted it. And besides, it was always more fun to make him pay for smart-ass remarks when he least expected it.

She watched from the darkness as Celluci climbed into Dave Graham's car. Then, with the taillights disappearing in the distance, she dug out his spare set of car keys and proceeded to leave tangled entrails of Highway Traffic Act strewn from Downsview to the heart of Toronto.

It took no supernatural ability to find the scene of the crime. What with the police, the press, and the morbidly curious, the area seethed with people. Vicki slipped past the constable stationed at the far end of the alley and followed the paths of shadow until she stood just outside the circle of police around the body.

Mac Eisler had been a somewhat attractive, not very all, white male Caucasian. Eschewing the traditional clothing excesses of his profession, he was dressed simply in designer jeans and an olive-green raw silk jacket. At the moment, he wasn't looking his best. A pair of rusty nails had been shoved through each manicured hand, securing his body upright across the back entrance of a trendy restaurant. Although the pointed toes of his tooled leather cowboy boots indented the wood of the door, Eisler's head had been turned completely around so that he stared, in apparent astonishment, out into the alley.

The smell of death fought with the stink of urine and garbage. Vicki frowned. There was another scent, a pungent predator scent that raised the hair on the back of her neck and drew her lips up off her teeth. Surprised by the strength of her reaction, she stepped silently into a deeper patch of night lest she give herself away.

"Why the hell would I have a comment?"

Preoccupied with an inexplicable rage, she hadn't heard Celluci arrive until he greeted the press. Shifting position slightly, she watched as he and his partner moved in off the street and got their first look at the body.

"Jesus H. Christ."

"On crutches," agreed the younger of the two detectives already on the scene.

"Who found him?"

"Dishwasher, coming out with the trash. He was obviously meant to be found; they nailed the bastard right across the door."

"The kitchen's on the other side and no one heard hammering?"

"I'll go you one better than that. Look at the rust on the head of those nails—they haven't *been* hammered."

"What? Someone just pushed the nails through Eisler's hands and into solid wood?"

"Looks like."

Celluci snorted. "You trying to tell me that Superman's gone bad?"

Under the cover of their laughter, Vicki bent and picked up a piece of planking. There were four holes in the unbroken end and two remaining three-inch spikes. She pulled a spike out of the wood and pressed it into the wall of the building by her side. A smut of rust marked the ball of her thumb, but the nail looked no different.

She remembered the scent.

Vampire.

". . . unable to come to the phone. Please leave a message after the long beep."

"Henry? It's Vicki. If you're there, pick up." She stared across the dark kitchen, twisting the phone cord between her fingers. "Come on, Fitzroy, I don't care what you're doing, this is important." Why wasn't he home writing? Or chewing on Tony? Or something? "Look, Henry, I need some information. There's another one of, of us, hunting my territory and I don't know what I should do. I know what I want to do . . ." The rage remained interlaced with the knowledge of *another*. ". . . but I'm new at this bloodsucking undead stuff, maybe I'm overreacting. Call me. I'm still at Mike's."

She hung up and sighed. Vampires didn't share territory. Which was why Henry had stayed in Vancouver and she'd come back to Toronto.

Well, all right, it's not the only reason I came back. She tossed Celluci's spare car keys into the drawer in the phone table and wondered if she should write him a note to explain the mysterious emptying of his gas tank. "Nah. He's a detective, let him figure it out."

Sunrise was at 5:12. Vicki didn't need a clock to tell her that it was almost time. She could feel the sun stroking the edges of her awareness.

"It's like that final instant, just before someone hits you from behind, when you know it's going to happen, but you can't do a damn thing about it." She crossed her arms on Celluci's chest and pillowed her head on them, adding, *"Only it lasts longer."*

"And this happens every morning?"

"Just before dawn."

"And you're going to live forever?"

"That's what they tell me."

Celluci snorted. "You can have it."

Although Celluci had offered to light-proof one of the two unused bedrooms, Vicki had been uneasy about the concept. At four and a half centuries, maybe Henry Fitzroy could afford to be blasé about immolation, but Vicki still found the whole idea terrifying and had no intention of being both helpless and exposed. Anyone could walk into a bedroom.

No one would accidentally walk into an enclosed plywood box, covered in a blackout curtain, at the far end of a five-foot-high crawl space—but just to be on the safe side, Vicki dropped two by fours into iron brackets over the entrance. Folded nearly in half, she hurried to her sanctuary, feeling the sun drawing closer, closer. Somehow she resisted the urge to turn.

"There's nothing behind me," she muttered, awkwardly stripping off her clothes. Her heart slamming against her ribs, she crawled under the front flap of the box, latched it behind her, and squirmed into her sleeping bag, stretched out ready for dawn.

"Jesus H. Christ, Vicki," Celluci had said squatting at one end while she'd wrestled the twin bed mattress inside. *"At least a coffin would have a bit of historical dignity."*

"You know where I can get one?"

"I'm not having a coffin in my basement."

"Then quit flapping your mouth."

She wondered, as she lay there waiting for oblivion, where the *other* was. Did they feel the same near panic knowing that they had no control over the hours from dawn to dusk? Or had they, like Henry, come to accept the daily death that governed an immortal life? There should, she supposed, be a sense of kinship between them, but all she could feel was a possessive fury. No one hunted in *her* territory.

"Pleasant dreams," she said as the sun teetered on the edge of the horizon. "And when I find you, you're toast."

Celluci had been and gone by the time the darkness returned. The note he'd left about the car was profane and to the point. Vicki added a couple of words he'd missed and stuck it under a refrigerator magnet in case he got home before she did.

She'd pick up the scent and follow it, the hunter becoming the hunted and, by dawn, the streets would be hers again.

The yellow police tape still stretched across the mouth of the alley. Vicki ignored it. Wrapping the night around her like a cloak, she stood outside the restaurant door and sifted the air.

Apparently, a pimp crucified over the fire exit hadn't been enough to close the place and Tex Mex had nearly obliterated the scent of a death not yet twenty-four hours old. Instead of the predator, all she could smell was fajitas.

"Goddamn it," she muttered, stepping closer and sniffing the wood. "How the hell am I supposed to find . . . ?"

She sensed his life the moment before he spoke.

"What are you doing?"

Vicki sighed and turned. "I'm sniffing the door frame. What's it look like I'm doing?"

"Let me be more specific," Celluci snarled. "What are you doing *here?*"

"I'm looking for the person who offed Mac Eisler," Vicki began. She wasn't sure how much more explanation she was willing to offer.

"No, you're not. You are not a cop. You aren't even a P.I. anymore. And how the hell am I going to explain you if Dave sees you?"

Her eyes narrowed. "You don't have to explain me, Mike."

"Yeah? He thinks you're in Vancouver."

"Tell him I came back."

"And do I tell him that you spend your days in a box in my basement? And that you combust in sunlight? And what do I tell him about your eyes?"

Vicki's hand rose to push at the bridge of her glasses but her fingers touched only air. The retinitis pigmentosa that had forced her from the Metro Police and denied her the night had been reversed when Henry'd changed her. The darkness held no secrets from her now. "Tell him they got better."

"RP doesn't get better."

"Mine did."

"Vicki, I know what you're doing." He dragged both hands up through his hair. "You've done it before. You had to quit the force. You were half-blind.

So what? Your life may have changed, but you were still going to prove that you were 'Victory' Nelson. And it wasn't enough to be a private investigator. You threw yourself into stupidly dangerous situations just to prove you were still who you wanted to be. And now your life has changed again and you're playing the same game."

She could hear his heart pounding, see a pulsing vein framed in the white vee of his open collar, feel the blood surging just below the surface in reach of her teeth. The Hunger rose and she had to use every bit of control Henry had taught her to force it back down. This wasn't about that.

Since she'd returned to Toronto, she'd been drifting, feeding, hunting, relearning the night, relearning her relationship with Michael Celluci. The early morning phone call had crystallized a subconscious discontent and, as Celluci pointed out, there was really only one thing she knew how to do.

Part of his diatribe was based on concern. After all their years together playing cops and lovers, she knew how he thought: if something as basic as sunlight could kill her, what else waited to strike her down? It was only human nature for him to want to protect the people he loved—for him to want to protect her.

But that was only the basis for *part* of the diatribe.

"You can't have been happy with me lazing around your house. I can't cook and I don't do windows." She stepped toward him. "I should think you'd be thrilled that I'm finding my feet again."

"Vicki."

"I wonder," she mused, holding tight to the Hunger, "how you'd feel about me being involved in this if it wasn't your case. I am, after all, better equipped to hunt the night than, oh, detective-sergeants."

"Vicki . . ." Her name had become a nearly inarticulate growl.

She leaned forward until her lips brushed his ear. "Bet you I solve this one first." Then she was gone, moving into shadow too quickly for mortal eyes to track.

"Who you talking to, Mike?" Dave Graham glanced around the empty alley. "I thought I heard . . ." Then he caught sight of the expression on his partner's face. "Never mind."

Vicki couldn't remember the last time she felt so alive. *Which, as I'm now a card-carrying member of the bloodsucking undead, makes for an interesting feeling.* She strode down Queen Street West, almost intoxicated by the lives surrounding her, fully aware of crowds parting to let her through and the admiring glances that traced her path. A connection had been made between her old life and her new one.

"You must surrender the day," Henry had told her, *"but you need not surrender anything else."*

"So what you're trying to tell me," she'd snarled, *"is that we're just normal people who drink blood?"*

Henry had smiled. *"How many* normal *people do you know?"*

She hated it when he answered a question with a question, but now she recognized his point. Honesty forced her to admit that Celluci had a point as well. She did need to prove to herself that she was still herself. She always had. The more things changed, the more they stayed the same.

"Well, now we've got that settled—" She looked around for a place to sit and think. In her old life, that would have meant a donut shop or the window seat in a cheap restaurant and as many cups of coffee as it took. In this new life, being enclosed with humanity did not encourage contemplation. Besides, coffee, a major component of the old equation, made her violently ill, a fact she deeply resented.

A few years back, CITY TV, a local Toronto station, had renovated a deco building on the corner of Queen and John. They'd done a beautiful job and the six-story, white building with its ornately molded modern windows had become a focal point of the neighborhood. Vicki slid into the narrow walkway that separated it from its more down-at-the-heels neighbor and swarmed up what effectively amounted to a staircase for one of her kind.

When she reached the roof a few seconds later, she perched on one crenellated corner and looked out over the downtown core. These were her streets, not Celluci's and not some out-of-town bloodsucker's. It was time she took them back. She grinned and fought the urge to strike a dramatic pose.

All things considered, it wasn't likely that the Metropolitan Toronto Police Department—in the person of Detective-Sergeant Michael Celluci—would be willing to share information. Briefly, she regretted issuing the challenge, then she shrugged it off. As Henry said, the night was too long for regrets.

She sat and watched the crowds jostling about on the sidewalks below, clumps of color indicating tourists among the Queen Street regulars. On a Friday night in August, this was the place to be as the Toronto artistic community rubbed elbows with wannabes and never-woulds.

Vicki frowned. Mac Eisler had been killed before midnight on a Thursday night in an area that never completely slept. Someone had to have seen or heard something. Something they probably didn't believe and were busy denying. Murder was one thing, creatures of the night were something else again.

"Now then," she murmured, "where would a person like that—and considering the time of day we're assuming a regular not a tourist—where would that person be tonight?"

She found him in the third bar she checked, tucked back in a corner, trying desperately to get drunk, and failing. His eyes darted from side to side, both hands were locked around his glass, and his body language screamed *I'm dealing with some bad shit here, leave me alone.*

Vicki sat down beside him and for an instant let the Hunter show. His reaction was everything she could have hoped for.

He stared at her, frozen in terror, his mouth working, but no sound coming out.

"Breathe," she suggested.

The ragged intake of air did little to calm him, but it did break the paralysis. He shoved his chair back from the table and started to stand.

Vicki closed her fingers around his wrist. "Stay."

He swallowed and sat down again.

His skin was so hot it nearly burned and she could feel his pulse breathing against it like a small wild creature struggling to be free. The Hunger clawed at her and her own breathing became a little ragged. "What's your name?"

"Ph . . . Phil."

She caught his gaze with hers and held it. "You saw something last night."

"Yes." Stretched almost to the breaking point, he began to tremble.

"Do you live around here?"

"Yes."

Vicki stood and pulled him to his feet, her tone half command, half caress. "Take me there. We have to talk."

Phil stared at her. "Talk?"

She could barely hear the question over the call of his blood. "Well, talk first."

"It was a woman. Dressed all in black. Hair like a thousand strands of shadow, skin like snow, eyes like black ice. She chuckled, deep in her throat, when she saw me and licked her lips. They were painfully red. Then she vanished, so quickly that she left an image on the night.

"Did you see what she was doing?"

"No. But then, she didn't have be doing anything to be terrifying. I've spent the last twenty-four hours feeling like I met my death."

Phil had turned out to be a bit of a poet. *And* a bit of an athlete. All in all, Vicki considered their time together well spent. Working carefully after he fell asleep, she took away his memory of her and muted the meeting in the alley. It was the least she could do for him.

Description sounds like someone escaped from a Hammer film: The Bride of Dracula Kills a Pimp.

She paused, key in the lock, and cocked her head. Celluci was home, she could feel his life and if she listened very hard, she could hear the regular rhythm of breathing that told her he was asleep. Hardly surprising as it was only three hours to dawn.

There was no reason to wake him as she had no intention of sharing what she'd discovered and no need to feed, but after a long, hot shower, she found herself standing at the door of his room. And then at the side of his bed.

Mike Celluci was thirty-seven. There were strands of gray in his hair and although sleep had smoothed out many of the lines, the deeper creases around his eyes remained. He would grow older. In time, he would die. What would she do then?

She lifted the sheet and tucked herself up close to his side. He sighed and without completely waking scooped her closer still.

"Hair's wet," he muttered.

Vicki twisted, reached up, and brushed the long curl back off his forehead. "I had a shower."

"Where'd you leave the towel?"

"In a sopping pile on the floor."

Celluci grunted inarticulately and surrendered to sleep again.

Vicki smiled and kissed his eyelids. "I love you, too."

She stayed beside him until the threat of sunrise drove her away.

"Irene MacDonald."

Vicki lay in the darkness and stared unseeing up at the plywood. The sun was down and she was free to leave her sanctuary, but she remained a moment longer, turning over the name that had been on her tongue when she woke. She remembered facetiously wondering if the deaths of Irene MacDonald and her pimp were connected.

Irene had been found beaten nearly to death in the bathroom of her apartment. She'd died two hours later in the hospital.

Celluci said that he was personally certain Mac Eisler was responsible. That was good enough for Vicki.

Eisler could've been unlucky enough to run into a vampire who fed on terror as well as blood—Vicki had tasted terror once or twice during her first year when the Hunger occasionally slipped from her control and she knew how addictive it could be—or he could've been killed in revenge for Irene.

Vicki could think of one sure way to find out.

"Brandon? It's Vicki Nelson."

"Victoria?" Surprise lifted most of the Oxford accent off Dr. Brandon Singh's voice. "I thought you'd relocated to British Columbia."

"Yeah, well, I came back."

"I suppose that might account for the improvement over the last month or so in a certain detective we both know."

She couldn't resist asking. "Was he really bad while I was gone?"

Brandon laughed. "He was unbearable and, as you know, I am able to bear a great deal. So, are you still in the same line of work?"

"Yes, I am." Yes, she was. God, it felt good. "Are you still the assistant coroner?"

"Yes, I am. As I think I can safely assume you didn't call me, at home, long after office hours, just to inform me that you're back on the job, what do you want?"

Vicki winced. "I was wondering if you'd had a look at Mac Eisler."

"Yes, Victoria, I have. And I'm wondering why you

can't call me during regular business hours. You must know how much I enjoy discussing autopsies in front of my children."

"Oh, God, I'm sorry, Brandon, but it's important."

"Yes. It always is." His tone was so dry it crumbled. "But since you've already interrupted my evening, try to keep my part of the conversation to a simple yes or no."

"Did you do a blood volume check on Eisler?"

"Yes."

"Was there any missing?"

"No. Fortunately, in spite of the trauma to the neck, the integrity of the blood vessels had not been breached."

So much for yes or no; she knew he couldn't keep to it. "You've been a big help, Brandon, thanks."

"I'd say *anytime,* but you'd likely hold me to it." He hung up abruptly.

Vicki replaced the receiver and frowned. She—the *other*—hadn't fed. The odds moved in favor of Eisler killed because he murdered Irene.

"Well, if it isn't Andrew P." Vicki leaned back against the black Trans Am and adjusted the pair of nonprescription glasses she'd picked up just after sunset. With her hair brushed off her face and the window-glass lenses in front of her eyes, she didn't look much different than she had a year ago. Until she smiled.

The pimp stopped dead in his tracks, bluster fading before he could get the first obscenity out. He swallowed, audibly. "Nelson. I heard you were gone."

Listening to his heart race, Vicki's smile broadened. "I came back. I need some information. I need the name of one of Eisler's other girls."

"I don't know." Unable to look away, he started to shake. "I didn't have anything to do with him. I don't remember."

Vicki straightened and took a slow step toward him. "Try, Andrew."

There was a sudden smell of urine and a darkening stain down the front of the pimp's cotton drawstring pants. "Uh, D . . . D . . . Debbie Ho. That's all I can remember. Really."

"And she works?"

"Middle of the track." His tongue tripped over the words in the rush to spit them at her. "Jarvis and Carlton."

"Thank you." Sweeping a hand toward his car, Vicki stepped aside.

He dove past her and into the driver's seat, jabbing the key into the ignition. The powerful engine roared to life and with one last panicked look into the shadows, he screamed out of the driveway, ground his way through three gear changes, and hit eighty before he reached the corner.

The two cops, quietly sitting in the parking lot of the donut shop on that same corner, hit their siren and took off after him.

Vicki slipped the glasses into the inner pocket of the tweed jacket she'd borrowed from Celluci's closet and grinned. "To paraphrase a certain adolescent crime-fighting amphibian, I *love* being a vampire."

"I need to talk to you, Debbie."

The young woman started and whirled around, glaring suspiciously at Vicki. "You a cop?"

Vicki sighed. "Not anymore." Apparently, it was easier to hide the vampire than the detective. "I'm a private investigator and I want to ask you some questions about Irene MacDonald."

"If you're looking for the shithead who killed her, you're too late. Someone already found him."

"And that's who I'm looking for."

"Why?" Debbie shifted her weight to one hip.

"Maybe I want to give him a medal."

The hooker's laugh held little humor. "You got that right. Mac got everything he deserved."

"Did Irene ever do women?"

Debbie snorted. "Not for free," she said pointedly.

Vicki handed her a twenty.

"Yeah, sometimes. It's safer, medically, you know?"

Editing out Brandon's more ornate phrases, Vicki repeated his description of the woman in the alley.

Debbie snorted again. "Who the hell looks at their faces?"

"You'd remember this one if you saw her. She's . . ." Vicki weighed and discarded several possibilities and finally settled on, ". . . powerful."

"Powerful." Debbie hesitated, frowned, and continued in a rush. "There was this person Irene was seeing a lot but she wasn't charging. That's one of the things that set Mac off, not that the shithead needed much encouragement. We knew it was gonna happen, I mean, we've all felt Mac's temper, but Irene wouldn't stop. She said that just being with this person was a high better than drugs. I guess it could've been a woman. And since she was sort of the reason Irene died, well, I know they used to meet in this bar on Queen West. Why are you hissing?"

"Hissing?" Vicki quickly yanked a mask of composure down over her rage. The other hadn't come into her territory only to kill Eisler—she was definitely Hunting it. "I'm not hissing. I'm just having a little trouble breathing."

"Yeah, tell me about it." Debbie waved a hand ending in three-inch scarlet nails at the traffic on Jarvis. "You should try standing here sucking carbon monoxide all night."

In another mood, Vicki might have reapplied the verb to a different object, but she was still too angry. "Do you know which bar?"

"What, now I'm her social director? No, I don't know which bar." Apparently they'd come to the end of the information twenty dollars could buy as Debbie turned her attention to a prospective client in a gray sedan. The interview was clearly over.

Vicki sucked the humid air past her teeth. There weren't that many bars on Queen West. Last night she'd found Phil in one. Tonight, who knew?

*   *   *

Now that she knew enough to search for it, minute traces of the other predator hung in the air—diffused and scattered by the paths of prey. With so many lives masking the trail, it would be impossible to track her. Vicki snarled. A pair of teenagers, noses pierced, heads shaved, and Doc Martens laced to the knee, decided against asking for change and hastily crossed the street.

It was Saturday night, minutes to Sunday. The bars would be closing soon. If the *other* was Hunting, she would have already chosen her prey.

I wish Henry had called back. Maybe over the centuries they've—we've—evolved ways to deal with this. Maybe we're supposed to talk first. Maybe it's considered bad manners to rip her face off and feed it to her if she doesn't agree to leave.

Standing in the shadow of a recessed storefront, just beyond the edge of the artificial safety the streetlight offered to the children of the sun, she extended her senses the way she'd been taught and touched death within the maelstrom of life.

She found Phil, moments later, lying in yet another of the alleys that serviced the business of the day and provided a safe haven for the darker business of the night. His body was still warm, but his heart had stopped beating and his blood no longer sang. Vicki touched the tiny, nearly closed wound she'd made in his wrist the night before and then the fresh wound in the bend of his elbow. She didn't know how he had died, but she knew who had done it. He stank of the *other*.

Vicki no longer cared what was traditionally "done" in these instances. There would be no talking. No negotiating. It had gone one life beyond that.

"I rather thought that if I killed him you'd come and save me the trouble of tracking you down. And here you are, charging in without taking the slightest of precautions." Her voice was low, not so much threatening as in itself a threat. "You're Hunting in my territory, child."

Still kneeling by Phil's side, Vicki lifted her head. Ten feet away, only her face and hands clearly visible, the other vampire stood. Without thinking—unable to think clearly through the red rage that shrieked for release—Vicki launched herself at the snow-white column of throat, finger hooked to talons, teeth bared.

The Beast Henry had spent a year teaching her to control was loose. She felt herself lost in its raw power and she reveled in it.

The *other* made no move until the last possible second then she lithely twisted and slammed Vicki to one side.

Pain eventually brought reason back. Vicki lay panting in the fetid damp at the base of a Dumpster, one eye swollen shut, a gash across her forehead still sluggishly bleeding. Her right arm was broken.

"You're strong," the other told her, a contemptuous gaze pinning her to the ground. "In another hundred years you might have stood a chance. But you're an infant. A child. You haven't the experience to control what you are. This will be your only warning. Get out of my territory. If we meet again, I *will* kill you."

Vicki sagged against the inside of the door and tried to lift her arm. During the two and a half hours it had taken her to get back to Celluci's house, the bone had begun to set. By tomorrow night, provided she fed in the hours remaining until dawn, she should be able to use it.

"Vicki?"

She started. Although she'd known he was home, she'd assumed—without checking—that because of the hour he'd be asleep. She squinted as the hall light came on and wondered, listening to him pad down the stairs in bare feet, whether she had the energy to make it into the basement bathroom before he saw her.

He came into the kitchen, tying his bathrobe belt around him, and flicked on the overhead light. "We need to talk," he said grimly as the shadows that might have hidden her fled. "Jesus H. Christ. What the hell happened to you?"

"Nothing much." Eyes squinted nearly shut, Vicki gingerly probed the swelling on her forehead. "You should see the other guy."

Without speaking, Celluci reached over and hit the play button on the telephone answering machine.

"Vicki? Henry. If someone's Hunting your territory, whatever you do, don't challenge. Do you hear me? *Don't* challenge. You can't win. They're going to be older, able to overcome the instinctive rage and remain in full command of their power. If you won't surrender the territory . . ." The sigh the tape played back gave a clear opinion of how likely he thought that was to occur. ". . . you're going to have to negotiate. If you can agree on boundaries, there's no reason why you can't share the city." His voice suddenly belonged again to the lover she'd lost with the change. "Call me, please, before you do anything."

It was the only message on the tape.

"Why," Celluci asked as it rewound, his gaze taking in the cuts and the bruising and the filth, "do I get the impression that it's 'the other guy' Fitzroy's talking about?"

Vicki tried to shrug. Her shoulders refused to cooperate. "It's my city, Mike. It always has been. I'm going to take it back."

He stared at her for a long moment then he shook his head. "You heard what Henry said. You can't win. You haven't been . . . what you are, long enough. It's only been fourteen months."

"I know." The rich scent of his life prodded the Hunger and she moved to put a little distance between them.

He closed it up again. "Come on." Laying his hand in the center of her back, he steered her toward the stairs. *Put it aside for now,* his tone told her. *We'll argue about it later.* "You need a bath."

"I need . . ."

"I know. But you need a bath first. I just changed the sheets."

The darkness wakes us all in different ways, Henry had told her. *We were all human once and we carried our differences through the change.*

For Vicki, it was like the flicking of a switch; one moment she wasn't, the next she was. This time, when she returned from the little death of the day, an idea returned with her.

Four-hundred-and-fifty-odd years a vampire, Henry had been seventeen when he changed. The *other* had walked the night for perhaps as long—her gaze had carried the weight of several lifetimes—but her physical appearance suggested that her mortal life had lasted even less time than Henry's had. Vicki allowed that it made sense. Disaster may have precipitated *her* change, but passion was the usual cause.

And no one does that kind of never-say-die passion like a teenager.

It would be difficult for either Henry or the other to imagine a response that came out of a mortal rather than a vampiric experience. They'd both had centuries of the latter and not enough of the former to count.

Vicki had been only fourteen months a vampire, but she'd been human thirty-two years when Henry'd saved her by drawing her to his blood to feed. During those thirty-two years, she'd been nine years a cop— two accelerated promotions, three citations, and the best arrest record on the force.

There was no chance of negotiation.

She couldn't win if she fought.

She'd be damned if she'd flee.

"Besides . . ." For all she realized where her strength had to lie, Vicki's expression held no humanity. ". . . she owes me for Phil."

Celluci had left her a note on the fridge.

Does this have anything to do with Mac Eisler?

Vicki stared at it for a moment then scribbled her answer underneath.

Not anymore.

It took three weeks to find where the *other* spent her days. Vicki used old contacts where she could and made new ones where she had to. Any modern Van Helsing could have done the same.

For the next three weeks, Vicki hired someone to watch the *other* come and go, giving reinforced instructions to stay in the car with the windows closed and the air-conditioning running. Life had an infinite number of variations, but one piece of machinery smelled pretty much like any other. It irritated her that she couldn't sit stakeout herself, but the information she needed would've kept her out after sunrise.

"How the hell did you burn your hand?"

Vicki continued to smear ointment over the blister. Unlike the injuries she'd taken in the alley, this would heal slowly and painfully. "Accident in a tanning salon."

"That's not funny."

She picked up the roll of gauze from the counter. "You're losing your sense of humor, Mike."

Celluci snorted and handed her the scissors. "I never had one."

"Mike, I wanted to warn you, I won't be back by sunrise."

Celluci turned slowly, the TV dinner he'd just taken from the microwave held in both hands. "What do you mean?"

She read the fear in his voice and lifted the edge of the tray so that the gravy didn't pour out and over his shoes. "I mean I'll be spending the day somewhere else."

"Where?"

"I can't tell you."

"Why? Never mind." He raised a hand as her eyes

narrowed. "Don't tell me. I don't want to know. You're going after that other vampire, aren't you? The one Fitzroy told you to leave alone."

"I thought you didn't want to know."

"I already know," he grunted. "I can read you like a book. With large type. And pictures."

Vicki pulled the tray from his grip and set it on the counter. "She's killed two people. Eisler was a scumbag who may have deserved it, but the other . . ."

"Other?" Celluci exploded. "Jesus H. Christ, Vicki, in case you've forgotten, murder's against the law! Who the hell painted a big vee on your long johns and made you the vampire vigilante?"

"Don't you remember?" Vicki snapped. "You were there. I didn't make this decision, Mike. You and Henry made it for me. You'd just better learn to live with it." She fought her way back to calm. "Look, you can't stop her, but I can. I know that galls, but that's the way it is."

They glared at each other, toe to toe. Finally Celluci looked away.

"I can't stop you, can I?" he asked bitterly. "I'm only human after all."

"Don't sell yourself short," Vicki snarled. "You're quintessentially human. If you want to stop me, you face me and ask me not to go and *then* you remember it every time *you* go into a situation that could get your ass shot off."

After a long moment, he swallowed, lifted his head, and met her eyes. "Don't die. I thought I lost you once and I'm not strong enough to go through that again."

"Are you asking me not to go?"

He snorted. "I'm asking you to be careful. Not that you ever listen."

She took a step forward and rested her head against his shoulder, wrapping herself in the beating of his heart. "This time, I'm listening."

The studios in the converted warehouse on King Street were not supposed to be live-in. A good 75 percent of the tenants ignored that. The studio Vicki wanted was at the back on the third floor. The heavy steel door—an obvious upgrade by the occupant—had been secured by the best lock money could buy.

New senses and old skills got through it in record time.

Vicki pushed open the door with her foot and began carrying boxes inside. She had a lot to do before dawn.

"She goes out every night between ten and eleven, then she comes home every morning between four and five. You could set your watch by her."

Vicki handed him an envelope.

He looked inside, thumbed through the money, then grinned up at her. "Pleasure doing business for you. Any time you need my services, you know where to call."

"Forget it," she told him.

And he did.

Because she expected her, Vicki knew the moment the *other* entered the building. The Beast stirred and she tightened her grip on it. To lose control now would be disaster.

She heard the elevator, then footsteps in the hall.

"You know I'm in here," she said silently, *"and you know you can take me. Be overconfident, believe I'm a fool, and walk right in."*

"I thought you were smarter than this." The *other* stepped into the apartment, then casually turned to lock the door. "I told you when I saw you again I'd kill you."

Vicki shrugged, the motion masking her fight to remain calm. "Don't you even want to know why I'm here?"

"I assume you've come to negotiate." She raised ivory hands and released thick, black hair from its bindings. "We went past that when you attacked me." Crossing the room, she preened before a large ornate mirror that dominated one wall of the studio.

"I attacked you because you murdered Phil."

"Was that his name?" The other laughed. The sound had razored edges. "I didn't bother to ask it."

"Before you murdered him."

"Murdered? You *are* a child. They are prey, we are predators—their deaths are ours if we desire them. You'd have learned that in time." She turned, the patina of civilization stripped away. "Too bad you haven't any time left."

Vicki snarled but somehow managed to stop herself from attacking. Years of training whispered, *Not yet.* She had to stay exactly where she was.

"Oh, yes." The sibilants flayed the air between them. "I almost forgot. You wanted me to ask you why you came. Very well. Why?"

Given the address and the reason, Celluci could've come to the studio during the day and slammed a stake through the *other's* heart. The vampire's strongest protection would be of no use against him. Mike Celluci believed in vampires.

"I came," Vicki told her, "because some things you have to do yourself."

The wire ran up the wall, tucked beside the surface-mounted cable of a cheap renovation, and disappeared into the shadows that clung to a ceiling sixteen feet from the floor. The switch had been stapled down beside her foot. A tiny motion, too small to evoke attack, flipped it.

Vicki had realized from the beginning that there were a number of problems with her plan. The first involved placement. Every living space included an area where the occupant felt secure—a favorite chair, a window . . . a mirror. The second problem was how to mask what she'd done. While the *other* would not be able to sense the various bits of wiring and equipment, she'd be fully aware of Vicki's scent *on* the wiring and equipment. Only if Vicki remained in the studio, could that smaller trace be lost in the larger.

The third problem was directly connected with the second. Given that Vicki had to remain, how was she to survive?

Attached to the ceiling by sheer brute strength, positioned so that they shone directly down into the space in front of the mirror, were a double bank of lights cannibalized from a tanning bed. The sun held a double menace for the vampire—its return to the sky brought complete vulnerability and its rays burned.

Henry had a round scar on the back of one hand from too close an encounter with the sun. When her burn healed, Vicki would have a matching one from a deliberate encounter with an imitation.

The *other* screamed as the lights came on, the sound pure rage and so inhuman that those who heard it would have to deny it for sanity's sake.

Vicki dove forward, ripped the heavy brocade off the back of the couch, and burrowed frantically into its depths. Even that instant of light had bathed her skin in flame and she moaned as, for a moment, the searing pain became all she was. After a time, when it grew no worse, she managed to open her eyes.

The light couldn't reach her, but neither could she reach the switch to turn it off. She could see it, three feet away, just beyond the shadow of the couch. She shifted her weight and a line of blister rose across one leg. Biting back a shriek, she curled into a fetal position, realizing her refuge was not entirely secure.

Okay, genius, now what?

Moving very, very carefully, Vicki wrapped her hand around the one by two that braced the lower edge of the couch. From the tension running along it, she suspected that breaking it off would result in at least a partial collapse of the piece of furniture.

And if it goes, I very well may go with it.

And then she heard the sound of something dragging itself across the floor.

Oh, shit! She's not dead!

The wood broke, the couch began to fall in on itself, and Vicki, realizing that luck would have a large part to play in her survival, smacked the switch and rolled clear in the same motion.

The room plunged into darkness.

Vicki froze as her eyes slowly readjusted to the night. Which was when she finally became conscious of the smell. It had been there all along, but her senses had refused to acknowledge it until they had to.

Sunlight burned.

Vicki gagged.

The dragging sound continued.

The hell with this! She didn't have time to wait for her eyes to repair the damage they'd obviously taken. She needed to see *now*. Fortunately, although it hadn't seemed fortunate at the time, she'd learned to maneuver without sight.

She threw herself across the room.

The light switch was where they always were, to the right of the door.

The thing on the floor pushed itself up on fingerless hands and glared at her out of the blackened ruin of a face. Laboriously it turned, hate radiating off it in palpable waves and began to pull itself toward her again.

Vicki stepped forward to meet it.

While the part of her that remembered being human writhed in revulsion, she wrapped her hands around its skull and twisted it in a full circle. The spine snapped. Another full twist and what was left of the head came off in her hands.

She'd been human for thirty-two years, but she'd been fourteen months a vampire.

"No one hunts in *my* territory," she snarled as the *other* crumbled to dust.

She limped over to the wall and pulled the plug supplying power to the lights. Later, she'd remove them completely—the whole concept of sunlamps gave her the creeps.

When she turned, she was facing the mirror.

The woman who stared out at her through bloodshot eyes, exposed skin blistered and red, was a hunter. Always had been, really. The question became, who was she to hunt?

Vicki smiled. Before the sun drove her to use her

inherited sanctuary, she had a few quick phone calls to make. The first to Celluci; she owed him the knowledge that she'd survived the night. The second to Henry for much the same reason.

The third call would be to the eight hundred line that covered the classifieds of Toronto's largest alternative newspaper. This ad was going to be a little different than the one she'd placed upon leaving the force. Back then, she'd been incredibly depressed about leaving a job she loved for a life she saw as only marginally useful. This time, she had no regrets.

Victory Nelson, Investigator: Otherworldly Crimes a Specialty.

What Manner of Man

Shortly after three o'clock in the morning, Henry Fitzroy rose from the card table, brushed a bit of ash from the sleeve of his superbly fitting coat, and inclined his head toward his few remaining companions. "If you'll excuse me, gentlemen, I believe I'll call it a night."

"Well, I won't excuse you." Sir William Wyndham glared up at Fitzroy from under heavy lids. "You've won eleven hundred pounds off me tonight, damn your eyes, and I want a chance to win it back."

His gaze flickering down to the cluster of empty bottles by Wyndham's elbow, Henry shook his head. "I don't think so, Sir William, not tonight."

"You don't think so?" Wyndham half rose in his chair, dark brows drawn into a deep vee over an aristocratic arc of nose. His elbow rocked one of the bottles. It began to fall.

Moving with a speed that made it clear he had not personally been indulging over the course of the evening's play, Henry caught the bottle just before it hit the floor. "Brandy," he chided softly, setting it back on the table, "is no excuse for bad manners."

Wyndham stared at him for a moment, confusion replacing the anger on his face, instinct warning him of a danger reason couldn't see. "Your pardon," he said at last. "Perhaps another night." He watched as the other man bowed and left, then muttered, "Insolent puppy."

"Who is?" asked another of the players, dragging his attention away from the brandy.

"Fitzroy." Raising his glass to his mouth, his hand surprisingly steady considering how much he'd already drunk, Wyndham tossed back the contents. "He speaks to me like that again and he can name his seconds."

"Well, *I* wouldn't fight him."

"No one's asking you to."

"He's just the sort of quiet chap who's the very devil when pushed too far. I've seen that look in his eyes, I tell you—the very devil when pushed too far."

"Shut up." Opening a fresh deck, Wyndham sullenly pushed Henry Fitzroy from his thoughts and set about trying to make good his losses.

His curly-brimmed beaver set at a fashionably rakish angle on his head, Henry stood on the steps of his club and stared out at London. Its limits had expanded since the last time he'd made it his principal residence, curved courts of elegant townhouses had risen where he remembered fields, but, all in all, it hadn't changed much. There was still something about London—a feel, an atmosphere—shared by no other city in the world.

One guinea-gold brow rose as he shot an ironic glance upward at the haze that hung over the buildings, the smoke from a thousand chimney pots that blocked the light of all but the brightest stars. Atmosphere was, perhaps, a less than appropriate choice of words.

"Shall I get you a hackney or a chair, Mr. Fitzroy?"

"Thank you, no." He smiled at the porter, his expression calculated to charm, and heard the elderly man's heart begin to beat a little faster. The Hunger rose in response, but he firmly pushed it back. It would be the worst of bad *ton* to feed so close to home. It would also be dangerous but, in the England of the Prince Regent, safety came second to social approval. "I believe I'll walk."

"If you're sure, sir. There's some bad'uns around after dark."

"I'm sure." Henry's smile broadened. "I doubt I'll be bothered."

The porter watched as the young man made his way down the stairs and along St. James Street. He'd watched a lot of gentlemen during the years he'd worked the clubs—first at Boodles, then at Brook's, and finally here at White's—and Mr. Henry Fitzroy had the unmistakable mark of Quality. For all he was so polite and soft-spoken, something about him spoke strongly of power. It would, the porter decided, take a desperate man, or a stupid one, to put Mr. Fitzroy in any danger. *Of course, London has no shortage of either desperate or stupid men.*

"Take care, sir," he murmured as he turned to go inside.

Henry quelled the urge to lift a hand in acknowledgment of the porter's concern, judging that he'd moved beyond the range of mortal hearing. As the night air held a decided chill, he shoved his hands deep in the pockets of his many-caped greatcoat, even though it would have to get a great deal colder before he'd feel it. A successful masquerade demanded attention to small details.

Humming under his breath, he strode down Brook Street to Grosvenor Square, marveling at the new technological wonder of the gaslights. The long lines of little brightish dots created almost as many shadows as they banished, but they were still a big improvement over a servant carrying a lantern on a stick. That he had no actual need of the light Henry considered unimportant in view of the achievement.

Turning toward his chambers in Albany, he heard the unmistakable sounds of a fight. He paused, head cocked, sifting through the lives involved. Three men beating a fourth.

"Not at all sporting," he murmured, moving forward so quickly that, had anyone been watching, it would have seemed he simply disappeared.

"Be sure that he's dead." The man who spoke held a narrow sword in one hand and the cane it had come out of in the other. The man on the ground groaned and the steel point moved around. "Never mind, I'll take care of it myself."

Wearing an expression of extreme disapproval, Henry stepped out of the shadows, grabbed the swordsman by the back of his coat, and threw him down the alley. When the other two whirled to face him, he drew his lips back off his teeth and said, in a tone of polite but inarguable menace, "Run."

Prey recognized predator. They ran.

He knelt by the wounded man, noted how the heartbeat faltered, looked down, and saw a face he knew. Captain Charles Evans of the Horse Guards, the nephew of the current Earl of Whitby. Not one of his few friends—friends were chosen with a care honed by centuries of survival—but Henry couldn't allow him to die alone in some dark alley like a stray dog.

A sudden noise drew his attention around to the man with the sword-cane. Up on his knees, his eyes unfocused, he groped around for his weapon. Henry snarled. The man froze, whimpered once, then, face twisted with fear, scrambled to his feet, and joined his companions in flight.

The sword had punched a hole high in the captain's left shoulder, not immediately fatal, but bleeding to death was a distinct possibility.

"Fitz . . . roy?"

"So you're awake, are you?" Taking the other man's chin in a gentle grip, Henry stared down into pain-filled eyes. "I think it might be best if you trusted me and slept," he said quietly.

The captain's lashes fluttered, then settled down to rest against his cheeks like fringed shadows.

Satisfied that he was unobserved, Henry pulled aside the bloodstained jacket—like most military men,

Captain Evans favored Scott—and bent his head over the wound.

"You cut it close. Sun's almost up."

Henry pushed past the small, irritated form of his servant. "Don't fuss, Varney, I've plenty of time."

"Plenty of time is it?" Closing and bolting the door, the little man hurried down the short hall in Henry's shadow. "I was worried sick, I was, and all you can say is don't fuss?"

Sighing, Henry shrugged out of his greatcoat—a muttering Varney caught it before it hit the floor—and stepped into his sitting room. There was a fire lit in the grate, heavy curtains over the window that opened onto a tiny balcony, and a thick oak slab of a door replacing the folding doors that had originally led to the bedchamber. The furniture was heavy and dark, as close as Henry could come to the furniture of his youth. It had been purchased in a fit of nostalgia and was now mostly ignored.

"You've blood on your cravat!"

"It's not mine," Henry told him mildly.

Varney snorted. "Didn't expect it was, but you're usually neater than that. Probably won't come out. Blood stains, you know."

"I know."

"Mayhap if I soak it . . ." The little man quivered with barely concealed impatience.

Henry laughed and unwound the offending cloth, dropping it over the offered hand. After thirty years of unique service, certain liberties were unavoidable. "I won eleven hundred pounds from Lord Wyndham tonight."

"You and everyone else. He's badly dipped. Barely a feather to fly with so I hear. Rumor has it he's getting a bit desperate."

"And I returned a wounded Charlie Evans to the bosom of his family."

"Nice bosom, so I hear."

"Don't be crude, Varney." Henry sat down and

lifted one foot after the other to have the tight Hessians pulled gently off. "I think I may have prevented him from being killed."

"Robbery?"

"I don't know."

"How many did you kill?"

"No one. I merely frightened them away."

Setting the gleaming boots to one side, Varney stared at his master with frank disapproval. "You merely frightened them away?"

"I did consider ripping their throats out, but as it wasn't actually necessary, it wouldn't have been . . ." He paused and smiled. ". . . polite."

"Polite!? You risked exposure so as you can be polite?"

The smile broadened. "I am a creature of my time."

"You're a creature of the night! You know what'll come of this? Questions, that's what. And we don't need questions!"

"I have complete faith in your ability to handle whatever might arise."

Recognizing the tone, the little man deflated. "Aye and well you might," he muttered darkly. "Let's get that jacket off you before I've got to carry you in to your bed like a sack of meal."

"I *can* do it myself," Henry remarked as he stood and turned to have his coat carefully peeled from his shoulders.

"Oh, aye, and leave it lying on the floor no doubt." Folding the coat in half, Varney draped it over one skinny arm. "I'd never get the wrinkles out. You'd go about looking like you dressed out of a ragbag if it wasn't for me. Have you eaten?" He looked suddenly hopeful.

One hand in the bedchamber door, Henry paused. "Yes," he said softly.

The thin shoulders sagged. "Then what're you standing about for?"

A few moments later, the door bolted, the heavy shutter over the narrow window secured, Henry Fitzroy, vampire, bastard son of Henry the VIII, once Duke of Richmond and Somerset, Earl of Nottingham, and Lord President of the Council of the North, slid into the day's oblivion.

"My apologies, Mrs. Evans, for not coming by sooner, but I was out when your husband's message arrived." Henry laid his hat and gloves on the small table in the hall and allowed the waiting footman to take his coat. "I trust he's in better health than he was when I saw him last night?"

"A great deal better, thank you." Although there were purple shadows under her eyes and her cheeks were more than fashionably pale, Lenore Evans' smile lit up her face. "The doctor says he lost a lot of blood, but he'll recover. If it hadn't been for you . . ."

As her voice trailed off, Henry bowed slightly. "I was happy to help." Perhaps he *had* taken a dangerous chance. Perhaps he should have wiped all memory of his presence from the captain's mind and left him on his own doorstep like an oversized infant. Having become involved, he couldn't very well ignore the message an obviously disapproving Varney had handed him at sunset with a muttered, *I told you so*.

It appeared that there were indeed going to be questions.

Following Mrs. Evans up the stairs, he allowed himself to be ushered into a well-appointed bedchamber and left alone with the man in the bed.

Propped up against his pillows, recently shaved but looking wan and tired, Charles Evans nodded a greeting. "Fitzroy. I'm glad you've come."

Henry inclined his own head in return, thankful that the bloodscent had been covered by the entirely unappetizing smell of basilicum powder. "You're looking remarkably well, all things considered."

"I've you to thank for that."

"I really did very little."

"True enough, you *only* saved my life." The captain's grin was infectious and Henry found himself re-

WHAT MANNER OF MAN 35

turning it in spite of an intention to remain aloof.
"Mind you, Dr. Harris did say he'd never seen such
a clean wound." One hand rose to touch the bandages
under his nightshirt. "He said I was healing faster than
any man he'd ever examined."

As his saliva had been responsible for that accelerated healing, Henry remained silent. It had seemed
foolish to resist temptation when there'd been so
much blood going to waste.

"Anyway . . ." The grin disappeared and the expres-
sive face grew serious. "I owe you my life and I'm
very grateful you came along, but that's not why I
asked you to visit. I can't get out of this damned bed
and I have to trust someone." Shadowed eyes lifted
to Henry's face. "Something tells me that I can trust
you."

"You barely know me," Henry murmured, inwardly
cursing his choice of words the night before. He'd told
Evans to trust him and now it seemed he was to play
the role of confidant. He could remove the trust as
easily as he'd placed it, but something in the man's
face made him hesitate. Whatever bothered him involved life and death—Henry had seen the latter too
often to mistake it now. Sighing, he added, "I can't
promise anything, but I'll listen."

"Please." Gesturing at a chair, the captain waited
until his guest had seated himself, then waited a little
longer, apparently searching for a way to begin. After
a few moments, he lifted his chin. "You know I work
at the Home Office?"

"I had heard as much, yes." In the last few years,
gossip had become the preferred entertainment of *all*
classes, and Varney was a devoted participant.

"Well, for the last little while—just since the start of
the Season, in fact—things have been going missing."

"Things?"

"Papers. Unimportant ones for the most part, until
now." His mouth twisted up into a humorless grin. "I
can't tell you exactly what the latest missing document
contained—in spite of everything we'd still rather it

wasn't common knowledge—but I can tell you that if it gets into the wrong hands, into French hands, a lot of British soldiers are going to die."

"Last night you were following the thief?"

"No. The man we think is his contact. A French spy named Yves Bouchard."

Henry shook his head, intrigued in spite of himself. "The man who stabbed you last night was no Frenchman. I heard him speak, and he was as English as you or I. English, and though I hesitate to use the term, a gentleman."

"That's Bouchard. He's the only son of an old emigre family. They left France during the revolution—Yves was a mere infant at the time, and now he dreams of restoring the family fortunes under Napoleon."

"One would have thought he'd be more interested in defeating Napoleon and restoring the rightful king."

Evans shrugged, winced, and said, "Apparently not. Anyway, Bouchard's too smart to stay around after what happened last night. I kept him from getting his hands on the document; now we have to keep it from leaving England by another means."

"We?" Henry asked, surprised into ill-mannered incredulity. "You and I?"

"Mostly you. The trouble is, we don't know who actually took the document, although we've narrowed it down to three men who are known to be in Bouchard's confidence and who have access to the Guard's offices."

"One moment, please." Henry raised an exquisitely manicured hand. "You want me to find your spy for you?"

"Yes."

"Why?"

"Because I can't be certain of anyone else in my office and because I trust you."

Realizing he had only himself to blame, Henry sighed. "And I suppose you can't bring the three in for questioning because two of them are innocent?"

Evans' pained expression had nothing to do with his wound. "Only consider the scandal. I will if I must, but as this is Wednesday and the information must be in France by Friday evening or it won't get to Napoleon in time for it to be of any use, one of those three will betray himself in the next two days."

"So the document must be recovered with no public outcry?"

"Exactly."

"I would have thought the Bow Street Runners . . ."

"No. The Runners may be fine for chasing down highwaymen and murderers, but my three suspects move in the best circles; only a man of their own class could get near them without arousing suspicion." He lifted a piece of paper off the table beside the bed and held it out to Henry, who stared at it for a long moment.

Lord Ruthven, Mr. Maxwell Aubrey, and Sir William Wyndham. Frowning, Henry looked up to meet Captain Evans' weary gaze. "You're sure about this?"

"I am. Send word when you're sure, I'll do the rest."

The exhaustion shading the other man's voice reminded Henry of his injury. Placing the paper back beside the bed, he stood. "This is certainly not what I expected."

"But you'll do it?"

He could refuse, could make the captain forget that this conversation had ever happened, but he had been a prince of England and, regardless of what he had become, he could not stand back and allow her to be betrayed. Hiding a smile at the thought of what Varney would have to say about such melodrama, he nodded. "Yes, I'll do it."

The sound of feminine voices rising up from the entryway caused Henry to pause for a moment on the landing.

". . . so sorry to arrive so late, Mrs. Evans, but we

were passing on our way to dinner before Almack's and my uncle insisted we stop and see how the captain was doing."

Carmilla Amworth. There could be no mistaking the faint country accent not entirely removed by hours of lessons intended to erase it. She had enough fortune to be considered an heiress and that, combined with a dark-haired, pale-skinned, waiflike beauty, brought no shortage of admirers. Unfortunately, she also had disturbing tendency to giggle when she felt herself out of her depth.

"My uncle," she continued, "finds it difficult to get out of the carriage and so sent me in his place."

"I quite understand." The smile in the answering voice suggested a shared amusement. "Please tell your uncle that the captain is resting comfortably and thank him for his consideration."

A brief exchange of pleasantries later, Miss Amworth returned to her uncle's carriage and Henry descended the rest of the stairs.

Lenore Evans turned and leaped backward, one hand to her heart, her mouth open. She would have fallen had Henry not caught her wrist and kept her on her feet.

He could feel her pulse racing beneath the thin sheath of heated skin. The Hunger rose, and he hurriedly broke the contact. Self-indulgence, besides being vulgar, was a sure road to the stake.

"Heavens, you startled me." Cheeks flushed, she increased the distance between them. "I didn't hear you come down."

"My apologies. I heard Miss Amworth and didn't wish to break in on a private moment."

"Her uncle works with Charles and wanted to know how he was, but her uncle is *also* a dear friend of His Royal Highness and is, shall we say, less than able to climb in and out of carriages. Is Charles . . . ?"

"I left him sleeping."

"Good." Her right hand wrapped around the place where Henry had held her. She swallowed, then, as though reminded of her duties by the action, stammered, "Can I get you a glass of wine?"

"Thank you, no. I must be going."

"Good. That is, I mean . . ." Her flush deepened. "You must think I'm a complete idiot. It's just that with Charles injured . . ."

"I fully understand." He smiled, careful not to show teeth.

Lenore Evans closed the door behind her husband's guest and tried to calm the pounding of her heart. Something about Henry Fitzroy spoke to a part of her she'd thought belonged to Charles alone. Her response might have come out of gratitude for the saving of her husband's life, but she didn't think so. He was a handsome young man, and she found the soft curves of his mouth a fascinating contrast to the gentle strength in his grip.

Shaking her head in self-reproach, she lifted her skirts with damp hands and started up the stairs. "I'm beginning to think," she sighed, "that Aunt Georgette was right. Novels are a bad influence on a young woman."

What she needed now was a few hours alone with her husband but, as his wound made that impossible, she'd supposed she'd have to divert her thoughts with a book of sermons instead.

Almack's Assembly Rooms were the exclusive temple of the beau monde, and vouchers to the weekly ball on Wednesday were among the most sought-after items in London. What matter that the assembly rooms were plain, the dance floor inferior, the anterooms unadorned, and the refreshments unappetizing—this was the seventh heaven of the fashionable world, and to be excluded from Almack's was to be excluded from the upper levels of society.

Henry, having discovered that a fashionable young man could live unremarked from dark to dawn, had effortlessly risen to the top.

After checking with the porter that all three of Captain Evans' potential spies were indeed in attendance, Henry left hat, coat, and gloves and made his way up into the assembly rooms. Avoiding the gaze of Princess Esterhazy, who he considered to be rude and overbearing, he crossed the room and made his bow to the Countess Lieven.

"I hear you were quite busy last night, Mr. Fitzroy."

A little astonished by how quickly the information had made its way to such august ears, he murmured he had only done what any man would have.

"Indeed. Any *man*. Still, I should have thought the less of you had you expected a fuss to be made." Tapping her closed fan against her other hand, she favored him with a long, level look. "I have always believed there was more to you than you showed the world."

Fully aware that the countess deserved her reputation as the cleverest woman in London, Henry allowed a little of his mask to slip.

She smiled, satisfied for the moment with being right and not overly concerned with what she had been right about. "Appearances, my dear Mr. Fitzroy, are everything. And now, I believe they are beginning a country dance. Let me introduce you to a young lady in need of a partner."

Unable to think of a reason why she shouldn't, Henry bowed again. A few moments later, as he moved gracefully through the pattern of the dance, he wondered if he should pay the countess a visit some night, had not made a decision by the time the dance ended, and put it off indefinitely as he escorted the young woman in his care back to her waiting mama.

Well aware that he looked, at best, in his early twenties, Henry could only be thankful that a well-crafted reputation as a man who trusted to the cards for the finer things in life took him off the marriage mart. No matchmaking mama would allow her daughter to become shackled to someone with such narrow prospects. As he had no interest in giggling young damsels just out of the schoolroom, he could only be thankful. The older women he spent time with were much more . . . appetizing.

Trying not to stare, one of the young damsels so summarily dismissed in Henry's thoughts leaned foward a second and whispered, "I wonder what Mr. Fitzroy is smiling about."

The second glanced up, blushed rosily, and ducked her head. "He looks *hungry*."

The first, a little wiser in the ways of the world than her friend, sighed and laid silent odds that the curve of Mr. Henry Fitzroy's full lips had nothing to do with bread and butter.

Hearing a familiar voice, Henry searched through the moving couples and spotted Sir William Wyndham dancing with Carmilla Amworth. Hardly surprising if he'd lost as much money lately as Varney suggested. While Henry wouldn't have believed the fragile, country-bred heiress to his taste—it was a well-known secret that he kept a yacht off Dover for the express purpose of entertaining the women of easy virtue he preferred—upon reflection he supposed Sir William would consider her inheritance sufficiently alluring. And a much safer way of recovering his fortune than selling state secrets to France.

With one of Captain Evans' suspects accounted for, Henry began to search for the other two, moving quietly and unobtrusively from room to room. As dancing was the object of the club and no high stakes were allowed, the card rooms contained only dowagers and those gentlemen willing to play whist for pennies. Although he found neither of the men he looked for, he did find Carmilla Amworth's uncle, Lord Beardsley. One of the Prince Regent's cronies, he was a stout and somewhat foolish middle-aged gentleman who smelled strongly of scent and creaked alarmingly when he moved. Considering the bulwark of his stays, Henry was hardly surprised that he'd been less than able to get out of the carriage to ask after Captain Evans.

". . . cupped and felt much better," Lord Beardsley was saying as Henry entered the room. "His Royal Highness swears by cupping, you know. Must've had gallons taken out over the years."

Henry winced, glanced around, and left. As much as he deplored the waste involved in frequent cupping, he had no desire to avail himself of the Prince Regent's blood—which he strongly suspected would be better than 90 percent Madeira.

When he returned to the main assembly room, he found Aubrey on the dance floor and Lord Ruthven brooding in a corner. Sir William had disappeared, but he supposed a two-for-one trade couldn't be considered bad odds and wondered just how he was expected to watch all three men at once. Obviously, he'd have to be more than a mere passive observer. The situation seemed to make it necessary he tackle Ruthven first.

Dressed in funereal black, the peer swept the room with a somber gaze. He gave no indication that he'd noticed Henry's approach and replied to his greeting with a curt nod.

"I'm surprised to see you here, Lord Ruthven." Henry locked eyes with the lord and allowed enough power to ensure a reply. "It is well known you do not dance."

"I am here to meet someone."

"Who, if I may be so bold as to ask? I've recently come from the card rooms and may have seen him."

A muscle jumped under the sallow skin of Ruthven's cheek. To Henry's surprise, he looked away, sighed deeply, and said, "It is of no account as he is not yet here."

Impressed by the man's willpower—if unimpressed by his theatrical melancholy—Henry bowed and moved away. The man's sullen disposition and cold, corpse-gray eyes isolated him from the society his wealth and title gave him access to. Could he be taking revenge against those who shunned him by selling secrets to the French? Perhaps. This was not the time, nor the place, for forcing an answer.

Treading a careful path around a cluster of turbaned dowagers—more dangerous amass than a crowd of angry peasants with torches and pitchforks—Henry made his way to the side of a young man he knew from White's and asked for an introduction to Mr. Maxwell Aubrey.

"Good lord, Henry, whatever for?"

Henry smiled disarmingly. "I hear he's a damnably bad card player."

"He is, but if you think to pluck him, you're a year too late or two years too early. He doesn't come into his capital until he's twenty-five and after the chicken incident, his trustees keep a tight hold of the purse strings."

"Chicken incident?"

"That's right. It happened before you came to London. You see, Aubrey fell in with this fellow named Bouchard."

"Yves Bouchard?"

"That's right. Anyway, Bouchard had Aubrey wrapped around his little finger. Dared him to cluck like a chicken in the middle of the dance floor. I thought Mrs. Drummond-Burrell was going to have spasms. Neither Bouchard nor Aubrey were given vouchers for the rest of the Season."

"And this Season?"

He nodded at Aubrey who was leading his partner off the dance floor. "This Season, all is forgiven."

"And Bouchard?" Henry asked.

"Bouchard, too. Although he doesn't seem to be here tonight."

"So Aubrey was wrapped around Bouchard's little finger. *Wrapped tightly enough to spy for the French?* Henry wondered.

The return of a familiar voice diverted his attention. He turned to see Sir William once again paying court to Carmilla. When she giggled and looked away, it only seemed to inspire Sir William the more. Henry moved closer until he could hear her protests. She sounded both flattered and frightened.

Now that's a combination impossible to resist, Henry thought, watching Wyndham respond. With a predator's fluid grace, he deftly inserted himself between them. "I believe this dance is mine." When Carmilla giggled but made no objection, there was nothing Wyndham could do but quietly seethe.

Once on the floor, Henry smiled down into cornflower blue eyes. "I hope you'll forgive me for interfering, Miss Amworth, but Sir William's attentions seemed to be bothering you."

She dropped her gaze to the vicinity of his waistcoat. "Not bothering, but a bit overwhelming. I'm glad of the chance to gather my thoughts."

"I feel I should warn you that he has a bad reputation."

"He *is* a very accomplished flirt."

"He is a confirmed rake, Miss Amworth."

"Do you think he is more than merely flirting, then?" Her voice held a hint of hope.

Immortality, Henry mused, *would not provide time enough to understand women.* Granted, Sir William had been blessed with darkly sardonic good looks and an athletic build, but he was also—the possibility of his being a spy aside—an arrogant, self-serving libertine. Some women were drawn to that kind of danger; he had not thought Carmilla Amworth to be one of them. His gaze dropped to the pulse beating at an ivory temple, and he wondered just how much danger she dared to experience.

Obviously aware that she should be at least attempting conversation, she took a deep breath and blurted, "I heard you saved Captain Evans last night."

Had everyone heard about it? Varney would not be pleased. "It was nothing."

"My maid says that he was set upon by robbers and you saved his life."

"Servants' gossip."

A dimple appeared beside a generous mouth. "Servants usually know."

Considering his own servant, Henry had to admit the truth of that.

"Were they robbers?"

"I didn't know you were so bloodthirsty, Miss Amworth." When she merely giggled and shook her head, he apologized and added, "I don't know what they were. They ran off as I approached."

"Surely Captain Evans knew."

"If he did, he didn't tell me."

"It must have been so exciting." Her voice grew stronger, and her chin rose, exposing the soft flesh of her throat. "There are times I long to just throw aside all this so-called polite society."

I should have fed before I came. After a brief struggle with his reaction, Henry steered the conversation to safer grounds. It wasn't difficult as Carmilla, apparently embarrassed by her brief show of passion, answered only yes and no for the rest of the dance.

As he escorted her off the floor, Wyndham moved possessively toward her. While trying to decide just how far he should extend his protection, Henry saw Aubrey and Ruthven leave the room together. He heard the younger man say "Bouchard" and lost the rest of their conversation in the surrounding noise.

Good lord, are they both involved?

"My dance this time, I believe, Fitzroy." Shooting Henry an obvious warning, Sir William captured Carmilla's hand and began to lead her away. She seemed fascinated by him and he, for his part, clearly intended to have her.

Fully aware that the only way to save the naive young heiress was to claim her himself, Henry reluctantly went after Aubrey and Ruthven.

By the time he reached King Street, the two men were distant shadows, almost hidden by the night. Breathing deeply in an effort to clear his head of the warm, meaty odor of the assembly rooms, Henry fol-

lowed, his pace calculated to close the distance between them without drawing attention to himself. An
experienced hunter knew better than to spook his
prey.

He could hear Aubrey talking of a recent race meeting, could hear Ruthven's monosyllabic replies, and
heard nothing at all that would link them to the missing document or to Yves Bouchard. Hardly surprising.
Only fools would speak of betraying their country so
publicly.

When they went into Aubrey's lodgings near Portman Square, Henry wrapped himself in the darkness
and climbed to the small balcony off the sitting room.
He felt a bit foolish, skulking about like a common
house-breaker. Captain Evans' desire to avoid a scandal, while admirable, was becoming irritating.

"Here it is."

"Are you sure?" Ruthven's heart pounded as though
he'd been running. It all but drowned out the sound of
paper rustling.

"Why would Bouchard lie to me?"

Why, indeed? A door opened, and closed, and
Henry was on the street waiting for Ruthven when he
emerged from the building. He was about to step forward when a carriage rumbled past, reminding him
that, in spite of the advanced hour, the street was far
from empty.

Following close on Ruthven's heels—and noting
that wherever the dour peer was heading it wasn't
toward home—Henry waited until he passed the
mouth of a dark and deserted mews, then made his
move. With one hand around Ruthven's throat and
the other holding him against a rough stone wall, his
lips drew back off his teeth in involuntary anticipation
of the other man's terror.

To his astonishment, Ruthven merely declared with
gloomy emphasis. "Come, Death, strike. Do not keep
me waiting any longer."

His own features masked by the night, Henry
frowned. Mouth slightly open to better taste the air,

he breathed in an acrid odor he recognized. "You're drunk!" Releasing his grip, he stepped back.

"Although it is none of your business, I am always drunk." Under his customary scowl, Ruthven's dull gray eyes flicked from side to side, searching the shadows.

That explained a great deal about Ruthven's near legendary melancholy, and perhaps it explained something else as well. "Is that why you're spying for France?"

"The only thing I do for France is drink their liquor." The peer drew himself up to his full height. "And Death or not, I resent your implication."

His protest held the ring of truth. "Then what do you want with Yves Bouchard?"

"He said he could get me . . ." All at once he stopped and stared despondently into the night. "That also is none of your business."

Beginning to grow irritated, Henry snarled.

Ruthven pressed himself back against the wall. "I ordered a cask of brandy from him. Don't ask me how he smuggles it through the blockade because I don't know. He was to meet me tonight at Almack's, but he never came."

"What did Maxwell Aubrey give you?"

"Bouchard's address." As the wine once again overcame his fear—imitation willpower, Henry realized— Ruthven's scowl deepened. "I don't believe you *are* Death. You're nothing but a common cutpurse." His tone dripped disdain. "I shall call for the Watch."

"Go right ahead." Henry's hand darted forward, patted Ruthven's vest, and returned clutching Bouchard's address. Slipping the piece of paper into an inner pocket, he stepped back and merged with the night.

Varney would probably insist that Ruthven should die, but Henry suspected that nothing he said would be believed. Besides, if he told everyone he'd met Death in an alley, he wouldn't be far wrong.

As expected, Bouchard was not in his rooms.

And neither, upon returning to Portman Square, was Maxwell Aubrey. Snarling softly to himself, Henry listened to a distant watchman announce it was a fine night. At just past two, it was certainly early enough for Aubrey to have gone to one of his clubs, or to a gaming hall, or to a brothel. Unfortunately, all Henry knew of him was that he was an easily influenced young man. Brow furrowed, he'd half decided to head back toward St. James Street when he heard the crash of breaking branches coming from the park the square enclosed.

Curious, he walked over to the wrought-iron fence and peered up into an immense old oak. Believing himself familiar with every nuance of the night, he was astonished to see Aubrey perched precariously on a swaying limb, arms wrapped tightly around another, face nearly as white as his crumpled cravat.

"What the devil are you doing up there?" Henry demanded, beginning to feel that Captain Evans had sent him on a fool's mission. The night was rapidly taking on all the aspects of high farce.

Wide-eyed gaze searching the darkness for the source of the voice, Aubrey flashed a nervous smile in all directions. "Seeber dared me to spend a night in one of these trees," he explained ingenuously. Then he frowned. "You're not the Watch, are you?"

"No, I'm not the Watch."

"Good. That is, I imagine it would be hard to explain this to the Watch."

"I imagine it would be," Henry repeated dryly.

"You see, it's not as easy as it looks like it would be." He shifted position slightly and squeezed his eyes closed as the branch he sat on bobbed and swayed.

The man was an idiot and obviously not capable of being a French spy. Bouchard would have to be a *greater* idiot to trust so pliable a tool.

"I don't suppose you could help me down."

Henry considered it. "No," he said at last and walked away.

* * *

He found Sir William Wyndham, the last name on the list, and therefore the traitor by default, at White's playing deep basset. Carefully guarding his expression after Viscount Hanely had met him in a dimly lit hall and leaped away in terror, Henry declined all invitations to play. Much like a cat at a mouse hole, he watched and waited for Sir William to leave.

Unfortunately, Sir William was winning.

At five, lips drawn back off his teeth, Henry left the club. He could feel the approaching dawn and had to feed before the day claimed him. He had intended to feed upon Sir William, leaving him weak and easy prey for the captain's men—but Sir William obviously had no intention of leaving the table while his luck held.

The porter who handed Mr. Fitzroy his greatcoat and hat averted his gaze and spent the next hour successfully convincing himself that he hadn't seen what he knew he had.

Walking quickly through the dregs of the night, Henry returned to Albany but, rather than enter his own chambers, he continued to where he could gain access to the suite on the second floor. Entering silently through the large window, he crossed to the bed and stared down at its sleeping occupant.

George Gordon, the sixth Lord Byron, celebrated author of *Childe Harold's Pilgrimage,* was indeed a handsome young man. Henry had never seen him as having the ethereal and poignant beauty described by Caroline Lamb, but then, he realized, Caroline Lamb had never seen the poet with his hair in paper curlers.

His bad mood swept away by the rising Hunger, Henry sat down on the edge of the bed and softly called Byron's name, drawing him up but not entirely out of sleep.

The wide mouth curved into an anticipatory smile, murmuring, "Incubus," without quite waking.

"I don't like you going to see that poet," Varney muttered, carefully setting the buckled shoes to one side. "You're going to end up in trouble there, see if you don't."

"He thinks I'm a dream." Henry ran both hands back through his hair and grinned, remembering the curlers. So much for Byron's claim that the chestnut ringlets were natural. "What could possibly happen?"

"You could end up in one of his stories, that's what." Unable to read, Varney regarded books with a superstitious awe that bordered on fear. "The secret'd be out and some fine day it'd be the stake sure as I'm standing here." The little man drew himself up to his full height and fixed Henry with an indignant glare. "I told you before and I'll tell you again, you got yourself so mixed up in this society thing you're forgetting what you are! You got to stop taking so many chances." His eyes glittered. "Try and remember, most folks don't look kindly on the bloodsucking undead."

"I'll try and remember." Glancing up at his servant over steepled fingers, Henry added, "I've something for you to do today. I need Sir William Wyndham watched. If he's visited by someone named Yves Bouchard, go immediately to Captain Evans; he'll know what to do. If he tries to leave London, stop him."

Brows that crossed above Varney's nose in a continuous line lifted. "How stopped?"

"Stopped. Anything else, I want to be told at sunset."

"So, what did this bloke do that he's to be stopped?" Varney raised his hand lest Henry get the wrong idea. "Not that I won't stop him, mind, in spite of how I feel about you suddenly taking it into your head to track down evil doers. You know me, give me an order and I'll follow it."

"Which is why I found you almost dead in a swamp outside Plassey while the rest of your regiment was *inside* Plassey?"

"Not the same thing at all," the ex-soldier told him, pointedly waiting for the answer to his question.

"He sold out Wellington's army to the French."
Varney grunted. "Stopping's too good for him."

"Sir William Wyndham got a message this after-noon. Don't know what was in it, but he's going to be taking a trip to the coast tonight."

"Damn him!" Henry dragged his shirt over his head. "He's taking the information to Napoleon *him-self!*"

Varney shrugged and brushed invisible dust off a green-striped waistcoat. "I don't know about that, but if his coachman's to be trusted, he's heading for the coast right enough, as soon as the moon lights the road."

Henry stood on the steps of Sir William's town-house, considered his next move and decided the ris-ing moon left him no time to be subtle.

The butler who answered the imperious summons of the polished brass knocker opened his mouth to deny this inopportune visitor entry, but closed it again without making a sound.

"Take me to Sir William," Henry commanded.

Training held, but only just. "Very good, sir. If you would follow me." The butler's hand trembled slightly, but his carefully modulated voice gave no indication that he had just been shown his own mortality. "Sir William is in the library, sir. Through this door here. Shall I announce you?"

With one hand on the indicated door, Henry shook his head. "That won't be necessary. In fact, you should forget I was ever here."

Lost in the surprising dark depths of the visitor's pale eyes, the butler shuddered. "Thank you, sir. I will."

Three sets of branched candelabra lit the library, more than enough for Henry to see that the room held two large leather chairs, a number of hunting trophies, and very few books.

Sir William, dressed for travel in breeches and top

boots, stood leaning on the mantlepiece reading a single sheet of paper. He turned when he heard the door open and scowled when he saw who it was. "Fitzroy! What the devil are you doing here? I told Babcock I was not to be . . ."

Then his voice trailed off as he got a better look at Henry's face. There were a number of men in London he considered to be dangerous, but until this moment, he would not have included Henry Fitzroy among them. Forcing his voice past the growing panic he stammered, "W-what?"

"You dare to ask when you're holding *that!*" A pale hand shot forward to point at the paper in Wyndham's hand.

"This?" Confusion momentarily eclipsed the fear. "What has this to do with you?"

Henry charged across the room, grabbed a double handful of cloth, and slammed the traitor against the wall. "It has everything to do with me!"

"I didn't know! I swear to God I didn't know!" Hanging limp in Henry's grasp, Sir William made no struggle to escape. Every instinct screamed "RUN!" but a last vestige of reason realized he wouldn't get far. "If I'd known you were interested in her . . ."

"Who?"

"Carmilla Amworth."

Sir William crashed to his knees as Henry released him and stepped back. "So that's how you were going to hide it," he growled. "A seduction on your fabled yacht. Was a French boat to meet you in the channel?"

"A French boat?"

"Or were you planning on finding sanctuary with Napoleon? And what of Miss Amworth, compromised both by your lechery and your treason?"

"Treason?"

"Forcing her to marry you would gain you her fortune, but tossing her overboard would remove the only witness." Lips drawn back off his teeth, Henry buried his hand in Sir William's hair and forced his head back. Cravat and collar were thrown to the floor, exposing the muscular column of throat. "I don't know how you convinced her to accompany you, but it doesn't really matter now."

With the last of his strength, Sir William shoved the crumpled piece of paper in Henry's face, his life saved by the faint scent of a familiar perfume clinging to it.

Henry managed to turn aside only because he'd fed at dawn. His left hand clutching the note, his right still holding Sir William's hair, he straightened.

"*. . . I can no longer deny you but it must be tonight for reasons I cannot disclose at this time.*" It was signed, C. Amworth.

Frowning, he looked down into Sir William's face. If Carmilla had insisted that they leave for the yacht tonight, there could be only one answer. "Did Yves Bouchard suggest you seduce Miss Amworth?"

"I do not seduce young woman on the suggestion of acquaintances," Sir William replied as haughtily as possible under the circumstances. "However," he added hurriedly as the hazel eyes locked onto his began to darken, "Bouchard may have mentioned she was not only rich but ripe for the plucking."

So, there was the Bouchard connection. Caught between the two men, Carmilla Amworth was being used by both. By Bouchard to gain access to Wyndham's yacht and therefore France. By Wyndham to gain access to her fortune. And that seemed to be all that Sir William was guilty of. Still frowning, Henry stepped back. "Well, if you didn't steal the document," he growled, "who did?"

"I did." As he turned, Carmilla pointed a small but eminently serviceable pistol at him. "I've been waiting in Sir William's carriage these last few moments and when no one emerged, I let myself in. Stay right where you are, Mr. Fitzroy," she advised, no longer looking either fragile or waiflike. "I am held to be a very good shot." Her calm gaze took in the positions of the two men and she suddenly smiled, dimples appearing in both cheeks. "Were you fighting for my honor?"

Lips pressed into a thin line, Henry bowed his head. "Until I discovered you had none."

The smile disappeared. "I was raised a republican, Mr. Fitzroy, and I find the thought of that fat fool returning to the throne of France to be ultimately distasteful. In time . . ." Her eyes blazed. ". . . I'll help England be rid of her own fat fool."

"You think the English will rise and overthrow the royal family?"

"I know they will."

"If they didn't rise when m . . ." About to say, *my father,* he hastily corrected himself. ". . . when King Henry burned Catholic and Protestant indiscriminately in the street, what makes you think they'll rise now?"

Her delicate chin lifted. "The old ways are finished. It's long past time for things to change."

"And does your uncle believe as you do?"

"My uncle knows nothing. His little niece would come visiting him at his office and little bits of paper would leave with her." The scornful laugh had as much resemblance to the previous giggles as night to day. "I'd love to stand around talking politics with you, but I haven't the time." Her lavender kid glove tightened around the butt of one of Manton's finest. "There'll be a French boat meeting Sir William's yacht very early tomorrow morning, and I have information I must deliver."

"You used me!" Scowling, Sir William got slowly to his feet. "I don't appreciate being used." He took a step forward, but Henry stopped him with a raised hand.

"You're forgetting the pistol."

"The pistol?" Wyndham snorted. "No woman would have the fortitude to kill a man in cold blood."

Remembering how both his half-sisters had held the throne, Henry shook his head. "You'd be surprised. However," he fixed Carmilla with an inquiring stare, "we seem to be at a standstill as you certainly can't shoot both of us."

"True. But I'm sure both of you *gentlemen* . . ." The emphasis was less than complimentary. ". . . will cooperate lest I shoot the other."

"I'm afraid you're going to shoot no one." Suddenly behind her, Henry closed one hand around her wrist and the other around the barrel of the gun. He had moved between one heartbeat and the next; impossible to see, impossible to stop.

"What are you?" Carmilla whispered, her eyes painfully wide in a face blanched of color.

His smile showed teeth. "A patriot." He'd been within a moment of killing Sir William, ripping out his throat and feasting on his life. His anger had been kicked sideways by Miss Amworth's entrance and he supposed he should thank her for preventing an unredeemable faux pas. "Sir William, if you could have your footman go to the house of Captain Charles Evans on Charges Street, I think he'll be pleased to know we've caught his traitor."

". . . so they came and took the lady away, but that still doesn't explain where you've been 'til nearly sunup."

"I was with Sir William. We had unfinished business."

Varney snorted, his disapproval plain. "Oh. It was like that, was it?"

Henry smiled as he remembered the feel of Sir William's hair in his hand and the heat rising off his kneeling body.

Well aware of what the smile meant, Varney snorted again. "And did Sir William ask what you were?"

"Sir William would never be so impolite. He thinks we fought over Carmilla, discovered she was a traitor, drank ourselves nearly senseless, and parted the best of friends." Feeling the sun poised on the horizon, Henry stepped into his bedchamber and turned to close the door on the day. "Besides, Sir William doesn't *want* to know what I am."

*   *   *

"Got some news for you." Varney worked up a lather on the shaving soap. "Something happened today."

Resplendent in a brocade dressing gown, Henry leaned back in his chair and reached for the razor. "I imagine that something happens every day."

"Well *today,* that Carmilla Amworth slipped her chain and run off."

"She escaped from custody?"

"That's what I said. Seems they underestimated her, her being a lady and all. Still, she's missed her boat, so even if she gets to France, she'll be too late. You figure that's where she's heading?"

"I wouldn't dare to hazard a guess." Henry frowned and wiped the remaining lather off his face. "Is everyone talking about it?"

"That she was a French spy? Not likely, they're all too busy talking about how she snuck out of Lady Glebe's party and into Sir William's carriage." He clucked his tongue. "The upper classes have got dirty minds, that's what I say."

"Are you including me in that analysis?"

Varney snorted. "Ask your poet. All I say about you is that you've got to take more care. So you saved Wellington's army. Good for you. Now . . ." he held out a pair of biscuit-colored pantaloons. ". . . do you think you could act a little more suitable to your condition?"

"I don't recall ever behaving *unsuitably.*"

"Oh, aye, dressing up so fine and dancing and going to the theater and sitting about playing cards at clubs for *gentlemen.*" His emphasis sounded remarkably like that of Carmilla Amworth.

"Perhaps you'd rather I wore grave clothes and we lived in a mausoleum?"

"No, but . . ."

"A drafty castle somewhere in the mountains of eastern Europe?"

Varney sputtered incoherently.

Henry sighed and deftly tied his cravat. "Then let's hear no more about me forgetting who and what I am. I'm very sorry if you wanted someone a little more darkly tragic. A brooding, mythic persona who only emerges to slake his thirst on the fair throats of helpless virgins . . ."

"Here now! None of that!"

"But I'm afraid you're stuck with me." Holding out his arms, he let Varney help him into his jacket. "And I am almost late for an appointment at White's. I promised Sir William a chance to win back his eleven hundred pounds."

His sensibilities obviously crushed, Varney ground his teeth.

"Now, what's the matter?"

The little man shook his head. "It just doesn't seem right that you, with all you could be, should be worried about being late for a card game."

His expression stern, Henry took hold of Varney's chin, and held the servants' gaze with his. "I think *you* forget who I am." His fingertips dimpled stubbled flesh. "I am a Lord of Darkness, a Creature of the Night, an Undead Fiend with Unnatural Appetites, indeed a *Vampyre;* but all of that . . ." His voice grew deeper and Varney began to tremble. ". . . is no excuse for bad manners."

Author's Note:

The real Henry Fitzroy, Duke of Richmond, bastard son of Henry VIII, died at seventeen on July 22, 1536, of what modern medicine thinks was probably tuberculosis. Modern medicine, however, has no explanation for why the Duke of Norfolk was instructed to smuggle the body out of St. James's Palace and bury it secretly.

All things considered, who's to say he stayed buried?

The Cards Also Say

Surveying Queen Street West from her favorite perch on the roof of the six-story CITY TV Building, Vicki Nelson fidgeted as she watched the pre-theater crowds spill from trendy restaurants. Usually able to sit, predator-patient, for hours on end, she had no idea why she was suddenly so restless.

Old instincts honed by eight years with the Metropolitan Toronto Police and two years on her own as a PI suggested there was something wrong, something she'd seen or heard. Something was out of place, and it nagged at her subconscious, demanding first recognition then action.

Apparently, observation wouldn't tell her what she needed to know; she had to participate in the night.

Crossing to the rear of the building, she climbed swiftly down the art deco ornamentation until she could drop the last ten feet into the alley below. Barely noticing the familiar stink of old urine, she straightened her clothes and stepped out onto John Street.

A dark-haired young man who'd been leaning on the side of the building straightened and turned toward her. *Hooker,* Vicki thought, then, as she drew closer and realized there was nothing of either sex or commerce in the young man's expression, revised her opinion.

"My grandmother wants to see you," he said matter-of-factly as she came along beside him.

Vicki stopped and stared. "To see me?"

"Yeah. You." Running the baby fingernail on his

right hand over the fuzzy beginning of a mustache, he avoided her gaze and in a bored tone recited, "Tall, fair, dressed like a man . . ."

Brows raised, Vicki glanced down at her black corduroy jacket, faded jeans, and running shoes.

". . . coming out of the alley behind the white TV station." Finished, he shrugged and added, "Looks like you. Looks like the place. You coming or not?" His posture clearly indicated that he didn't care either way. "She says if you don't want to come with me, I've got to say night walker."

Not night walker as he pronounced it, two separate words, but Nightwalker.

Vampire.

"Do you have a car?"

In answer, he nodded toward an old Camaro parked under the NO PARKING sign, continuing to avoid her gaze so adroitly, it seemed he'd been warned.

They made the trip up Bathurst Street to Bloor in complete silence. Vicki waited until she could ask her questions of someone more likely to know the answers. The young man seemed to have nothing to say.

He stopped the car just past Bloor and Euclid and, oblivious to the horns beginning to blow behind him, jerked his head toward the north side of the street. "In there."

At the other end of the gesture was a small storefront. Painted in brilliant yellow script over a painting of a classic horse-drawn Gypsy caravan were the words: *Madame Luminitsa, Fortune Teller. Sees Your Future in Cards, Palms, or Tea Leaves.* Behind the glass, a crimson curtain kept the curious from attempting to glimpse the future for free.

The door was similarly curtained and held a sign that listed business hours as well as an explanation that Madame Luminitsa dealt only in cash, having seen too many bad credit cards. As Vicki pushed it open and stepped into a small waiting room, she heard a buzzer sound in the depths of the building.

The waiting room reminded her of a baroque doctor's office, with, she noted, glancing down at the glass-topped coffee table, one major exception—the magazines were current. The place was empty not only of customers but also of the person who usually sat behind the official-looking desk in the corner of the room. There were two interior doors: one behind the desk, one in the middle of the back wall. Soft background music with an Eastern European sound, combined with three working incense burners, set the mood.

Vicki sneezed and listened for the nearest heartbeat.

A group in the back of the building caught her attention but couldn't hold it when she became aware of the two lives just behind the back wall. One beat slowly and steadily, the other raced, caught in the grip of some strong emotion. As Vicki listened, the second heartbeat began to calm.

It sounded very nearly post-coital.

"Must've got good news," she muttered, crossing to the desk.

The desktop had nothing on it but a phone and half a pad of yellow legal paper. About to start searching the drawers, Vicki moved quickly away when she heard the second door begin to open.

A slim man with a distinctly receding hairline and slightly protuberant eyes emerged first, a sheet of crumpled yellow paper clutched in one hand. "You don't know what this means to me," he murmured.

"I have a good idea." The middle-aged woman behind him smiled broadly enough to show a gold-capped molar. "I'm pleased that I could help."

"Help?" he repeated. "You've done more than help. You've opened my eyes. I've got to get home and get started."

He rushed past Vicki without seeing her. As the outer door closed behind him, she took a step forward. "Madame Luminitsa, I presume?"

Flowered skirt swirling around her calves, the woman strode purposefully toward the desk. "Do you have an appointment?"

Vicki shook her head. Under other circumstances, she'd have been amused by the official trappings to what was, after all, an elaborate way to exploit the unlimited ability of people to be self-deluded. "Someone's grandmother wants to see me."

"Ah. So you're the one." She showed no more interest than the original messenger had. "Wait here."

Since it seemed to be the only way she'd find out what was going on, Vicki dropped down onto a corner of the desk and waited while Madame Luminitsa went back into the rear of the building. Although strange things seemed to be afoot, she'd learned to trust her instincts and she didn't think she was in danger.

The Romani, as a culture, were more than willing to exploit the greed and/or stupidity of the *gadje,* or non-Rom, but they were also culturally socialized to avoid violence whenever possible. During the eight years she'd spent on the police force, Vicki had never heard of an incident where one of Toronto's extensive Romani communities had started a fight. Finished a couple, yes, but never started one.

Still, someone here had named her Nightwalker.

When the door opened again, the woman framed within it bore a distinct family resemblance to Madame Luminitsa. There were slight differences in height and weight and coloring—a little shorter, a little rounder, a little grayer—but a casual observer would have had difficulty telling them apart. Vicki was not a casual observer, and she slowly stood as the dark gaze swept over her. The Hunger rose in recognition of a challenging power.

"Good. Now we know who we are, we can put it aside and get on with things." The woman's voice held a faint trace of Eastern Europe. "You'd best come in." She stepped aside, leaving the way to the inner room open.

Curiosity overcoming her instinctive reaction, Vicki slipped a civilized mask back into place and did as suggested.

The inner room was a quarter the size of the outer.

The ceiling had been painted navy blue and sprinkled with day-glo stars. Multicolored curtains fell from the stars to the floor and on each wall an iron bracket supporting a round light fixture thrust through the folds. In the center of the room, taking up most of the available floor space, was a round table draped in red between two painted chairs. Shadows danced in every corner and every fold of fabric.

"Impressive," Vicki acknowledged. "Definitely sets the mood. But I'm not here to have my fortune told."

"We'll see." Indicating the second chair, the woman sat down.

Vicki sat as well. "Your grandson neglected to give me your name."

"You can call me Madame Luminitsa."

"Another one?"

The fortune teller shrugged. "We are all Madame Luminitsa if business is good enough. My sister, our daughters, their daughters . . ."

"You?"

"Not usually."

"Why not?" Vicki asked dryly. "Your predictions don't come true?"

"On the contrary." She folded her hands on the table, the colored stones in the rings that decorated six of eight fingers flashing in the light. "Some people can't take a dump without asking advice—Madame Luminitsa gives them a glimpse of the future they want. I give them the future they're going to get."

Arms crossed, Vicki snorted. "You're telling me you can really see the future?"

"I saw you, Nightwalker. I saw where you'd be this evening. I sent for you and you came."

Which was, undeniably, unpleasantly, true. "For all that, you seem pretty calm about what I am."

"I'm used to seeing what others don't." Her expression darkened again for a moment as though she were gazing at a scene she'd rather not remember, then she shook her head and half-smiled. "If you know your

history, Nightwalker—my people and your people
have worked together in the past."

Vicki had a sudden vision of Gypsies filling boxes
of dirt to keep their master safe on his trip to England.
The memory bore the distinctive stamp of an old Hammer film. She returned the half-smile, another fraction
of trust gained. "The one who changed me said that
Bram Stoker was a hack."

"He got a few things right. The Romani were en-
slaved in that part of the world for many years and
we had masters who made Bram Stoker's count seem
like a lovely fellow." Her voice held no bitterness at
the history. It was over, done; they'd moved on and
wouldn't waste the energy necessary to hold a grudge.
"I've seen you're no danger to me, Nightwalker. As
for the others . . ." The deliberate pause held a clear
warning. ". . . they don't know."

"All right." It was an acknowledgment more than
agreement. "So why did you send for me?"

"I saw something."

"In my future?"

"Yes."

Vicki snorted, attempting to ignore the hair lifting
off the back of her neck. "A tall, dark stranger?"

"Yes."

Good cops learned to tell when people were lying.
It wasn't a skill vampires needed; no one lied to them.
So far, Vicki had been told only the truth—or at least
the truth as Madame Luminitsa believed it. Unfortu-
nately, truth tended to be just a tad fluid when spoken
Romani to *gadje*.

The other woman sighed. "Would you feel better if
I said that I saw a short, fair stranger?"

"Did you?"

"No. The stranger that I saw was tall and dark, and
he is dangerous. To you and to my family."

Now this meeting began to make sense. Intensely
loyal to their extended families and clans, the Romani
would never go to this much trouble for a mere *gadje*,

even, or especially, if that *gadje* was a member of the
bloodsucking undead. Self-interest, however, Vicki understood. "I'm listening."

"It isn't easy to always see, so I look only enough
to keep my family safe. This afternoon I laid out the
cards, and I saw you and I saw danger approaching
as a tall, dark man. Cliché," she shrugged, "but true.
If you fall, this stranger will grow so strong that when
he turns his hate on other targets, he will be almost
invincible."

"And the danger to you?"

"He hates you because you're different. You haven't
hurt him or anyone near him, but neither are you like
him." Madame Luminitsa paused, glanced around the
room, and spread her hands. "We are also different,
and we work hard at keeping it that way. In the old
days, we could have taken to the roads, but now we,
as much as you, are sitting targets."

"You're sure he's just a man?" Vicki asked, twisting
a pinch of the tablecloth between thumb and forefinger. She'd met a demon once and didn't want to again.

"*Just* a man? Men do by choice what demons do
by nature."

Vicki'd spent too much time in Violent Crimes to
argue with that. "You've got to give me more to go
on than tall, dark, and male."

From a pocket in her skirt or perhaps a shelf under
the table, Madame Luminitsa pulled out a deck of
tarot cards. "I can."

"Oh, come on . . ."

Shuffling the cards with a dexterity that spoke of
long practice, the older woman ignored her. She placed
the shuffled deck in the center of the table. "With
your left hand, cut the cards into three piles to your
left," she said.

Vicki stared down at the cards, then up at the fortune teller. "I don't think so."

"Cut the cards if you want to live."

Put like that, it was pretty hard to refuse.

Tarot cards had made a brief surge into popular culture while Vicki'd been a university student. A number of the girls she knew laid out patterns at every opportunity. Vicki'd considered it more important to maintain her average than to take the time to learn the symbolism. She also considered most of the kerchiefed, sandaled, skirted amateur fortune tellers to be complete flakes. As a history major, she was fully aware of the persecutions the Romani had gone through for centuries, persecutions that had started up with renewed vigor after the fall of the Iron Curtain, and she was at a loss to understand why anyone would consider the life of the caravans to be romantic.

The pattern Madame Luminitsa laid out was a familiar one. "Aren't you supposed to start by picking a card out to stand for me?"

"Do I tell you your business?"

"Uh, no."

"Then don't tell me mine." She laid down the tenth card, set the unused part of the deck carefully to one side, and sat back in her chair, her eyes never leaving the brightly colored rectangles spread out in front of her. "The Three of Swords sets an atmosphere of loss. Reversed, the Emperor covers it; a weak man but one who will take action. In his past, the star reversed; physical or mental illness."

"Wait a minute, I thought this was my reading."

"It's a reading to help you find the stranger before he can strike."

"Oh." Vicki reached into the inside pocket of her jacket for the small notebook and pen. She carried the old massive shoulder bag less and less these days. Somehow a purse, even one of luggage dimensions, just didn't seem vampiric. "Maybe I should be writing this down."

Madame Luminitsa waited until the first three cards had been recorded and then went on. "He has just set aside his material life."

"Fired from his job?"

"I don't know, but now he does other, more spiritual things."

"How can destroying me be spiritual?"

"He believes he's removing evil from the world."

"And what will be believe when he goes after your people?"

"For some, different is enough to be considered evil. He's about to come to a decision; you haven't much time."

"Or much information."

"You're here, in his recent past. I suspect you took his blood and the mental illness kept the shadows you command from blotting the memory. The Page of Swords—here—means he's watching you. Spying, learning your patterns before he strikes."

She remembered the feeling that something was wrong, out of place. "Great. Like I've only ever fed off one tall dark man, unstable and unemployed."

"There's only one watching you."

"That makes me feel so much better."

"Ace of Wands, reversed. He's likely to make one unsuccessful attempt before you're in any actual danger. He's afraid of being alone, and he's created this purpose to fill the void. He has no family. No friends. But look here . . ."

Vicki obediently bent forward.

". . . the Nine of Wands. He has prepared for this. In the final outcome, he is dead to reason. Don't argue with him, stop him."

"Kill him?"

Madame Luminitsa shuffled the cards back into the deck. "That's up to you, Nightwalker."

Tapping her pen against the paper, Vicki glanced over her list. "So I'm looking for a tall, dark, unstable, unemployed, lonely man with sawdust in his cuffs from sharpening stakes, who remembers me feeding from him and has been spying on me ever since. He'll make an attempt he won't carry through all the way, but when push comes to shove, I won't be able to talk him out of destroying me and may have to destroy him first." When she looked up, her eyes had silvered slightly. "How do I know you're not setting me up to destroy an enemy of yours?"

"You don't."

"How do I know you didn't deliberately mislead me so that you can destroy me yourself?"

"You don't."

"So, essentially, what you're saying is, I have to trust that you, and this whole fortune-telling thing, are on the level."

The Romani's eyes reflected bits of silver; the physical manifestation of Vicki's power stopped at the surface. "Yes."

"Vicki, get real! These are Gypsies, they live for the elaborate scam."

"Not this time, Mike." Swiveling out into the room, she tipped back her desk chair and frowned up at him. "Even if your stereotyping was accurate, this wasn't a scam. Madame Luminitsa needs me to protect her family. That's the only possible reason strong enough for her to even deal with me. If my danger wasn't her danger as well, I'd be facing it on my own."

"So she wants something from you."

Beginning to wish she'd never told him how she'd spent her evening, Vicki closed her eyes and counted to ten. "Yes, she does. And so she's no different than any of my other clients who want something from me except that she's paid in full, in advance, by warning me of the danger that I'm in."

"You want to know what danger you're in?" Detective-Sergeant Michael Celluci stopped pacing and turned to glare at the woman in the chair. He'd loved her when they'd been together on the police force, he'd loved her when a degenerative eye disease had forced her to quit a job she'd excelled at and start over as a private investigator, and he'd continued to love her even after she'd become an undead, blood-sucking creature of the night—*but* there were times, and this was one of them, when he wanted to wring her neck. "This fortune teller knows what you are, and what one Gypsy knows, they all do."

"Romani."

"What?"

"Most prefer to be called Romani, not Gypsy."

He threw up his hands. "What difference does that make?"

"Well, let's see . . ." Her voice dripped sarcasm. "How would you like to be called a dumb, bigoted wop?"

Celluci's eyes narrowed and, over the angry pounding of his heart, Vicki could hear him breathing heavily through his nose. "Fine. Romani. Whatever. They still know what you are, and therefore they know you're completely helpless during the day. I want you to move back in with me."

"So you can protect me?"

"Yes!" He spat out the word, defying the reaction he knew she'd have.

To his surprise, there was no explosion.

As much touched as irritated by his concern, Vicki sighed impatiently and said, "Mike, do you honestly think that a plywood box in your basement is safer than this apartment?" The converted warehouse space boasted a barred window, a steel door, industrial strength locks, and an enclosed loft with an access so difficult even Celluci didn't attempt it on his own. The safety features had been designed by a much older vampire who'd made one fatal error—she hadn't realized that the territory was already taken.

Slowly, Celluci sank down onto the arm of the sofa. "No. I don't."

"And it's not like you're home all day."

"I know. It's just . . ."

Vicki rolled her office chair out from under the edge of the loft, stopping only when they were knee to knee. She reached out and pushed an overlong curl of hair back off his face. "I'm not saying that I won't ever move back, Mike, just not now. Not because a mentally unstable, unemployed blood donor thinks he's a modern Van Helsing."

He caught her hand, the skin cool against his palm. "And the Gy . . . the Romani?"

"From what I understand about their culture, Madame Luminitsa's abilities make her a bit of an outsider already, and she won't risk being named *marhime* . . . a kind of social/cultural exile," she added when Mike's brows went up, "by telling her family she's dealing with a vampire."

"All right." Releasing his grip, he pushed her chair far enough away to give him room to stand. "So how do we stop this Van Helsing of yours?"

"I love it when you get all macho," she purred, rubbing her foot up his inseam. Before he could react, she scooted back to the office, the chair's wheels protesting her speed. "According to the cards, he's prepared. You could check with the B&E guys to see if anyone's reported stolen holy water."

"Holy water?"

"Madame Luminitsa said he thinks of me as evil and holy water is one of the traditional, albeit ineffectual, ways to melt a vampire."

"How the hell would someone steal holy water?"

"Don't you ever watch movies, Mike?" She mimed filling a water pistol. "Ask them about communion wafers, too."

"Communion wafers?" He sighed and looked at his watch. "Fine. Whatever. Patterson's on evenings this week and he owes me a favor. It's only a quarter past eleven, so if I leave in the next few minutes, I'll catch him at Headquarters before he heads home."

"Great—I'll make this next bit quick. Since the cards also pointed out that our stalker's recently unemployed, a homicide detective with an open case involving the shooting of two counselors at a Canada Manpower center last month would have a reason to ask for a printout of everyone who'd recently applied for unemployment insurance."

"The guy who did the shooting could've been unemployed for years."

"You don't know that."

"Okay, let's say I come up with a plausible story and get the list—would you recognize the name of a . . ." He paused. This aspect of her life wasn't something they spoke about. Intellectually, Celluci knew he couldn't fulfill all her needs, but he chose to ignore what that actually meant. ". . . dinner companion."

"I don't know. Do you remember what you had for dinner every night for the last month?"

His lip curled into an expression approximating a smile. "Any other time, I'd be pleased you thought so little of them; this time, it's damned inconvenient. If you won't recognize his name, why do you want to see the list?"

"I *might* recognize his name," Vicki corrected. "But mostly I want to see the list to compare it to . . ." She paused and decided Detective-Sergeant Michael Celluci would be happier not knowing about the list she planned on comparing it to.

Unlike the unemployment office, the Queen Street Mental Health Center was open more or less twenty-four hours a day—recent government cutbacks having redefined the word open.

Vicki watched from the shadows as the old woman wearing a plastic hospital bracelet shuffled into the circle of light by the glass doors, cringed as the street-car went by, pushed a filthy palm against the buzzer, and left it there. She'd been easy enough to find—this part of the city had an embarrassment of riches when it came to the lost—but less than easy to control. Those parts of the human psyche that responded to the danger, to the forbidden sensuality that the vampire represented, were so inaccessible they might as well not have existed. Vicki'd finally given her ten bucks and told her, in words of one syllable, what she needed done.

Sometimes, the old ways worked best.

Eventually, an orderly appeared, shaking his head as if the motion would disconnect the incessant buzzing. Peering through the wired glass, his frown segued into annoyed recognition. "Damn it, Helen," he muttered as he opened the door. "Stop leaning on the fucking buzzer."

Vicki slipped inside while he dealt with the old woman.

When he turned, the door closing behind him, she was there: her eyes silver, her smile very white, the Hunger rising.

"I need you to do me a favor," she said.

He swallowed convulsively as she ran her thumb lightly down the muscles of his throat.

Sometimes, the new ways worked best.

When the approaching dawn drove her home, Vicki carried a list of recent discharges from Queen Street and a similar list from the Clark Institute. All she needed was Celluci's list from UIC to make comparisons. With luck there'd be names in common, names with addresses she could visit until she recognized the distinctive signature of a life she'd fed on.

Her pair of lists were depressingly long and, given the current economic climate in Mike Harris' Ontario, she expected the third to be no shorter. Searching them would take most of a night and checking the names in common could easily take another two or three nights after that.

Unlocking her door, Vicki hoped they'd have the time. Madame Luminitsa had seemed convinced the wacko in the cards was about to make his move.

The apartment was dark, but the shadows were familiar. Nothing lurked in the corners except dust bunnies not quite big enough to be a danger.

After locking and then barring the door with a two by four painted to match the wall—unsophisticated safety measures were often the most effective—Vicki hurried toward the loft, fighting to keep her shoulders from hunching forward as she felt the day creep up behind her. Almost safe within her sanctuary, she looked down and saw the light flashing on her answering machine. She hesitated. The sun inched closer toward the horizon.

"Oh, damn." Unable to let it go, she swung back down to the floor.

"Vicki, Mike. St. Paul's Anglican on Bloor reported a break-in last Tuesday afternoon. The only thing missing was a box of communion wafers. If he drained the holy water as well, they didn't bother reporting it. Looks like you were right." His sigh seemed to take up a good ten seconds of tape. "There's no point in telling you to be careful but could you please . . ."

She couldn't wait for the end of the message. The sun was too close. Throwing herself up and into the loft, she barred that door as well and sank back onto the bed.

The seconds, moving so quickly a moment before, slowed.

There were sounds, all around her, Vicki couldn't remember ever hearing before. Outside, in the alley— was that someone climbing toward her window?

No. Pigeons.

That vibration in the wall—a drill?

No. The distant ring of a neighbor's alarm.

In spite of her vulnerability, she had never faced the dawn wondering if she'd see the dusk—until today. She didn't like the feeling.

"Maybe I *should* move back into Celluci's ba . . ."

Vicki hated spending the day in her clothes. She had a long hot shower to wash away the creases and listened to another message from Celluci suggesting she check out the church as he'd be at work until after midnight. ". . . and don't bother feeding, you can grab a bite when I get there."

"Like *that's* going to speed things up?" she muttered, shrugging into her jacket as the tape rewound. "Feeding from you isn't exactly fast food."

Quite the contrary.

Deciding to grab a snack on the street, or they'd

never get to those lists, Vicki set aside the two by four and opened her door. Out in the hallway, key in hand, she stared down at the lower of the two locks. It smelled like latex. Like a glove intended to hide fingerprints.

She jumped as the door opened across the hall.

"Hey, sweetie. Did he scratch the paint?"

"Did who scratch the paint, Lloyd?"

"Well, when I got home this P.M. I saw some guy on his knees foolin' with your lock. I yelled, and he fled." Ebony arms draped in a blue silk kimono, crossed over a well-muscled chest. "I knocked, but you didn't wake up."

"I've told you before, Lloyd, I work nights and I'm a heavy sleeper." It seemed that pretty soon she'd have to reinforce the message. "Can you tell me what this guy looked like?"

Lloyd shrugged. "White guy. Tall, dark, dressed all in black, but not like he was makin' a fashion statement, you know? I didn't get a good look at his face, but I can tell you, I've never seen him before." He paused and suddenly smiled. "I guess he was a tall, dark stranger. Pretty funny, eh?"

"Not really."

"He's likely to make one unsuccessful attempt before you're in any actual danger."

He'd made his attempt.

"The Page of Swords—here—means he's watching you."

He knew what she was, and he knew where she lived.

"Well, that sucks," Vicki muttered, standing on the front step of the converted factory, scanning the street.

Something was out of place, and it nagged at her subconscious, demanding first recognition then action.

At some point during the last few nights, she'd seen him, or been aware of him watching her. A little desperately, she searched for the touch of a life she'd shared, however briefly, but the city defeated her.

There were a million lives around and such a tenuous familiarity got lost in the roar.

Another night, she'd have walked to St. Paul's. Tonight, she flagged a cab and hoped her watching stranger had to run like hell to keep up.

It had been some years since churches in the city had been able to leave their doors unlocked after dark; penitent souls looking for God had to make do with twenty-four-hour donut shops. Ignoring the big double doors that faced the bright lights of Bloor Street, Vicki slipped around to the back of the old stone building and one of the less obvious entrances. To her surprise, the door was unlocked.

When she pulled it open, she realized why. Choir practice. Keeping to the shadows, she made her way up and into the back of the church. There were bodies in the pews, family and friends of those singing, and, standing off to one side, an elderly minister—or perhaps St. Paul's was high enough Anglican that they called him a priest.

Vicki waited until the hymn ended, then tapped the minister on the shoulder and asked if she could have a quiet word. She used only enough power to get the information she wanted—when he assumed she was with the police, she encouraged him to think it.

The communion wafers had been kept in a locked cupboard in the church office. Time and use had erased any scent Vicki might have recognized.

"No, nothing else," the minister said confidently when she asked if anything else had been taken.

"What about holy water?"

He glanced up at her in some surprise. "Funny you should mention that." Relocking the cupboard, he led the way out of the office. "We had a baptism on Thursday evening—three families, two babies and an adult—or I might never have noticed. When I took the lid off the font, just before the service, the water level was lower than it should have been—I knew because I'd been the one to fill it, you see—and I found a cuff button caught on the lip." Opening the door to his own office, he crossed to the desk. "It's a heavy lid and anyone trying to scoop the water out, for heaven only knows what reason, would have to hold it up one-handed. Easy enough to get your shirt caught, I imagine. Ah, here it is."

Plucking a white button out of an empty ashtray, he turned and dropped it in Vicki's palm. "The sad thing is, you know, this probably makes the thief one of ours."

"Why?"

"Well, the Catholics keep holy water by the door; it's a whole lot easier to get to. If he went to all this trouble, he was probably on familiar ground. Will that button help you catch him, do you think?"

Vicki smiled, forgetting for a moment the effect it was likely to have. "Oh, yes, I think it will."

She had the cab wait out front while she ran into her apartment for the pair of lists, then had it drop her off in front of Madame Luminitsa's.

Which was closed.

Fortunately, there were lights on upstairs and there could be no mistaking the unique signature of the fortune teller's life. Fully aware she was not likely to be welcomed with open arms and not really caring, Vicki went around back.

She'd never seen so many large cars in so many states of disrepair as were parked in the alley that theoretically provided delivery access for the stores. Squeezing between an old blue delivery van and a cream-colored caddy, she stood at the door and listened: eight heartbeats, upstairs and down, three of them children, one of them the woman she was looking for. There were a number of ways she could gain an audience—Stoker had been wrong about that, she no more needed to be invited in than an encyclopedia salesman—but, deciding it might be best to cause the least amount of offense, she merely knocked on the door.

The man who opened it was large. Not tall exactly, nor exactly fat—large. A drooping mustache, almost too black to be real, covered his upper lip and he stroked it with the little finger of his right hand as he looked her up and down, waiting for her to speak.

"I'm looking for Madame Luminitsa," Vicki told him, masks carefully in place. "It's very important."

"Madame Luminitsa is not available. The shop is closed."

She could feel the Hunger beginning to rise, remembered she'd intended to feed and hadn't. "I saw her last night; she sent for me."

"Ah. You." His expression became frankly speculative, and Vicki wondered just how much Madame Luminitsa *had* told her family. Without turning his head, he raised his voice. "One of you, fetch your grandmother."

Vicki heard a chair pushed out and the sound of small feet running up a flight of stairs. "Thank you."

He shrugged. "She may not come. In the meantime, do you own a car?"

"Uh, no."

"Then I can sell you one of these." An expansive gesture and a broad smile reserved for prospective customers indicated the vehicles crowding the alley. "You won't find a better price in all of Toronto, and I will personally vouch for the quality of each and every one." A huge hand reached out and slapped the hood of the blue van. "Brand new engine, eight cylinders, more power than . . ."

"Look, I'm not interested." Not unless that tall, dark stranger gave her a chance to run him over.

"Later then, after the cards have been played out."

A small, familiar hand covered in rings reached out into the doorway and shoved the big man aside. He glanced down at the woman Vicki knew as Madame Luminitsa and hurriedly stepped back into the building, closing the door behind him.

"You haven't stopped him," the fortune teller said bluntly.

"Give me a break," Vicki snorted. "I have to find him first. And I think you can help me with that."

"The cards . . ."

"Not the cards." She pulled the lists from her shoulder bag and fished the button out of a pocket. "This was his. If his name's here, shouldn't it help you find him?"

The dark brows rose. "You watch too much television, Nightwalker." But she took the pile of fanfold and the button. "Has he made his first attempt?"

"Yeah. He has."

"Then there's a need to hurry."

"No shit, Sherlock," Vicki muttered as the fortune teller slipped back inside.

She acted as though she hadn't heard, declaring imperiously as the door closed, "I'll let you know what I find."

The door was unlocked, but since Vicki could hear Celluci's heartbeat inside her apartment, she wasn't concerned. She *was* surprised to hear another life besides his, both hearts beating hard and fast. They'd obviously been arguing; not an unusual occurrence around the detective.

He'd probably pulled a late duty and, when she hadn't answered his calls, had thought she was in trouble and brought his partner in with him for backup, just in case. It wasn't hard for Vicki to follow his logic. If they were too late to save her, explanations wouldn't matter. If they were in time, she could easily clear up the confusion he'd caused poor Detective-Sergeant Graham.

Stepping into the apartment, she froze just over the threshold, eyes widening in disbelief. "You've got to be kidding."

"Snuck up on me in the parking lot," Celluci growled, glaring up at the man holding his own gun to his head. "Shoved a pad of chloroform under my nose and jabbed me with a pin so I'd inhale." Muscles strained as he fought to free his hands from the frame of the chair. "Used my own goddamed handcuffs, too."

"Shut up! Both of you!" He was probably in his midforties, with short black hair and a beard lightly dusted with gray, tall enough from the fortune teller's point of view. White showed all around the brown eyes locked on Vicki's face. His free hand pointed toward the door, trembling slightly with the effect of strong emotions. "Close it."

Without turning, she pushed it shut, gently so that the latch didn't quite catch; then she let the Hunger rise. He'd made a big mistake not attacking her in the day when she was vulnerable. Her eyes grew paler than his, and her voice went past command to compulsion. "Let him go."

Celluci shuddered, but the man with the gun only laughed shrilly. "You have no power over me! You never have! You never will!" He met her gaze and, even through the Hunger, she saw that he was right. Like the woman she'd used to gain access to Queen Street, he had no levels of darkness or desire she could touch. Everything inside his head had been locked tightly away, and she didn't have the key. She couldn't command him, so in spite of Madame Luminitsa's belief that she couldn't reason with him, she reined in the Hunger and let the silver fade from her eyes.

"Let him go," she said again. "You have me."

"But I can't keep you without him." The muzzle of the gun dug a circle into Celluci's cheek. "You can't leave, or I'll blow his freakin' head off."

She'd forgotten that she had another vulnerability besides the day. "If you kill him, I'll rip your living heart out of your chest, and I'll make you eat it while you . . ."

"Vicki."

He laughed again as Celluci protested. "You can't get to me, before I can pull the trigger. As long as I have him, I have you."

"So we have a standoff," she said. The silver rose

unbidden to her eyes. "Do you think you can out-wait me?"

His teeth flashed in the shadow of his beard. "I know I can. I only have to wait until dawn."

And he would, too. It was the one certainty Vicki could read in his eyes. She took an involuntary step forward.

He lifted a bright green water pistol. "Hold it right there, or I'll shoot."

"I don't think so." She took another step.

The holy water hit her full in the face. He was a good shot, she had to give him that—although under the circumstances, there wasn't much chance of him missing the target that mattered. Wiping the water from her eyes, she growled, "If this is how you plan to kill me, there's a flaw in the plan."

Appalled that the water hadn't had its intended effect, he recovered quickly. Throwing the plastic pistol onto the sofa, he reached down beside him and brought up a rough-hewn wooden stake. "The water was only intended to slow you down. This is what I'll kill you with."

Celluci cursed and began to struggle again.

The man with the gun ignored him, merely keeping the muzzle pressed tight into his face.

Vicki had no idea of how much damage she could take and survive but a stake through the heart had to count as a mortal wound, especially since he seemed to be the type to finish the job with a beheading and a mouthful of garlic. "What happens *after* I'm dead?"

"After?" He looked confused. "Then you'll be dead. And it'll be over." He checked his watch. "Less than five hours."

Desperately trying to remember everything she'd ever learned about defusing a hostage situation, Vicki took a deep breath and spread her arms, trying to appear as nonthreatening as possible. "Since we're going to be together for those five hours," she said quietly, forcing her lips down over her teeth, "why don't you explain why you've decided to kill me? I've never hurt you."

"You don't remember me, do you?"

"Not remember as such, no." She could tell that she'd fed from him and how long ago, but that was all.

"Do you spread your evil over so many?"

"What evil?" Vicki asked, trying to keep her tone level. It wasn't easy when all she could think of was rushing forward and ripping the hand holding the gun right off the end of his arm.

"You are evil by existing!" Tears glimmered against his lower lids and spilled over to vanish in his beard. "You mock their deaths by not dying."

"The Three of Swords sets an atmosphere of loss."

"Whose deaths?"

"My Angela, my Sandi."

Vicki exchanged a puzzled look with Celluci. "Whoever they are, I'm sorry for your loss, but I didn't kill them."

"Of course you didn't kill them." He had to swallow sobs before he could go on. In spite of his anguish, the hand holding the gun never wavered. "It was a car accident. They died and were buried, and now the worms devour their flesh. But you!" His voice rose to a shriek. "You live on, mocking their death with infinity. You will never die." Drawing in a long shuddering breath, he checked his watch again. "God sent you to me and gave me the power to resist you, so I could kill you and set things right."

"God doesn't work that way," Celluci objected.

His smile was almost beatific. "Mine does."

Uncertain of where to go next, Vicki was astonished to hear footsteps stop outside her door. A soft touch eased it open just enough for a breath to pass through.

"Nightwalker, his name is James Wause."

Then the footsteps went away again.

There was power in a name. Power enough to reach through the madness? Vicki didn't know, but it was their only chance. She let the Hunger rise again, this time let it push away the masks of civilization, and

when she spoke, her voice had all the primal cadences
of a storm.

"James Wause."

He jerked and shook his head. "No."

She caught his gaze with hers, saw the silver reflected in the dilated pupils as his madness kept her
out, then saw it abruptly vanish as she called his name
again, and it gave her the key to the locked places
inside. The cards had said she couldn't reason with
him, so she stopped trying. She called his name a third
and final time. When he crumpled forward, she caught
him. When he lifted his chin, she brought her teeth
down to his throat.

"Vicki."

There was power in a name.

But his blood throbbed warm and red beneath his
skin, and sobbing in a combination of sorrow and ec-
stasy, he was begging her to take him.

"Vicki, no."

More importantly, he had threatened one of hers.

"Vicki! Hey!" Celluci head-butted her in the elbow,
about all the contact the handcuffs allowed. "Stop it!
Now."

There was also power in the sheer pigheaded unwill-
ingness that refused to allow her to lose the humanity
she had remaining. Forcing the Hunger back under
fingertip control, she dropped the man she held and
turned to the one beside her. The cards hadn't
counted on Detective-Sergeant Michael Celluci.

Ignoring the Hunger still in her expression, he
snorted. "Nice you remembered I'm here. Now do you
think you could do something about the nine millime-
ter automatic—with, I'd like to add, the safety off—
that Mr. Wause dropped into my lap?"

Later, after Celluci had been released and James
Wause laid out on the sofa, put to sleep by a surprisingly gentle command, Vicki leaned against the loft
support and tried not think of how close it had all
come to ending.

When Celluci picked up the phone, she reached out and closed her hand around his wrist. "What are you doing?"

He looked at her, sighed, and set the receiver back in its cradle. "No police, right?"

"Would the courts understand what I am any better than he did?" She nodded toward Wause who stirred in his sleep as though aware of her regard.

Celluci sighed again and gathered her into the circle of his arms. "All right," he said, resting his cheek against her hair. "What do we do with him?"

"I've got an idea."

This time the back door was locked, but Vicki quickly picked the lock, slung James Wause over her shoulder, and carried him into the church. Celluci had wanted to come, but she'd made him wait in the car.

Laying him out in a front pew, she tucked the box of unused communion wafers under his hands and stepped back. His confession would be short a few details—this time she'd successfully removed all memory of her existence from his mind—but she hoped she'd opened the way for him to get the help he needed to cope with his grief.

"The vampire as therapist," she sighed. She nodded toward the altar as she passed. "If he's one of yours, you deal with him."

It didn't surprise her to see the beat-up old Camaro out in the church parking lot when she emerged. Lifting a hand to let Celluci know he should stay where he was, she walked over to the passenger side door.

"Did the cards tell you I'd be here?"

Madame Luminitsa nodded toward the church. "You gave him to God?"

"Seems like it."

"Alive."

"Didn't the cards say?"

"The cards weren't sure."

On the other side of the car, the grandson snorted.

Both women ignored him.

"Did the cards tell you where I lived?" Vicki asked.

"If they did, are you complaining?"

Without his name, she'd have never stopped him. "No. I guess I'm not."

"Good. You've less blood on your hands than I feared," the fortune teller murmured, taking Vicki's hands in hers and turning them. "Someday, I'll have to read your palms."

Vicki glanced over at Celluci, who was making it plain he wasn't going to wait patiently much longer. "I'll bet I have a really long life line."

An ebony brow rose as, across the parking lot, the car door opened. "How much?"

The Vengeful Spirit of Lake Nepeakea

"Camping?"

"Why sound so amazed?" Dragging the old turquoise cooler behind her, Vicki Nelson, once one of Toronto's finest and currently the city's most successful paranormal investigator, backed out of Mike Celluci's crawlspace.

"Why? Maybe because you've never been camping in your life. Maybe because your idea of roughing it is a hotel without room service. Maybe . . ." He moved just far enough for Vicki to get by then followed her out into the rec room. ". . . because you're a . . ."

"A?" Setting the cooler down beside two sleeping bags and a pair of ancient swim fins, she turned to face him. "A *what*, Mike?" Gray eyes silvered.

"Stop it."

Grinning, she turned her attention back to the cooler. "Besides, I won't be on vacation, I'll be working. You'll be the one enjoying the great outdoors."

"Vicki, my idea of the great outdoors is going to the Skydome for a Jays game."

"No one's forcing you to come." Setting the lid to one side, she curled her nose at the smell coming out of the cooler's depths. "When was the last time you used this thing?"

"Police picnic, 1992. Why?"

She turned it up on its end. The desiccated body of a mouse rolled out, bounced twice, and came to rest with its sightless little eyes staring up at Celluci. "I think you need to buy a new cooler."

"I think I need a better explanation than *'I've got a great way for you to use up your long weekend,'* " he sighed, kicking the tiny corpse under the rec room couch.

"So this developer from Toronto, Stuart Gordon, bought an old lodge on the shores of Lake Nepeakea and he wants to build a rustic timeshare resort so junior executives can relax in the woods. Unfortunately, one of the surveyors disappeared and local opinion seems to be that he's pissed off the lake's protective spirit . . ."

"The what?"

Vicki pulled out to pass a truck and deftly reinserted the van back into her own lane before replying. "The protective spirit. You know, the sort of thing that rises out of the lake to vanquish evil." A quick glance toward the passenger seat brought her brows in. "Mike, are you all right? You're going to leave permanent finger marks in the dashboard."

He shook his head. The truckload of logs coming down from northern Ontario had missed them by inches. Feet at the very most. *All right, maybe meters but not very many of them.* When they'd left the city, just after sunset, it had seemed logical that Vicki, with her better night vision, should drive. He was regretting that logic now, but realizing he didn't have a hope in hell of gaining control of the vehicle, he tried to force himself to relax. "The speed limit isn't just a good idea," he growled through clenched teeth, "it's the law."

She grinned, her teeth very white in the darkness. "You didn't used to be this nervous."

"I didn't used to have cause." His fingers wouldn't release their grip so he left them where they were. "So this missing surveyor, what did he . . ."

"She."

". . . she do to piss off the protective spirit?"

"Nothing much. She was just working for Stuart Gordon."

"The same Stuart Gordon you're working for."

"The very one."

Right. Celluci stared out at the trees and tried not to think about how fast they were passing them. *Vicki Nelson against the protective spirit of Lake Nepeakea. That's one for pay per view . . .*

"This is the place."

"No. In order for this to be 'the place' there'd have to be something here. It has to be '*a place*' before it can be '*the place*.' "

"I hate to admit it," Vicki muttered, leaning forward and peering over the arc of the steering wheel, "but you've got a point." They'd gone through the village of Dulvie, turned right at the ruined barn, and followed the faded signs to The Lodge. The road, if the rutted lanes of the last few kilometers could be called a road, had ended, as per the directions she'd received, in a small gravel parking lot—or more specifically in a hard-packed rectangular area that could now be called a parking lot because she'd stopped her van on it. "He said you could see the lodge from here."

Celluci snorted. "Maybe *you* can."

"No. I can't. All I can see are trees." At least she assumed they were trees; the high contrast between the area her headlights covered and the total darkness beyond made it difficult to tell for sure. Silently calling herself several kinds of fool, she switched off the lights. The shadows separated into half a dozen large evergreens and the silhouette of a roof steeply angled to shed snow.

Since it seemed they'd arrived, Vicki shut off the engine. After a heartbeat's silence, the night exploded into a cacophony of discordant noise. Hands over sensitive ears, she sank back into the seat. "What the hell is that?"

"Horny frogs."

"How do you know?" she demanded.

He gave her a superior smile. "PBS."

"Oh." They sat there for a moment, listening to the frogs. "The creatures of the night," Vicki sighed, "what music they make." Snorting derisively, she got out of the van. "Somehow, I expected the middle of nowhere to be a lot quieter."

Stuart Gordon had sent Vicki the key to the lodge's back door; once she switched on the main breaker, they found themselves in a modern stainless steel kitchen that wouldn't have looked out of place in any small, trendy restaurant back in Toronto. The sudden hum of the refrigerator turning on momentarily drowned out the frogs and both Vicki and Celluci relaxed.

"So now what?" he asked.

"Now we unpack your food from the cooler, we find you a room, and we make the most of the short time we have until dawn."

"And when does Mr. Gordon arrive?"

"Tomorrow evening. Don't worry, I'll be up."

"And I'm supposed to do what, tomorrow in the daytime?"

"I'll leave my notes out. I'm sure something'll occur to you."

"I thought I was on vacation."

"Then do what you usually do on vacation."

"Your footwork." He folded his arms. "And on my last vacation—which was also your idea—I almost lost a kidney."

Closing the refrigerator door, Vicki crossed the room between one heartbeat and the next. Leaning into him, their bodies touching between ankle and chest, she smiled into his eyes and pushed the long curl of hair back off of his forehead. "Don't worry, I'll protect you from the spirit of the lake. I have no intention of sharing you with another legendary being."

"Legendary?" He couldn't stop a smile. "Think highly of yourself, don't you?"

                          *   *   *

"Are you sure you'll be safe in the van?"

"Stop fussing. You know I'll be fine." Pulling her jeans up over her hips, she stared out the window and shook her head. "There's a whole lot of nothing out there."

From the bed, Celluci could see a patch of stars and the top of one of the evergreens. "True enough."

"And I really don't like it."

"Then why are we here?"

"Stuart Gordon just kept talking. I don't even remember saying yes but the next thing I knew, I'd agreed to do the job."

"He pressured *you?*" Celluci's emphasis on the final pronoun made it quite clear that he hadn't believed such a thing was possible.

"Not pressured, no. Convinced with extreme prejudice."

"He sounds like a prince."

"Yeah? Well, so was Machiavelli." Dressed, she leaned over the bed and kissed him lightly. "Want to hear something romantic? When the day claims me, yours will be the only life I'll be able to feel."

"Romantic?" His breathing quickened as she licked at the tiny puncture wounds on his wrist. "I feel like a box luuu . . . ouch! All right. It's romantic."

Although she'd tried to keep her voice light when she'd mentioned it to Celluci, Vicki really *didn't* like the great outdoors. Maybe it was because she understood the wilderness of glass and concrete and needed the anonymity of three million lives packed tightly around hers. Standing by the van, she swept her gaze from the first hints of dawn to the last lingering shadows of night and couldn't help feeling excluded, that there was something beyond what she could see that she wasn't a part of. She doubted Stuart Gordon's junior executives would feel a part of it either and wondered why anyone would want to build a resort in the midst of such otherness.

The frogs had stopped trying to get laid and the silence seemed to be waiting for something.

Waiting . . .

Vicki glanced toward Lake Nepeakea. It lay like a silver mirror down at the bottom of a rocky slope. Not a ripple broke the surface. Barely a mile away, a perfect reflection brought the opposite shore closer still.

Waiting . . .

Whippor-will!

Vicki winced at the sudden, piercing sound and got into the van. After locking both outer and inner doors, she stripped quickly—if she were found during the day, naked would be the least of her problems—laid down between the high, padded sides of the narrow bed and waited for the dawn. The birdcall, repeated with Chinese water torture frequency, cut its way through special seals and interior walls.

"Man, that's annoying," she muttered, linking her fingers over her stomach. "I wonder if Celluci can sleep through . . ."

As soon as he heard the van door close, Celluci fell into a dreamless sleep that lasted until just past noon. When he woke, he stared up at the inside of the roof and wondered where he was. The rough lumber looked like it'd been coated in creosote in the far distant past.

"No insulation, hate to be here in the winter . . ."

Then he remembered where *here* was and came fully awake.

Vicki had dragged him out to a wilderness lodge, north of Georgian Bay, to hunt for the local and apparently homicidal protective lake spirit.

A few moments later, his sleeping bag neatly rolled on the end of the old iron bed, he was in the kitchen making a pot of coffee. That kind of a realization upon waking needed caffeine.

On the counter next to the coffeemaker, right where he'd be certain to find it first thing, he found a file labeled LAKE NEPEAKEA in Vicki's unmistakable handwriting. The first few pages of glossy card stock had been clearly sent by Stuart Gordon along with the key. An artist's conception of the timeshare resort, they showed a large L-shaped building where the lodge now stood and three dozen "cottages" scattered through the woods, front doors linked by broad gravel paths. Apparently, the guests would commute out to their personal chalets by golf cart.

"Which they can also use on . . ." Celluci turned the page and shook his head in disbelief. ". . . the nine-hole golf course." Clearly, a large part of Mr. Gordon's building plan involved bulldozers. And right after the bulldozers would come the cappuccino. He shuddered.

The next few pages were clipped together and turned out to be photocopies of newspaper articles covering the disappearance of the surveyor. She'd been working with her partner in the late evening, trying to finish up a particularly marshy bit of shore destined to be filled in and paved over for tennis courts, when, according to her partner, she'd stepped back into the mud, announced something had moved under her foot, lost her balance, fell, screamed, and disappeared. The OPP, aided by local volunteers, had set up an extensive search but she hadn't been found. Since the area was usually avoided because of the sinkholes, sinkholes a distraught Stuart Gordon swore he knew nothing about—"Probably distraught about having to move his tennis courts," Celluci muttered— the official verdict allowed that she'd probably stepped in one and been sucked under the mud.

The headline on the next page declared *DEVEL-OPER ANGERS SPIRIT,* and in slightly smaller type, *Surveyor Pays the Price*. The picture showed an elderly woman with long gray braids and a hawklike profile staring enigmatically out over the water. First impressions suggested a First Nations elder. In actually reading the text, however, Celluci discovered that

Mary Joseph had moved out to Dulvie from Toronto in 1995 and had become, in the years since, the self-proclaimed keeper of local myth. According to Ms. Joseph, although there had been many sightings over the years, there had been only two other occasions when the spirit of the lake had felt threatened enough to kill. *"It protects the lake,"* she was quoted as saying, *"from those who would disturb its peace."*

"Two weeks ago," Celluci noted, checking the date. "Tragic but hardly a reason for Stuart Gordon to go to the effort of convincing Vicki to leave the city."

The final photocopy included a close-up of a car door that looked like it had been splashed with acid. *SPIRIT ATTACKS DEVELOPER'S VEHICLE.* During the night of May 13, the protector of Lake Nepeakea had crawled up into the parking lot of the lodge and secreted something corrosive and distinctly fishy against Stuart Gordon's brand new Isuzu Trooper. *A trail of dead bracken, a little over a foot wide and smelling strongly of rotting fish, leads back to the lake.* Mary Joseph seemed convinced it was a manifestation of the spirit, the local police were looking for anyone who might have information about the vandalism, and Stuart Gordon announced he was bringing in a special investigator from Toronto to settle it once and for all.

It was entirely probable that the surveyor had stepped into a mud hole and that local vandals were using the legends of the spirit against an unpopular developer. Entirely probable. But living with Vicki had forced Mike Celluci to deal with half a dozen improbable things every morning before breakfast so, mug in hand, he headed outside to investigate the crime scene.

Because of the screen of evergreens—although given their size barricade was probably the more descriptive word—the parking lot couldn't be seen from the lodge. Considering the impenetrable appearance of the overlapping branches, Celluci was willing to bet that not even light would get through. The spirit could have done anything it wanted to, up to and including changing the oil, in perfect secrecy.

Brushing one or two small insects away from his face, Celluci found the path they'd used the night before and followed it. By the time he reached the van, the one or two insects had become twenty-nine or thirty and he felt the first bite on the back of his neck. When he slapped the spot, his fingers came away dotted with blood.

"Vicki's not going to be happy about that," he grinned, wiping it off on his jeans. By the second and third bites, he'd stopped grinning. By the fourth and fifth, he really didn't give a damn what Vicki thought. By the time he'd stopped counting, he was running for the lake, hoping that the breeze he could see stirring its surface would be enough to blow the little bastards away.

The faint but unmistakable scent of rotting fish rose from the dead bracken crushed under his pounding feet and he realized that he was using the path made by the manifestation. It was about two feet wide and led down an uncomfortably steep slope from the parking lot to the lake. But not exactly all the way to the lake. The path ended about three feet above the water on a granite ledge.

Swearing, mostly at Vicki, Celluci threw himself backward, somehow managing to save both his coffee and himself from taking an unexpected swim. The following cloud of insects effortlessly matched the move. A quick glance through the bugs showed the ledge tapering off to the right. He bounded down it to the water's edge and found himself standing on a small, man-made beach staring at a floating dock that stretched out maybe fifteen feet into the lake. Proximity to the water *had* seemed to discourage the swarm, so he headed for the dock, hoping that the breeze would be stronger fifteen feet out.

It was. Flicking a few bodies out of his coffee, Celluci took a long grateful drink and turned to look back up at the lodge. Studying the path he'd taken, he was amazed he hadn't broken an ankle and had to admit a certain appreciation for who or what had created it. A graying staircase made of split logs offered a more conventional way to the water and the tiny patch of gritty sand, held in place by a stone wall. Stuart Gordon's plans had included a much larger beach and had replaced the old wooden dock with three concrete piers.

"One for papa bear, one for mama bear, and one for baby bear," Celluci mused, shuffling around on the gently rocking platform until he faced the water. Not so far away, the far shore was an unbroken wall of trees. He didn't know if there *were* bears in this part of the province, but there was certainly bathroom facilities for any number of them. Letting the breeze push his hair back off his face, he took another swallow of rapidly cooling coffee and listened to the silence. It was unnerving.

The sudden roar of a motorboat came as a welcome relief. Watching it bounce its way up the lake, he considered how far the sound carried and made a mental note to close the window should Vicki spend any significant portion of the night with him.

The moment distance allowed, the boat's driver waved over the edge of the cracked windshield and, in a great, banked turn that sprayed a huge fantail of water out behind him, headed toward the exact spot where Celluci stood. Celluci's fingers tightened around the handle of the mug, but he held his ground. Still turning, the driver cut his engines and drifted the last few meters to the dock. As empty bleach bottles slowly crumpled under the gentle impact, he jumped out and tied off his bowline.

"Frank Patton," he said, straightening from the cleat and holding out a calloused hand. "You must be the guy that developer's brought in from the city to capture the spirit of the lake."

"Detective Sergeant Mike Celluci." His own age or a little younger, Frank Patton had a workingman's grip that was just a little too forceful. Celluci returned pressure for pressure. "And I'm just spending a long weekend in the woods."

Patton's dark brows drew down. "But I thought . . ."

"You thought I was some weirdo psychic you could impress by crushing his fingers." The other man looked down at their joined hands and had the grace to flush. As he released his hold, so did Celluci. He'd played this game too often to lose at it. "I suggest, if you get the chance to meet the actual investigator, you don't come on quite so strong. She's liable to feed you your preconceptions."

"She's . . ."

"Asleep right now. We got in late and she's likely to be up . . . investigating tonight."

"Yeah. Right." Flexing his fingers, Patton stared down at the toes of his workboots. "It's just, you know, we heard that, well . . ." Sucking in a deep breath, he looked up and grinned. "Oh hell, talk about getting off on the wrong foot. Can I get you a beer, Detective?"

Celluci glanced over at the Styrofoam cooler in the back of the boat and was tempted for a moment. As sweat rolled painfully into the bug bites on the back of his neck, he remembered just how good a cold beer could taste. "No, thanks," he sighed with a disgusted glare into his mug. "I've, uh, still got coffee."

To his surprise, Patton nodded and asked, "How long've you been dry? My brother-in-law gets that exact same look when some damn fool offers him a drink on a hot almost-summer afternoon," he explained as Celluci stared at him in astonishment. "Goes to AA meetings in Bigwood twice a week."

Remembering all the bottles he'd climbed into during those long months Vicki had been gone, Celluci shrugged. "About two years now—give or take."

"I got generic cola . . ."

He dumped the dregs of cold, bug-infested coffee into the lake. The Ministry of Natural Resources could kiss his ass. "Love one," he said.

*   *   *

"So essentially everyone in town and everyone who owns property around the lake and everyone in a hundred-kilometer radius has reason to want Stuart Gordon gone."

"Essentially," Celluci agreed, tossing a gnawed chicken bone aside and pulling another piece out of the bucket. He'd waited to eat until Vicki got up, maintaining the illusion that it was a ritual they continued to share. "According to Frank Patton, he hasn't endeared himself to his new neighbors. This place used to belong to an Anne Kellough who . . . What?"

Vicki frowned and leaned toward him. "You're covered in bites."

"Tell me about it." The reminder brought his hand up to scratch at the back of his neck. "You know what Nepeakea means? It's an old Indian word that translates as 'I'm fucking sick of being eaten alive by black flies; let's get the hell out of here.' "

"Those old Indians could get a lot of mileage out of a word."

Celluci snorted. "Tell me about it."

"Anne Kellough?"

"What, not even one 'poor sweet baby'?"

Stretching out her leg under the table, she ran her foot up the inseam of his jeans. "Poor sweet baby."

"That'd be a lot more effective if you weren't wearing hiking boots." Her laugh was one of the things that hadn't changed when she had. Her smile was too white and too sharp and it made too many new promises, but her laugh remained fully human. He waited until she finished, chewing, swallowing, congratulating himself for evoking it, then said, "Anne Kellough ran this place as sort of a therapy camp. Last summer, after ignoring her for thirteen years, the Ministry of Health people came down on her kitchen. Renovations cost more than she thought, the bank foreclosed, and Stuart Gordon bought it twenty minutes later."

"That explains why she wants him gone—what about everyone else?"

"Lifestyle."

"They think he's gay?"

"Not his, theirs. The people who live out here, down in the village and around the lake—while not adverse to taking the occasional tourist for everything they can get—like the quiet, they like the solitude and, God help them, they even like the woods. The boys who run the hunting and fishing camp at the west end of the lake . . ."

"Boys?"

"I'm quoting here. The boys," he repeated, with emphasis, "say Gordon's development will kill the fish and scare off the game. He nearly got his ass kicked by one of them, Pete Wegler, down at the local gas station and then got tossed out on said ass by the owner when he called the place quaint."

"In the sort of tone that adds, 'and a Starbucks would be a big improvement'?" When Celluci raised a brow, she shrugged. "I've spoken to him, it's not that much of an extrapolation."

"Yeah, exactly that sort of tone. Frank also told me that people with kids are concerned about the increase in traffic right through the center of the village."

"Afraid they'll start losing children and pets under expensive sport utes?"

"That, and they're worried about an increase in taxes to maintain the road with all the extra traffic." Pushing away from the table, he started closing plastic containers and carrying them to the fridge. "Apparently, Stuart Gordon, ever so diplomatically, told one of the village women that this was no place to raise kids."

"What happened?"

"Frank says they got them apart before it went much beyond name calling."

Wondering how far "much beyond name calling" went, Vicki watched Mike clean up the remains of his meal. "Are you sure he's pissed off more than just these few people? Even if this was already a resort and he didn't have to rezone, local council must've agreed to his building permit."

"Yeah, and local opinion would feed local council to the spirit right alongside Mr. Gordon. Rumor has it, they've been bought off."

Tipping her chair back against the wall, she smiled up at him. "Can I assume from your busy day that you've come down on the mud hole/vandals' side of the argument?"

"It does seem the most likely." He turned and scratched at the back of his neck again. When his fingertips came away damp, he heard her quick intake of breath. When he looked up, she was crossing the kitchen. Cool fingers wrapped around the side of his face.

"You didn't shave."

It took him a moment to find his voice. "I'm on vacation."

Her breath lapped against him, then her tongue.

The lines between likely and unlikely blurred.

Then the sound of an approaching engine jerked him out of her embrace.

Vicki licked her lips and sighed. "Six cylinder, sport utility, four-wheel drive, *all* the extras, black with gold trim."

Celluci tucked his shirt back in. "Stuart Gordon told you what he drives."

"Unless you think I can tell all that from the sound of the engine."

"Not likely."

"A detective sergeant? I'm impressed." Pale hands in the pockets of his tweed blazer, Stuart Gordon leaned conspiratorially in toward Celluci, too many teeth showing in too broad a grin. "I don't suppose you could fix a few parking tickets."

"No."

Thin lips pursed in exaggerated reaction to the blunt monosyllable. "Then what do you *do,* detective sergeant?"

"Violent crimes."

Thinking that sounded a little too much like a suggestion, Vicki intervened. "Detective Celluci has agreed to assist me this weekend. Between us, we'll be able to keep a twenty-four-hour watch."

"Twenty-four hours?" The developer's brows drew in. "I'm not paying more for that."

"I'm not asking you to."

"Good." Stepping up onto the raised hearth as though it were a stage, he smiled with all the sincerity of a television infomercial. "Then I'm glad to have you aboard Detective, Mike—can I call you Mike?" He continued without waiting for an answer. "Call me Stuart. Together we'll make this a safe place for the weary masses able to pay a premium price for a premium week in the woods." A heartbeat later, his smile grew strained. "Don't you two have detecting to do?"

"Call me Stuart?" Shaking his head, Celluci followed Vicki's dark-on-dark silhouette out to the parking lot. "Why is he here?"

"He's bait."

"Bait? The man's a certified asshole, sure, but we are *not* using him to attract an angry lake spirit."

She turned and walked backward so she could study his face. Sometimes he forgot how well she could see in the dark and forgot to mask his expressions. "Mike, you don't believe that call-me-Stuart has actually pissed off some kind of vengeful spirit protecting Lake Nepeakea?"

"You're the one who said bait . . ."

"Because we're not going to catch the person, or persons, who threw acid on his car unless we catch them in the act. He understands that."

"Oh. Right."

Feeling the bulk of the van behind her, she stopped. "You didn't answer my question."

He sighed and folded his arms, wishing he could see her as well as she could see him. "Vicki, in the last four years I have been attacked by demons, mummies, zombies, werewolves . . ."

"That wasn't an attack, that was a misunderstanding."

"He went for my throat, I count it as an attack. I've offered my blood to the bastard son of Henry VIII and I've spent two years watching you hide from the day. There isn't anything much I don't believe in anymore."

"But . . ."

"I believe in you," he interrupted, "and from there, it's not that big a step to just about anywhere. Are you going to speak with Mary Joseph tonight?"

His tone suggested the discussion was over. "No, I was going to check means and opportunity on that list of names you gave me." She glanced down toward the lake, then up at him, not entirely certain what she was looking for in either instance. "Are you going to be all right out here on your own?"

"Why the hell wouldn't I be?"

"No reason." She kissed him, got into the van, and leaned out the open window to add, "Try and remember, Sigmund, that sometimes a cigar is just a cigar."

Celluci watched Vicki drive away. Then he turned on his flashlight and played the beam over the side of Stuart's car. Although it would have been more helpful to have seen the damage, he had to admit that the body shop had done a good job. And to give the man credit, however reluctantly, developing a wilderness property did provide more of an excuse than most of his kind had for the four-wheel drive.

Making his way over to an outcropping of rock where he could see both the parking lot and the lake but not be seen, Celluci sat down and turned off his light. According to Frank Patton, the black flies only fed during the day and the water was still too cold for mosquitoes. He wasn't entirely convinced, but since nothing had bitten him so far, the information seemed accurate. "I wonder if Stuart knows his little paradise is crawling with bloodsuckers." His right thumb stroking the puncture wound on his left wrist, he turned toward the lodge.

His eyes widened.

Behind the evergreens, the lodge blazed with light. Inside lights. Outside lights. Every light in the place. The harsh yellow-white illumination washed out the stars up above and threw everything below into such sharp relief that even the lush spring growth seemed manufactured. The shadows under the distant trees were now solid, impenetrable sheets of darkness.

"Well, at least Ontario Hydro's glad he's here." Shaking his head in disbelief, Celluci returned to his surveillance.

Too far away for the light to reach it, the lake threw up shimmering reflections of the stars and lapped gently against the shore.

Finally back on the paved road, Vicki unclenched her teeth and followed the southern edge of the lake toward the village. With nothing between the passenger side of the van and the water but a whitewashed guardrail and a few tumbled rocks, it was easy enough to look out the window and pretend she was driving on the lake itself. When the shoulder widened into a small parking area and a boat ramp, she pulled over and shut off the van.

The water moved inside its narrow channel like liquid darkness, opaque and mysterious. The part of the night that belonged to her ended at the water's edge.

"Not the way it's supposed to work," she muttered, getting out of the van and walking down the boat ramp. Up close, she could see through four or five inches of liquid to a stony bottom and the broken shells of freshwater clams, but beyond that, it was hard not believe she couldn't just walk across to the other side.

The ubiquitous spring chorus of frogs suddenly fell silent, drawing Vicki's attention around to a marshy cove off to her right. The silence was so complete she thought she could hear a half a hundred tiny amphibian hearts beating. One. Two . . .

"Hey, there."

She'd spun around and taken a step out into the lake before her brain caught up with her reaction. The feel of cold water filling her hiking boots brought her back to herself and she damped the hunter in her eyes before the man in the canoe had time to realize his danger.

Paddle in the water, holding the canoe in place, he nodded down at Vicki's feet. "You don't want to be doing that."

"Doing what?"

"Wading at night. You're going to want to see where you're going; old Nepeakea drops off fast." He jerked his head back toward the silvered darkness. "Even the ministry boys couldn't tell you how deep she is in the middle. She's got so much loose mud on the bottom it kept throwing back their sonar readings."

"Then what are you doing here?"

"Well, I'm not wading, that's for sure."

"Or answering my question," Vicki muttered stepping back out on the shore. Wet feet making her less than happy, she half hoped for another smartass comment.

"I often canoe at night. I like the quiet." He grinned at her, clearly believing he was too far away and there was too little light for her to see the appraisal that went with it. "You must be that investigator from Toronto. I saw your van when I was up at the lodge today."

"You must be Frank Patton. You've changed your boat."

"Can't be quiet in a 50-horsepower Evenrud, can I? You going in to see Mary Joseph?"

"No. I was going in to see Anne Kellough."

"Second house past the stop sign on the right. Little yellow bungalow with a carport." He slid backward so quietly even Vicki wouldn't have known he was moving had she not been watching him. He handled the big aluminum canoe with practiced ease. "I'd offer you a lift but I'm sure you're in a hurry."

Vicki smiled. "Thanks anyway." Her eyes silvered. "Maybe another time."

She was still smiling as she got into the van. Out on the lake, Frank Patton splashed about trying to retrieve the canoe paddle that had dropped from nerveless fingers.

"Frankly, I hate the little bastard, but there's no law against that." Anne Kellough pulled her sweater tighter and leaned back against the porch railing. "He's the one who set the health department on me, you know."

"I didn't."

"Oh yeah. He came up here about three months before it happened looking for land and he wanted mine. I wouldn't sell it to him so he figured out a way to take it." Anger quickened her breathing and flared her nostrils. "He as much as told me, after it was all over, with that big shit-eating grin and his, 'Rough, luck, Ms. Kellough, too bad the banks can't be more forgiving.' The patronizing asshole." Eyes narrowed, she glared at Vicki. "And you know what really pisses me off? I used to rent the lodge out to people who needed a little silence in their lives; you know, so they could maybe hear what was going on inside their heads. If Stuart Gordon has his way, there won't *be* any silence and the place'll be awash in brand names and expensive dental work."

"*If* Stuart Gordon has his way?" Vicki repeated, brows rising.

"Well, it's not built yet, is it?"

"He has all the paperwork filed; what's going to stop him?"

The other woman picked at a flake of paint, her whole attention focused on lifting it from the railing. Just when Vicki felt she'd have to ask again, Anne looked up and out toward the dark waters of the lake. "That's the question, isn't it," she said softly, brushing her hair back off her face.

The lake seemed no different to Vicki than it ever

had. About to suggest that the question acquire an answer, she suddenly frowned. "What happened to your hand? That looks like an acid burn."

"It is." Anne turned her arm so that the burn was more clearly visible to them both. "Thanks to Stuart fucking Gordon, I couldn't afford to take my car in to the garage and I had to change the battery myself. I thought I was being careful . . ." She shrugged.

"A new battery, eh? Afraid I can't help you miss." Ken, owner of Ken's Garage and Auto Body, pressed one knee against the side of the van and leaned, letting it take his weight as he filled the tank. "But if you're not in a hurry, I can go into Bigwood tomorrow and get you one." Before Vicki could speak, he went on. "No wait, tomorrow's Sunday, place'll be closed. Closed Monday too, seeing as how it's Victoria Day." He shrugged and smiled. "I'll be open but that won't get you a battery."

"It doesn't have to be a new one. I just want to make sure that when I turn her off on the way home I can get her started again." Leaning back against the closed driver's side door, she gestured into the work bay where a small pile of old batteries had been more or less stacked against the back wall. "What about one of them?"

Ken turned, peered, and shook his head. "Damn but you've got good eyes, miss. It's dark as bloody pitch in there."

"Thank you."

"None of them batteries will do you any good though, cause I drained them all a couple of days ago. They're just too dangerous, eh? You know, if kids get poking around?" He glanced over at the gas pump and carefully squirted the total up to an even thirty-two dollars. "You're that investigator working up at the lodge, aren't you?" he asked as he pushed the bills she handed him into a greasy pocket and counted out three dollars in change. "Trying to lay the spirit?"

"Trying to catch whoever vandalized Stuart Gordon's car."

"He, uh, get that fixed then?"

"Good as new." Vicki opened the van door and paused, one foot up on the running board. "I take it he didn't get it fixed here?"

"Here?" The slightly worried expression on Ken's broad face vanished to be replaced by a curled lip and narrowed eyes. "My gas isn't good enough for that pissant. He's planning to put his own tanks in if he gets that god damned yuppie resort built."

"If?"

Much as Anne Kellough had, he glanced toward the lake. "If."

About to swing up into the van, two five-gallon glass jars sitting outside the office caught her eye. The lids were off and it looked very much as though they were airing out. "I haven't seen jars like that in years," she said, pointing. "I don't suppose you want to sell them?"

Ken turned to follow her finger. "Can't. They belong to my cousin. I just borrowed them, eh? Her kids were supposed to come and get them but, hey, you know kids."

According to call-me-Stuart, the village was no place to raise kids.

Glass jars would be handy for transporting acid mixed with fish bits.

And where would they have gotten the fish, she wondered, pulling carefully out of the gas station. *Maybe from one of the* boys *who runs the hunting and fishing camp.*

Pete Wegler stood in the door of his trailer, a slightly confused look on his face. "Do I know you?"

Vicki smiled. "Not yet. Aren't you going to invite me in?"

Ten to twelve. The lights were still on at the lodge. Celluci stood, stretched, and wondered how much longer Vicki was going to be. *Surely everyone in Dulvie's asleep by now.*

Maybe she stopped for a bite to eat.

The second thought followed the first too quickly for him to prevent it so he ignored it instead. Turning his back on the lodge, he sat down and stared out at the lake. Water looked almost secretive at night, he decided as his eyes readjusted to the darkness.

In his business, secretive meant guilty.

"And if Stuart Gordon has gotten a protective spirit pissed off enough to kill, what then?" he wondered aloud, glancing down at his watch.

Midnight.

Which meant absolutely nothing to that ever-expanding catalog of things that went bump in the night. Experience had taught him that the so-called supernatural was just about as likely to attack at two in the afternoon as at midnight, but he couldn't not react to the knowledge that he was as far from the dubious safety of daylight as he was able to get.

Even the night seemed affected.

Waiting . . .

A breeze blew in off the lake and the hair lifted on both his arms.

Waiting for *something* to happen.

About fifteen feet from shore, a fish broke through the surface of the water like Alice going the wrong way through the looking glass. It leaped up, up, and was suddenly grabbed by the end of a glistening, gray tube as big around as his biceps. Teeth, or claws, or something back inside the tube's opening sank into the fish and together they finished the arch of the leap. A hump, the same glistening gray, slid up and back into the water, followed by what could only have been the propelling beat of a flat tail. From teeth to tail the whole thing had to be at least nine feet long.

"Jesus H. Christ." He took a deep breath and added, "On crutches."

"I'm telling you, Vicki, I saw the spirit of the lake manifest."

"You saw something eat a fish." Vicki stared out at the water but saw only the reflection of a thousand stars. "You probably saw a bigger fish eat a fish. A long, narrow pike leaping up after a nice fat bass."

About to deny he'd seen any such thing, Celluci suddenly frowned. "How do you know so much about fish?"

"I had a little talk with Pete Wegler tonight. He provided the fish for the acid bath, provided by Ken the garageman, in glass jars provided by Ken's cousin, Kathy Boomhower—the mother who went much beyond name calling with our boy Stuart. Anne Kellough did the deed—she's convinced Gordon called in the Health Department to get his hands on the property—having been transported quietly to the site in Frank Patton's canoe." She grinned. "I feel like Hercule Poirot on the Orient Express."

"Yeah? Well, I'm feeling a lot more Stephen King than Agatha Christie."

Sobering, Vicki laid her hand on the barricade of his crossed arms and studied his face. "You're really freaked by this, aren't you?"

"I don't know exactly what I saw, but I didn't see a fish get eaten by another fish."

The muscles under her hand were rigid and he was staring past her, out at the lake. "Mike, what is it?"

"I told you, Vicki. I don't know exactly what I saw." In spite of everything, he still liked his world defined. Reluctantly transferring his gaze to the pale oval of her upturned face, he sighed. "How much, if any, of this do you want me to tell Mr. Gordon tomorrow?"

"How about none? I'll tell him myself after sunset."

"Fine. It's late, I'm turning in. I assume you'll be staking out the parking lot for the rest of the night."

"What for? I guarantee the vengeful spirits won't be back." Her voice suggested that in a direct, one-on-one confrontation, a vengeful spirit wouldn't stand a chance. Celluci remembered the thing that rose up out of the lake and wasn't so sure.

"That doesn't matter, you promised twenty-four-hour protection."

"Yeah, but . . ." His expression told her that if she

wasn't going to stay, he would. "Fine, I'll watch the car. Happy?"

"That you're doing what you said you were going to do? Ecstatic." Celluci unfolded his arms, pulled her close enough to kiss the frown lines between her brows, and headed for the lodge. *She had a little talk with Pete Wegler, my ass.* He knew Vicki had to feed off others, but he didn't have to like it.

Should never have mentioned Pete Wegler. She settled down on the rock, which was still warm from Celluci's body heat, and tried unsuccessfully to penetrate the darkness of the lake. When something rustled in the underbrush bordering the parking lot, she hissed without turning her head. The rustling moved away with considerably more speed than it had used to arrive. The secrets of the lake continued to elude her.

"This isn't mysterious, it's irritating."

As Celluci wandered around the lodge, turning off lights, he could hear Stuart snoring through the door of one of the two main floor bedrooms. In the few hours he'd been outside, the other man had managed to leave a trail of debris from one end of the place to the other. On top of that, he'd used up the last of the toilet paper on the roll and hadn't replaced it, he'd put the almost empty coffee pot back in the coffeemaker with the machine still on so that the dregs had baked onto the glass, and he'd eaten a piece of Celluci's chicken, tossing the gnawed bone back into the bucket. Celluci didn't mind him eating the piece of chicken, but the last thing he wanted was Stuart Gordon's spit over the rest of the bird.

Dropping the bone into the garbage, he noticed a crumpled piece of paper and fished it out. Apparently the resort was destined to grow beyond its current boundaries. Destined to grow all the way around the lake, devouring Dulvie as it went.

"Which would put Stuart Gordon's spit all over the rest of the area."

*   *   *

Bored with watching the lake and frightening off
the local wildlife, Vicki pressed her nose against the
window of the sports ute and clicked her tongue at
the dashboard full of electronic displays, willing to bet
that call-me-Stuart didn't have the slightest idea of
what most of them meant.

"Probably has a trouble light if his air freshener
needs . . . hello."

Tucked under the passenger seat was the unmistakable edge of a laptop.

"And how much to you want to bet this thing'll
scream bloody blue murder if I try and jimmy the
door . . ." Turning toward the now dark lodge, she
listened to the sound of two heartbeats. To the slow,
regular sound that told her both men were deeply
asleep.

Stuart slept on his back with one hand flung over
his head and a slight smile on his thin face. Vicki
watched the pulse beat in his throat for a moment.
She'd been assured that, if necessary, she could feed
off lower life-forms—pigeons, rats, developers—but
she was just as glad she'd taken the edge off the Hunger down in the village. Scooping up his car keys, she
went out of the room as silently as she'd come in.

Celluci woke to a decent voice belting out a Beatles
tune and came downstairs just as Stuart came out of
the bathroom fingercombing damp hair.

"Good morning, Mike. Can I assume no vengeful
spirits of Lake Nepeakea trashed my car in the
night?"

"You can."

"Good. Good. Oh, by the way . . ." His smile could
have sold attitude to Americans. ". . . I've used all
the hot water.

"I guess it's true what they say about so many of
our boys in blue."

"And what's that?" Celluci growled, fortified by two

cups of coffee made only slightly bitter by the burned carafe.

"Well, you know, Mike." Grinning broadly, the developer mimed tipping a bottle to his lips. "I mean, if you can drink that vile brew, you've certainly got a drinking problem." Laughing at his own joke, he headed for the door.

To begin with, they're not your boys in blue and then, you can just fucking well drop dead. You try dealing with the world we deal with for a while, asshole, it'll chew you up and spit you out. But although his fist closed around his mug tightly enough for it to creak, all he said was, "Where are you going?"

"Didn't I tell you? I've got to see a lawyer in Bigwood today. Yes, I know what you're going to say, Mike; it's Sunday. But since this is the last time I'll be out here for a few weeks, the local legal beagle can see me when I'm available. Just a few loose ends about that nasty business with the surveyor." He paused, with his hand on the door, voice and manner stripped of all pretensions. "I told them to be sure and finish that part of the shoreline before they quit for the day—I know I'm not, but I feel responsible for that poor woman's death and I only wish there was something I could do to make up for it. You can't make up for someone dying though, can you, Mike?"

Celluci growled something noncommittal. Right at the moment, the last thing he wanted was to think of Stuart Gordon as a decent human being.

"I might not be back until after dark, but hey, that's when the spirit's likely to appear so you won't need me until then. Right, Mike?" Turning toward the screen where the black flies had settled, waiting for their breakfast to emerge, he shook his head. "The first thing I'm going to do when all this is settled is drain every stream these little bloodsuckers breed in."

The water levels in the swamp had dropped in the two weeks since the death of the surveyor. Drenched in the bug spray he'd found under the sink, Celluci followed the path made by the searchers, treading carefully on the higher hummocks no matter how solid the ground looked. When he reached the remains of the police tape, he squatted and peered down into the water. He didn't expect to find anything, but after Stuart's confession, he felt he had to come.

About two inches deep, it was surprisingly clear.

"No reason for it to be muddy now, there's nothing stirring it . . ."

Something metallic glinted in the mud.

Gripping the marsh grass on his hummock with one hand, he reached out with the other and managed to get thumb and forefinger around the protruding piece of . . .

"Stainless steel measuring tape?"

It was probably a remnant of the dead surveyor's equipment. One end of the six inch piece had been cleanly broken, but the other end, the end that had been down in the mud, looked as though it had been dissolved.

When Anne Kellough had thrown the acid on Stuart's car, they'd been imitating the spirit of Lake Nepeakea.

Celluci inhaled deeply and spit a mouthful of suicidal black flies out into the swamp. "I think it's time to talk to Mary Joseph."

"Can't you feel it?"

Enjoying the first decent cup of coffee he'd had in days, Celluci walked to the edge of the porch and stared out at the lake. Unlike most of Dulvie, separated from the water by the road, Mary Joseph's house was right on the shore. "I can feel *something*," he admitted.

"You can feel the spirit of the lake, angered by this man from the city. Another cookie?"

"No, thank you." He'd had one and it was without question the worst cookie he'd ever eaten. "Tell me about the spirit of the lake, Ms. Joseph. Have you seen it?"

"Oh yes. Well, not exactly it, but I've seen the wake

of its passing." She gestured out toward the water but, at the moment, the lake was perfectly calm. "Most water has a protective spirit, you know. Wells and springs, lakes and rivers; it's why we throw coins into fountains, so that the spirits will exchange them for luck. Kelpies, selkies, mermaids, Jenny Greenteeth, Peg Powler, the Fideal . . . all water spirits."

"And one of them, is that what's out there?" Somehow he couldn't reconcile mermaids to that toothed trunk snaking out of the water.

"Oh no, our water spirit is a New World water spirit. The Cree called it a mantouche— surely you recognize the similarity to the word Manitou or Great Spirit? Only the deepest lakes with the best fishing had them. They protected the lakes and the area around the lakes and, in return . . ."

"Were revered?"

"Well, no, actually. They were left strictly alone."

"You told the paper that the spirit had manifested twice before?"

"Twice that we know of," she corrected. "The first recorded manifestation occurred in 1762 and was included in the notes on native spirituality that one of the exploring Jesuits sent back to France."

Product of a Catholic school education, Celluci wasn't entirely certain the involvement of the Jesuits added credibility. "What happened?"

"It was spring. A pair of white trappers had been at the lake all winter, slaughtering the animals around it. Animals under the lake's protection. According to the surviving trapper, his partner was coming out of a highwater marsh, just after sunset, when his canoe suddenly upended and he disappeared. When the remaining man retrieved the canoe, he found that bits had been burned away without flame and it carried the mark of all the dead they'd stolen from the lake."

"The mark of the dead?"

"The record says it stank, Detective. Like offal." About to eat another cookie, she paused. "You do know what offal is?"

"Yes, ma'am. Did the survivor see anything?"

"Well, he said he saw what he thought was a giant snake except that it had two stubby wings at the upper end. And you know what that is."

. . . *a glistening, gray tube as big around as his biceps.* "No."

"A wyvern. One of the ancient dragons."

"There's a dragon in the lake."

"No, of course not. The spirit of the lake can take many forms. When it's angry, those who facing its anger see a great and terrifying beast. To the trapper, who no doubt had northern European roots, it appeared as a wyvern. The natives would have probably seen a giant serpent. There are many so-called serpent mounds around deep lakes."

"But it couldn't just *be* a giant serpent?"

"Detective Celluci, don't you think that if there was a giant serpent living in this lake that someone would have gotten a good look at it by now? Besides, after the second death the lake was searched extensively with modern equipment—and once or twice since then as well—and nothing has ever been found. That trapper was killed by the spirit of the lake and so was Thomas Stebbing."

"Thomas Stebbing?"

"The recorded death in 1937. I have newspaper clippings . . ."

According to the newspaper, in the spring of 1937, four young men from the University of Toronto came to Lake Nepeakea on a wilderness vacation. Out canoeing with a friend at dusk, Thomas Stebbing saw what he thought was a burned log on the shore and they paddled in to investigate. As his friend watched in horror, the log "attacked" Stebbing, left him burned and dead, and "undulated into the lake" on a trail of dead vegetation.

The investigation turned up nothing at all, and the eyewitness account of a "kind of big worm thing" was summarily dismissed. The final, official verdict was that the victim had indeed disturbed a partially burned log, and as it rolled over him was burned by the embers and died. The log then rolled into the lake, burning a path as it rolled, and sank. The stench was dismissed as the smell of roasting flesh and the insistence by the friend that the burns were acid burns was completely ignored—in spite of the fact he was a chemistry student and should therefore know what he was talking about.

"The spirit of the *lake* came up on *land,* Ms. Joseph?"

She nodded, apparently unconcerned with the contradiction. "There were a lot of fires being lit around the lake that year. Between the wars this area got popular for a while and fires were the easiest way to clear land for summer homes. The spirit of the lake couldn't allow that, hence its appearance as a burned log."

"And Thomas Stebbing had done what to disturb its peace?"

"Nothing specifically. I think the poor boy was just in the wrong place at the wrong time. It is a vengeful spirit, you understand."

Only a few short years earlier, he'd have understood that Mary Joseph was a total nutcase. But that was before he'd willingly thrown himself into the darkness that lurked behind a pair of silvered eyes. He sighed and stood; the afternoon had nearly ended. It wouldn't be long now until sunset.

"Thank you for your help, Ms. Joseph. I . . . what?"

She was staring at him, nodding. "You've seen it, haven't you? You have that look."

"I've seen something," he admitted reluctantly and turned toward the water. "I've seen a lot of thi . . ."

A pair of jet skis roared around the point and drowned him out. As they passed the house, blanketing it in noise, one of the adolescent operators waved a cheery hello.

Never a vengeful lake spirit around when you really need one, he thought.

*   *   *

"He knew about the sinkholes in the marsh and he sent those surveyors out anyway." Vicki tossed a pebble off the end of the dock and watched it disappear into the liquid darkness.

"You're sure?"

"The information was all there on his laptop and the file was dated back in March. Now, although evidence that I just happened to have found in his computer will be inadmissible in court, I can go to the Department of Lands and Forests and get the dates he requested the geological surveys."

Celluci shook his head. "You're not going to be able to get him charged with anything. Sure, he should've told them, but they were both professionals, they should've been more careful." He thought of the crocodile tears Stuart had cried that morning over the death and his hands formed fists by his side. Being an irresponsible asshole was one thing; being a manipulative, irresponsible asshole was on another level entirely. "It's an ethical failure," he growled, "not a legal one."

"Maybe I should take care of him myself, then." The second pebble hit the water with considerably more force.

"He's your client, Vicki. You're supposed to be working for him, not against him."

She snorted. "So I'll wait until his check clears."

"He's planning on acquiring the rest of the land around the lake." Pulling the paper he'd retrieved from the garbage out of his pocket, Celluci handed it over.

"The rest of the land around the lake isn't for sale."

"Neither was this lodge until he decided he wanted it."

Crushing the paper in one hand, Vicki's eyes silvered. "There's got to be something we can . . . Shit!" Tossing the paper aside, she grabbed Celluci's arm as the end of the dock bucked up into the air and leaped back one section, dragging him with her. "What the fuck was that?" she demanded as they turned to watch the place they'd just been standing rock violently back and forth. The paper she'd dropped into the water was nowhere to be seen.

"Wave from a passing boat?"

"There hasn't been a boat past here in hours."

"Sometimes these long narrow lakes build up a standing wave. It's called a seiche."

"A seiche?" When he nodded, she rolled her eyes. "I've got to start watching more PBS. In the meantime . . ."

The sound of an approaching car drew their attention up to the lodge in time to see Stuart slowly and carefully pull into the parking lot, barely disturbing the gravel.

"Are you going to tell him who vandalized his car?" Celluci asked as they started up the hill."

"Who? Probably not. I can't prove it after all, but I will tell him it wasn't some vengeful spirit and it definitely won't happen again." At least not if Pete Wegler had anything to say about it. The spirit of the lake might be hypothetical, but she wasn't.

"A group of villagers, Vicki? You're sure?"

"Positive."

"They actually thought I'd believe it was an angry spirit manifesting all over the side of my vehicle?"

"Apparently." Actually, they hadn't cared if he believed it or not. They were all just so angry, they needed to do something, and since the spirit was handy . . . She offered none of that to call-me-Stuart.

"I want their names, Vicki." His tone made it an ultimatum.

Vicki had never responded well to ultimatums. Celluci watched her masks begin to fall and wondered just how far his dislike of the developer would let her go. He could stop her with a word, he just wondered if he'd say it. Or when.

To his surprise, she regained control. "Check the census lists, then. You haven't exactly endeared yourself to your neighbors."

For a moment, it seemed that Stuart realized how close he'd just come to seeing the definition of his own mortality but then he smiled and said, "You're right, Vicki, I haven't endeared myself to my neighbors. And do you know what; I'm going to do something about that. Tomorrow's Victoria Day, I'll invite them all to a big picnic supper with great food and fireworks out over the lake. We'll kiss and make up."

"It's Sunday evening and tomorrow's a holiday. Where are you going to find food and fireworks?"

"Not a problem, Mike. I'll e-mail my caterers in Toronto. I'm sure they can be here by tomorrow afternoon. I'll pay through the nose but hey, developing a good relationship with the locals is worth it. You two will stay, of course."

Vicki's lips drew back off her teeth but Celluci answered for them both. "Of course."

"He's up to something," he explained later, "and I want to know what that is."

"He's going to confront the villagers with what he knows, see who reacts, and make their lives a living hell. He'll find a way to make them the first part of his expansion."

"You're probably right."

"I'm always right." Head pillowed on his shoulder, she stirred his chest hair with one finger. "He's an unethical, immoral, unscrupulous little asshole."

"You missed annoying, irritating, and just generally unlikeable."

"I could convince him he was a combination of Mother Teresa and Lady Di. I could rip his mind out, use it for unnatural purposes, and stuff it back into his skull in any shape I damn well chose, but I can't."

Once you start down the dark side, forever will it dominate your destiny. But he didn't say it aloud because he didn't want to know how far down the dark side she'd been. He was grateful that she'd drawn any personal boundaries at all, that she'd chosen to remain someone who couldn't use terror for the sake of terror. "So what are we going to do about him?"

"I can't think of a damned thing. You?"

Suddenly he smiled. "Could you convince him that *you* were the spirit of the lake and that he'd better haul his ass back to Toronto unless he wants it dissolved off?"

She was off the bed in one fluid movement. "I knew there was a reason I dragged you out here this weekend." She turned on one bare heel then turned again and was suddenly back in the bed. "But I think I'll wait until tomorrow night. He hasn't paid me yet."

"Morning, Mike. Where's Vicki?"

"Sleeping."

"Well, since you're up, why don't you help out by carrying the barbecue down to the beach. I may be willing to make amends but I'm not sure they are, and since they've already damaged my car, I'd just as soon keep them away from anything valuable. Particularly when in combination with propane and open flames."

"Isn't Vicki joining us for lunch, Mike?"

"She says she isn't hungry. She went for a walk in the woods."

"Must be how she keeps her girlish figure. I've got to hand it to you, Mike, there aren't many men your age who could hold onto such a woman. I mean, she's really got that independent thing going, doesn't she?" He accepted a tuna sandwich with effusive thanks, took a bite and winced. "Not light mayo?"

"No."

"Never mind, Mike. I'm sure you meant well. Now, then, as it's just the two of us, have you ever considered investing in a timeshare . . ."

Mike Celluci had never been so glad to see anyone as he was to see a van full of bleary-eyed and stiff caterers arrive at four that afternoon. As Vicki had discovered during that initial phone call, Stuart Gordon was not a man who took no for an answer. He might have accepted "Fuck off and die!" followed by a fast exit, but since Vicki expected to wake up on the shores of Lake Nepeakea, Celluci held his tongue. Besides, it would be a little difficult for her to chase the developer away if they were halfway back to Toronto.

Sunset.

Vicki could feel maybe two dozen lives around her when she woke, and she laid there for a moment reveling in them. The last two evenings she'd had to fight the urge to climb into the driver's seat and speed toward civilization.

"Fast food."

She snickered, dressed, and stepped out into the parking lot.

Celluci was down on the beach talking to Frank Patton. She made her way over to them, the crowd opening to let her pass without really being aware she was there at all. Both men nodded as she approached and Patton gestured toward the barbecue.

"Burger?"

"No thanks, I'm not hungry." She glanced around. "No one seems to have brought their kids."

"No one wants to expose their kids to Stuart Gordon."

"Afraid they'll catch something," Celluci added.

"Mike here says you've solved your case and you're just waiting for Mr. Congeniality over there to pay you."

Wondering what Mike had been up to, Vicki nodded.

"He also says you didn't mention any names. Thank you." He sighed. "We didn't really expect the spirit of the lake thing to work but . . ."

Vicki raised both hands. "Hey, you never know. He could be suppressing."

"Yeah, right. The only thing that clown suppresses

is everyone around him. If you'll excuse me, I'd better go rescue Anne before she rips out his tongue and strangles him with it."

"I'm surprised she came," Vicki admitted.

"She thinks he's up to something and she wants to know what it is."

"Don't we all," Celluci murmured as he walked away.

The combined smell of cooked meat and fresh blood making her a little light-headed, Vicki started Mike moving toward the floating dock. "Have I missed anything?"

"No, I think you're just in time."

As Frank Patton approached, Stuart broke off the conversation he'd been having with Anne Kellough— or more precisely, Vicki amended, *at* Anne Kellough— and walked out to the end of the dock where a number of large rockets had been set up.

"He's got a permit for the damned things," Celluci muttered. "The son of a bitch knows how to cover his ass."

"But not his id." Vicki's fingers curved cool around Mike's forearm. "He'll get his, don't worry."

The first rocket went up, exploding red over the lake, the colors muted against the evening gray of sky and water. The developer turned toward the shore and raised both hands above his head. "Now that I've got your attention, there's a few things I'd like to share with you all before the festivities continue. First of all, I've decided not to press charges concerning the damage to my vehicle, although I'm aware that . . ."

The dock began to rock. Behind him, one of the rockets fell into the water.

"Mr. Gordon." The voice was Mary Joseph's. "Get to shore, now."

Pointing a finger toward her, he shook his head. "Oh no, old woman, I'm Stuart Gordon . . ."

No *call-me-Stuart* tonight, Celluci noted.

". . . and you don't tell me what to do, I tell . . ."

Arms windmilling, he stepped back, once, twice, and

hit the water. Arms and legs stretched out, he looked as though he was sitting on something just below the surface. "I have had enough of this," he began . . . . . . and disappeared.

Vicki reached the end of the dock in time to see the pale oval of his face engulfed by dark water. To her astonishment, he seemed to have gotten his cell phone out of his pocket and all she could think of was that old movie cut line, *Who you gonna call?*

One heartbeat, two. She thought about going in after him. The fingertips on her reaching hand were actually damp when Celluci grabbed her shoulder and pulled her back. She wouldn't have done it, but it was nice that he thought she would.

Back on the shore, two dozen identical wide-eyed stares were locked on the flat, black surface of the lake, too astounded by what had happened to their mutual enemy, Vicki realized, to notice how fast she'd made it to the end of the dock.

Mary Joseph broke the silence first. "Thus acts the vengeful spirit of Lake Nepeakea," she declared. Then as heads began to nod, she added dryly, "Can't say I didn't warn him."

Mike looked over at Vicki, who shrugged.

"Works for me," she said.

Someone to Share the Night

You write for a living, Henry reminded himself, staring at the form on the monitor. *A hundred and fifty thousand publishable words a year. How hard can this be?* Red-gold brows drawn in, he began to type.

"Single white male seeks . . . no . . ." The cursor danced back. "Single white male, mid-twenties, seeks . . ." That wasn't exactly his age, but he rather suspected that personals ads were like taxes, everybody lied. "Seeks . . ."

He paused, fingers frozen over the keyboard. *Seeks what?* he wondered, staring at the five words that, so far, made up the entire fax. Then he sighed and removed a word. He had no real interest in spending time with those who used race as a criteria for friendship. Life was too short. Even his.

"Single male, midtwenties, seeks . . ." He glanced down at the tabloid page spread out on his desk searching for inspiration. Unfortunately, he found wishful thinking, macho posturing, and, reading between the lines, a quiet desperation that made the hair rise off the back of his neck.

"What am I doing?" Rolling his eyes, he shoved his chair away from the desk. "I could walk out that door and have anyone I wanted."

Which was true.

But it wouldn't *be* what he wanted.

This is not an act of desperation, he reminded himself. Impatient, perhaps. Desperate, no.

"Single male, mid-twenties, not into the bar scene . . ." The phrase *meat market* was singularly apt in his case. ". . . seeks . . ."

What he'd had.

But Vicki was three thousand odd miles away with a man who loved her in spite of changes.

And Tony, freed from a life of mere survival on the streets, had defined himself and moved on.

They'd left a surprising hole in his life. Surprising and painful. Surprisingly painful. He found himself unwilling to wait for time and fate to fill it.

"Single male, midtwenties, not into the bar scene, out of the habit of being alone, seeks someone strong, intelligent, and adaptable."

Frowning, he added, "Must be able to laugh at life." Then he sent the fax before he could change his mind. The paper would add the electronic mailbox number when they ran it on Thursday.

Late Thursday or early Friday depending how the remaining hours of darkness were to be defined, Henry picked a copy of the paper out of a box on Davie Street and checked his ad. In spite of the horror stories he'd heard to the contrary, they'd not only gotten it right but placed it at the bottom of the first column of Alternative Lifestyles, where it had significantly more punch than if it had been buried higher up on the page.

Deadlines kept him from checking the mailbox until Sunday evening.

There were thirty-two messages. Thirty-two.

He felt flattered until he actually listened to them and then, even though no one else knew, he felt embarrassed about feeling flattered.

Twenty, he dismissed out of hand. A couple of the instant rejects had clearly been responding to the wrong mailbox. A few sounded interesting but had a change of heart in the middle of the message and left no actual contact information. The rest seemed to be laughing just a little *too* hard at life.

But at the end of a discouraging half an hour, he still had a dozen messages to choose from; seven women, five men. It wasn't thirty-two, but it wasn't bad.

Eleven of them had left him e-mail addresses.

One had left him a phone number.

He listened again to the last voice in the mailbox, the only one of the twelve who believed he wouldn't abuse the privilege offered by the phone company.

"Hi. My name is Lilah. I'm also in my mid-twenties—although which side of the midpoint I'd rather not say."

Henry could hear the smile in her voice. It was a half smile, a crooked smile, the kind of smile that could appreciate irony. He found himself smiling in response.

"Although I can quite happily be into the bar scene, I do think they're the worst possible place to meet someone for the first time. How about a coffee? I can probably be free any evening this week."

And then she left her phone number.

Still smiling, he called it.

If American troops had invaded Canada during the War of 1812 with half the enthusiasm Starbucks had exhibited when crossing the border, the outcome of the war would have been entirely different. While Henry had nothing actually against the chain of coffee shops, he found their client base to be just a little too broad. In the café on Denman that he preferred, there were never any children, rushing junior executives, or spandex shorts. Almost everyone wore black and, in spite of multiple piercings and overuse of profanity, the younger patrons were clearly imitating their elders.

Their elders were generally the kind of artists and writers who seldom made sales but knew how to look the part. They were among the very few in Vancouver without tans.

Using the condensation on a three-dollar bottle of water to make rings on the scarred tabletop, Henry

watched the door and worried about recognizing Lilah
when she arrived. Then he worried a bit that she wasn't
going to arrive. Then he went back to worrying about
recognizing her.

You are way too old for this nonsense, he told himself sternly. *Get a . . .*

The woman standing in the doorway was short,
vaguely Mediterranean with thick dark hair that
spilled halfway down her back in ebony ripples. If
she'd passed her midtwenties it wasn't by more than
a year or two. She'd clearly ignored the modern notion
that a woman should be so thin she looked like an
adolescent boy with breasts. Not exactly beautiful,
something about her drew the eye. Noting Henry's
regard, she smiled, red lips parting over very white
teeth and it was exactly the expression that Henry had
imagined. He stood as she walked to his table, enjoying the sensual way she moved her body across the
room and aware that everyone else in the room was
enjoying it, too.

"Henry?" Her voice was throatier in person, almost
a purr.

"Lilah." He gave her name back to her as confir-
mation.

She raised her head and locked her dark gaze to his.
They blinked in unison.

"Vampire."

Henry Fitzroy, bastard son of Henry VIII, once
Duke of Richmond and Somerset, dropped back into
his chair with an exhalation halfway between a sigh
and a snort. "Succubus."

"So are you saying you *weren't* planning to feed off
whoever answered your ad?"

"No, I'm saying it wasn't the primary reason I
placed it."

The overt sexual attraction turned off, Lilah swirled
a finger through a bit of spilled latté and rolled her
eyes. "So you're a better man than I am, Gunga Din,

but I personally don't see the difference between us. You don't kill anymore, I don't kill anymore."

"I don't devour years off my . . ." He paused and frowned, uncertain of how to go on.

"Victims? Prey? Quarry? Dates?" The succubus sighed. "We've got to come up with a new word for it."

Recognizing she had a point, Henry settled for the lesser of four evils. "I don't devour years off my date's life."

"Oh, please. So they spend less time having their diapers changed by strangers in a nursing home, less time drooling in their pureed mac and cheese. If they knew, they'd thank me. At least I don't violate their structural integrity."

"I hardly think a discreet puncture counts as a violation."

"Hey, you said puncture, not me. But . . ." She raised a hand to stop his protest. ". . . I'm willing to let it go."

"Gracious of you."

"Always."

In spite of himself, Henry smiled.

"You know, hon, you're very attractive when you do that."

"Do what?"

"When you stop looking so irritated about things not turning out the way you expected. Blind dates *never* turn out the way you expect." Dropping her chin she looked up at him through the thick fringe of her lashes. "Trust me, I've been on a million of them."

"A million?"

"Give or take."

"So you're a pro . . ."

A sardonic eyebrow rose. "A gentleman wouldn't mention that."

"True." He inclined his head in apology and took the opportunity to glance at his watch. "*Run Lola Run* is playing at the Caprice in ninety minutes; did you want to go?"

For the first time since entering the café, Lilah looked startled. "With you?"

A little startled himself, Henry shrugged, offering the only reason that explained the unusually impulsive invitation. "I'd enjoy spending some time just being myself, without all the implicit lies."

Dark brows drew in and she studied him speculatively. "I can understand that."

An almost comfortable silence filled the space between them.

"Well?" Henry asked at last.

"My German's a little rusty. I haven't used it for almost a century."

Henry stood and held out his hand. "There're subtitles."

Shaking her head, she pushed her chair out from the table and laid her hand in his. "Why not?"

Sunset. A slow return to awareness. The feel of cotton sheets against his skin. The pulse of the city outside the walls of his sanctuary. The realization he was smiling.

After the movie, they'd walked for hours in a soft mist, talking about the places they'd seen and when they'd seen them. A primal demon, the succubus had been around for millennia but politely restricted her observations to the four and a half centuries Henry could claim. Their nights had been remarkably similar.

When they parted about an hour before dawn, they parted as friends although it would never be a sexual relationship; sex was too tied to feeding for them both.

"World's full of warm bodies," Lilah had pointed out, *"but how many of them saw Mrs. Siddon play Lady Macbeth at Covent Garden Theater on opening night* and *felt the hand washing scene was way, way over the top?"*

How many indeed, Henry thought, throwing back the covers and swinging his legs out of bed. Rather than deal with the balcony doors in the master suite, he'd sealed the smallest room in the three bedroom condo against the light. He'd done the crypt thing once, and didn't see the attraction.

After his shower, he wandered into the living room and picked up the remote. With any luck he could catch the end of the news. He didn't often watch it but last night's . . . date? . . . had left him feeling reconnected to the world.

". . . when southbound travelers waited up to three hours to cross the border at the Peace Arch as U.S. customs officials tightened security checks as a precaution against terrorism."

"Canadian terrorists." Henry frowned as he toweled his hair. "Excuse me while I politely blow up your building?"

"Embarrassed Surrey officials had to shut down the city's Web site after a computer hacker broke into the system and rewrote the greeting, using less-than-flattering language. The hacker remains unknown and unapprehended.

"And in a repeat of our top story, police have identified the body found this morning on Wreck Beach as Taylor Johnston, thirty-two, of Haro Street. They still have no explanation for the condition of the body, although an unidentified constable commented that 'it looked like he had his life sucked out of him.'

"And now to Rajeet Singh with our new product report."

Jabbing at the remote, Henry cut Rajeet off in the middle of an animated description of a battery-operated cappuccino frother. Plastic cracked as his fingers tightened. A man found with the life sucked out of him. He didn't want to believe. . . .

As part of an ongoing criminal investigation, the body was at the City Morgue in the basement of Vancouver General Hospital. The previous time Henry'd made an after hours visit, he'd been searching for information to help identify the victim. This time, he needed to identify the murderer.

He walked silently across the dark room to the

drawer labeled TAYLOR JOHNSTON, pulled it open, and flipped back the sheet. LEDs on various pieces of machinery and the exit sign over the door provided more than enough light to see tendons and ligaments standing out in sharp relief under desiccated, parchment-colored skin. Hands and feet looked like claws and the features of the skull had overwhelmed the features of the face. The unnamed constable had made an accurate observation; the body did, indeed, look as if all the life had been sucked out of it.

Henry snarled softly and closed the drawer.

"You don't kill anymore, I don't kill anymore . . ."

He found the dead man's personal effects in a manila envelope in the outer office. A Post-it note suggested that the police should have picked the envelope up by six PM. The watch was an imitation Rolex—but not a cheap one. There were eight keys on his key ring. The genuine cowhide wallet held four high end credit cards, eighty-seven dollars in cash, a picture of a golden retriever, and half a dozen receipts. Three were out of bank machines. Two were store receipts. The sixth was for a credit card transaction.

Henry had faxed in both his personal ad and his credit information. It looked as though Taylor Johnston had dropped his off in person.

"Blind dates never turn out the way you expect. Trust me, I've been on a million of them."

In a city the size of Vancouver, a phone number and a first name provided no identification at all. Had Lilah answered when he called, Henry thought he'd be able to control his anger enough to arrange another meeting but she didn't, and when he found himself snarling at her voice mail, he decided not to leave a message.

"Although I can quite happily be into the bar scene . . ."

She'd told him she liked jazz. It was a place to start.

* * *

She wasn't at O'Doul's, although one of the waiters recognized her description. From the strength of his reacton, Henry assumed she'd fed—but not killed. Why kill Johnston and yet leave this victim with only pleasant memories? Henry added it to the list of questions he intended to have answered.

A few moments later, he parked his BMW, illegally, on Abbot Street and walked around the corner to Water Street, heading for The Purple Onion Cabaret. There were very few people on the sidewalks—a couple, closely entwined, a small clump of older teens, and a familiar form just about to enter the club.

Henry could move quickly when he needed to and he was in no mood for subtlety. He was in front of her before she knew he was behind her.

An ebony brow rose, but that was the only movement she made. "What brings you here, hon? I seem to recall you saying that jazz made your head ache."

He snarled softly, not amused.

The brow lowered, slowly. "Are you Hunting me, Nightwalker? Should I scream? Maybe that nice young man down the block will disentangle himself from his lady long enough to save me."

Henry's lips drew up off his teeth. "And who will save him as you add another death to your total?"

Lilah blinked, and the formal cadences left her voice. "What the hell are you talking about?"

Demons seldom bothered lying; the truth caused more trouble.

She honestly didn't know what he meant.

"You actually saw this body?" When Henry nodded, Lilah took a long swallow of mocha latte, carefully put the cup down on its saucer, and said, "Why do you care? I mean, I know why you cared when you thought it was me," she added before he could speak. "You thought I'd lied to you and you didn't like feeling dicked around. I can understand that. But it's not me. So why do you care?"

Henry let the final mask fall, the one he maintained even for the succubus. "Someone, something, is hunting in my territory."

Across the café, a mug slid from nerveless fingers and hit the Italian tile floor, exploding into a hundred shards of primary-colored porcelain. There was nervous·laughter, scattered applause, and all eyes thankfully left the golden-haired man with the night in his voice.

Lilah shrugged. "There're millions of people in the Greater Vancouver area, hon. Enough for all of us."

"It's the principle of the thing," he muttered, a little piqued by her lack of reaction.

"It's not another vampire."

It was almost a question so he answered it. "No. The condition of the corpse was classic succubus."

"Or incubus," she pointed out. "You don't know for certain those men weren't gay, and I sincerely doubt that you and I alone were shopping from the personals."

"I wasn't looking to feed," Henry ground out through clenched teeth.

"That's right. You were looking for a victimless relationship and . . ." Lilah spread her hands, fingernails drawing glistening scarlet lines in the air. ". . . ta dah, you found me. And if I'm not what you were looking for, then you were clearly planning to feed—if not sooner, then later—so you can just stop being so 'more ethical than thou' about it." She half turned in her chair, turning her gesture into a wave at the counter staff. "Sweetie, could I have another of these and a chocolate croissant? Thanks."

The café didn't actually have table service. Her smile created it.

Henry's smile sent the young man scurrying back behind the counter.

"Is there another succubus in the city?" He demanded.

"How should I know? I've never run into one, but that just means I've never run into one." The pointed tip of a pink tongue slowly licked foam off her upper lip.

Another mug shattered.

"Incubus?"

She sighed and stopped trying to provoke a reaction from the vampire. "I honestly don't know, Henry. We're not territorial like your lot, we pretty much keep racking up those frequent flyer miles—town to town, party to party . . ." Eyebrows flicked up then down. ". . . man to man. If this is your territory, can't *you* tell?"

"No. I can recognize a demon if I see one, regardless of form, but you have no part in the lives I Hunt or the blood I feed from." He shrugged. "A large enough demon might cause some sort of dissonance, but . . ."

"But you haven't felt any such disturbance in the Force."

"What?"

"You've got to get out to more movies without subtitles, hon." She pushed her chair out from the table and stood, lowering her voice dramatically. "Since you've been to the morgue, there's only one thing left for us to do."

"Us?" Henry interrupted, glancing around with an expression designed to discourage eavesdroppers. "This isn't your problem."

"Sweetie, it became my problem when you showed me your Prince of Darkness face."

He stood as well; she had a point. Since he'd been responsible for involving her, he couldn't then tell her she wasn't involved. "All right, what's left for us to do?"

Her smile suggested that a moonless romp on a deserted beach would be the perfect way to spend the heart of the night. "Why, visit the scene of the crime, of course."

Traffic on the bridge slowed them a little and it was almost two AM by the time they got to Wreck Beach.

Taylor Johnston's body had been found on the north side of the breakwater at Point Grey. Henry parked the car on one of the remaining sections of Old Marine Drive but didn't look too happy about it.

"Campus security," he replied when Lilah inquired. "This whole area is part of the University of British Columbia's endowment lands and they've really been cracking down on people parking by the side of the road."

"*You're* worried about campus security?" The succubus shook her head in disbelief as they walked away from the car. "You know, hon, there are times when you're entirely too human for a vampire."

He supposed he deserved that. "The police have been all over this area; what are we likely to find that they missed?"

"Something they weren't looking for."

"Ghoulies and ghosties and things that go bump in the night?"

"Takes one to know one." She stepped around the tattered end of a piece of yellow police tape. "Or in this case, takes two."

For a moment, Henry had the weirdest sense of déjà vu. It could have been Vicki he was following down to the sand, their partnership renewed. Then Lilah half turned, laughingly telling him to hurry, and she couldn't have been more different than his tall, blonde ex-lover.

Single male, midtwenties, seeks someone to share the night.

So what if it was a different someone. . . .

He knew when he stood on the exact spot the body had been found; the stink of the dying man's terror was so distinct that it had clearly been neither a fast nor a painless death.

"Not an incubus, then," Lilah declared dumping sand out of an expensive Italian pump. "We may like to take our time, but no one ever complains about the process."

Henry frowned and turned his face into the breeze coming in off the Pacific. There was no moon and except for the white lines of breakers at the seawall, the waves were very dark. "Can you smell the rot?"

"Sweetie, there's a great big dead fish not fifteen feet away. I'd have to be in the same shape as Mr. Johnston not to smell it."

"Not the fish." It smelled of the crypt. Of bones left to lie in the dark and damp. "There." He pointed toward the seawall. "It's in there."

Lilah looked up at Henry's pale face, then over at the massive mound of rock jutting out into the sea. "What is?"

"I don't know yet." Half a dozen paces toward the rock, he turned back toward the succubus. "Are you coming?"

"No, just breathing hard."

"Pardon?"

He looked so completely confused, she laughed as she caught up. "You really don't get out much, do you, hon?"

The night was no impediment to either of them, but the entrance was well hidden. If it hadn't been for the smell, they'd never have found it.

Dropping to her knees beside him, Lilah handed Henry a lighter. He stretched his arm to its full length under a massive block of stone, the tiny flame shifting all the shadows but one.

"You can take the lighter with you." Lilah rocked back onto her heels, shaking her head. "I, personally, am not going in there."

Henry understood. Succubi were only slightly harder to kill than the humans they resembled. "I don't think it's home," he muttered dropping onto his stomach and inching forward into the black line of the narrow crevice.

Lilah's voice drifted down to him. "Not a problem, hon, but I'd absolutely ruin this dress. Not to mention my manicure."

"Not to mention," Henry repeated, smiling in spite

of the conditions. There was an innate honesty in the succubus he liked. A lot.

Twice his body-length under the stone, after creeping through a puddle of saltwater at least an inch deep, the way opened up and, although he had to keep turning his shoulders, he could move forward in a crouch. The smell reminded him of the catacombs under St. Mark's Square in Venice where the sea had permeated both the rock and the ancient dead.

Three or four minutes later, he straightened cautiously as the roof rose away and drew Lilah's lighter out of his pocket, expecting to see bones piled in every corner. He saw, instead, a large crab scuttling away, a filthy nest of clothing, and a dark corner where the sucking sound of water moving up and down in a confined space overlaid the omnipresent roar of the sea. A closer inspection showed an almost circular hole down into the rock and, about ten or twelve feet away, the moving water of the Pacific Ocean. A line of moisture showed the high tide mark and another large crab peered out of a crevice just below it. It was obvious where the drained bodies were dumped and what happened to them after dumping.

The scent of death, or rot, hadn't come from the expected cache of corpses, so it had to have come from the creature who lacired here.

Which narrows it down considerably, Henry thought grimly as he closed the almost unbearably hot lighter with a snap.

Lilah and a young man were arranging their clothes as he crawled out from under the seawall. The succubus, almost luminescent by starlight, waved when she saw him.

"Hey, sweetie, you might want to hear this."

"Hear what?" The smell of sex and a familiar pungent smoke overlaid the smell of death.

The young man smiled in what Henry could only describe as a satiated way and said, "Like you know the dead guy they found here this morning, eh? I sort of like saw it happen."

Henry snarled. "Saw what?"

"Whoa, like what big teeth you have, Grandma. Anyway, I've been crashing on the beach when the weather's good, you know, and like last night I'm asleep and I hear this whimpering sort of noise and I think it's a dog in trouble, eh? But it's not. It's like two guys. I can't see them too good but I think, 'hey, go for the gusto, guys,' but one of them seems really pissed 'cause like the tide's really high and I guess he can't go to his regular nooky place in the rocks and he sort of throws himself on the other guy so I stop looking, you know."

"Why didn't you tell this to the police?"

The young man giggled. "Well, some mornings you don't want to talk to the police, you know. And I was like gone before they arrived anyhow. So, like, is this your old lady, 'cause she's one prime piece of . . . OW!"

Henry tightened his grip on the unshaven chin enough to dimple the flesh. He let the Hunter rise, and when the dilated pupils finally responded by dilating further, he growled, "Forget you ever saw us."

"Dude . . ."

"It's a wight," Henry said when they were back in the car. "From the pile of clothing, it looks like it's been there for a while. It probably lives on small animals most of the time, but every now and then people like your friend go missing off the beach or students disappear from the campus, but since they never find a body, no one ever goes looking for a killer.

"Last night, it went hunting a little farther from home only to get back and find the tide in and over the doorway. Which answers the question of why it left the body on the beach. It must've had to race the dawn to shelter."

"Wait a minute." Lilah protested, pausing in her

dusting of sand from crevices. "A wight wouldn't care about going through saltwater. Salted holy water, yes, but not just the sea."

"If it tried to drag its victim the rest of the way, he'd drown."

"And no more than the rest of us, wights don't feed from the dead," Lilah finished. "And all the pieces but one fall neatly into place. You don't honestly think a wight would pick its victim from the personal ads, do you, hon?"

Unclean creature of darkness seeks life essence to suck.

"I don't honestly think it can read," Henry admitted. "That whole personals thing had to have been a coincidence."

"And now that we've answered that question, why don't we head for this great after-hours club I know?"

"I don't have time for that, Lilah. I have a silver letter opener at home I can use for a weapon."

"Against?"

She sounded so honestly confused he turned to look at her. "Against the wight. I can't let it keep killing."

"Why not? Why should you care? Curiosity is satisfied, move on."

Traffic on Fourth Avenue turned his attention back to the road. "Is that the only reason you came tonight? Curiosity?"

"Of course. When a life gets sucked and it's not me doing the sucking, I like to know what is. You're not really . . . ?" He could feel the weight of her gaze as she studied him. "You're not seriously . . . ? You are, aren't you?"

"Yes, I am. It's getting careless."

"Good. Someday, it'll get caught by the dawn, problem solved."

"And when some forensic pathologist does an autopsy on the remains, what then?"

"I'm not a fortune-teller, hon. The only future I can predict is who's going to get lucky."

"Modern forensics will find something that shouldn't

exist. Most people will deny it, but some will start thinking."

"You do know that they moved *The X-Files* out of Vancouver?"

Henry kept his eyes locked on the taillights in front of him. The depth of his disappointment in her reaction surprised him. "Our best defense is that no one believes we exist so they don't look for us. If they start looking . . ." His voice trailed off into mobs with torches and laboratory dissection tables.

They drove in silence until they crossed the Burrard Bridge, then Lilah reached over and laid her fingers on Henry's arm. "That's a nice, pragmatic reason you've got there," she murmured, "but I don't believe you for a moment. You're going to destroy this thing because it's killing in your territory. But it has nothing to do with the territorial imperatives of a vampire," she added before he could speak. "Your territory. Your people. Your responsibility." She dropped her hand back onto her lap. "Let me out here, hon. I try to keep my distance from the overly ethical."

His fingers tightened on the steering wheel as he guided the BMW to the curb. "You *weren't* what I was looking for when I placed that ad," he said as she opened the door. "But I thought we . . ." Suddenly at a low for words, he fell back on the trite. ". . . had a connection."

Leaning over she kissed his cheek. "We did." Stepping out onto the sidewalk, she smiled back in through the open door. "You'll find your Robin, Batman. It just isn't me."

Henry returned to the beach just before high tide, fairly certain the wight hadn't survived so long by making the same mistake twice. He blocked the entrance to the lair with a silver chain and waited.

The fight didn't last long. Henry felt mildly embarrassed by taking his frustrations out on the pitiful creature, but he'd pretty much gotten over it by the time he fed the desiccated body to the crabs.

He broke a number of traffic laws getting home before dawn. Collapsing inside the door to his sanctuary, he woke at sunset stiff and sore from a day spent crumpled on a hardwood floor. He tried to call Lilah and tell her it was over, but whatever connection there'd been between them was well and truly broken. Her phone number was no longer in service.

The brief, aborted companionship made it even harder to be alone.

For two nights, he Hunted and fed and wondered if Lilah had been right and he should have been more specific.

Overly ethical creature of the night seeks sidekick.

The thought of who'd answer something like that frightened him the way nothing else had frightened him over the last four and a half centuries.

Finally, he picked up the list of e-mail addresses and started alphabetically.

The man who came in the door of the café was tall and dark and muscular. Shoulder-length hair had been caught back in a gold clasp. Gold rings flashed on every finger and dangled from both ears. He caught Henry's eye and strode across the café toward him, smiling broadly.

Stopped on the other side of the table.

Stopped smiling.

"Henry?"

"Abdula?"

They blinked in unison.

"Vampire."

Henry dropped back into his chair. "Djinn."

Perhaps he ought to have his ad placed somewhere *other* than Alternative Lifestyles.

Another Fine Nest

There were three other people in the small bookstore. Vicki hesitated to call them customers, since in the ten minutes she'd been standing in front of the new releases shelf ostensibly reading the staff reviews—her favorite the succinct *Trees died for this?*—none of them had given any indication they were planning to actually buy a book. Two were reading, the third attempting to engage the young woman behind the cash register in conversation but succeeding only in monologue.

Without ever having seen him before, Vicki easily identified her contact. Male Caucasian, five eight, dark hair and beard, carrying a good twenty kilos more than was healthy; she could hear his heart pounding as he stared down at the pages of the novel he held. Since he was holding it upside down, it seemed highly unlikely his growing excitement had anything to do with what he wasn't reading. He smelled strongly of garlic.

He was clearly waiting for the other two customers to leave before approaching her. *"They mustn't find out I've called you."*

"Who?"

"Them."

Screw that. Suddenly tired of amateur cloak and dagger theatrics, she walked deeper into the narrow store until she stood directly behind him. Unfortunately, a massive sneeze derailed the impression she'd intended to make. Up close, the smell of garlic was nearly overpowering.

He spun around, dark eyes wide, the heavy gold cross he wore bouncing between the open wings of his jacket.

"Hey." She rummaged in her pocket for a tissue. "Vicki Nelson. You have a job for me?"

Sitting at one of the coffee shop's small tables, Vicki took a drink from her bottle of water and waited for Duncan Travis to pull himself together. His hands, clasped reverently around the paper curves of his triple/triple, were still trembling. She stared at her reflection in the glass, beyond that to the bookstore now across the street, and wished he'd get to the freakin' point.

"I could see your reflection in the glass!"

So could she, but since the glass and her reflection were behind him . . .

"I checked everyone out as they came into the store."

Oh. Her reflection in the glass at the store. That made a little more sense.

"That's why I didn't know you were you."

"You didn't?"

"No." Duncan detached one hand from the paper cup just long enough to sketch a quick emphasis in the air. "I know, you know."

"You know what?"

"About you. What you are."

"I kind of assumed you did, since you called me." Her emphasis on the last three words didn't seem to make the intended impression.

"Not that! People talk, you know. And there's stuff, on the Web . . ." Grabbing the base of the cross, he thrust it toward her, the chain biting deep into the folds of his neck.

Vicki sighed. "People say I'm Catholic? Religious? What?"

"Vampire!" He dropped his voice as heads turned. "Nosferatu. A member of the bloodsucking undead."

"I knew what you meant." She sighed again. Maybe

keeping a lower profile over the last couple of years *would* have been a good idea. "I was just messing with your head. You've got garlic in your pockets, don't you?"

"I am not so desperate that I'd trust you not to drain me and cast my body aside. I have taken precautions." From his expression, Duncan clearly believed his tone sounded threatening. He was wrong.

"Okay." Vicki leaned back in her chair and massaged the bridge of her nose, attempting to forestall a burgeoning headache. "A quick lesson in reality as opposed to the vast amounts of television I suspect you watch. One. Garlic, crosses, holy water—not repelling. Except for maybe the garlic, because frankly, you reek. Two. A biological change does not suddenly start reversing the laws of physics. I had a reflection before I changed, I still have one now. Three. If that's a stake in your pocket and, trust me, I'd much prefer it to be a stake 'cause I don't want you that happy to see me, have you considered the actual logistics of using it? You'll be trying to thrust a not very sharp hunk of wood through clothing, skin, muscle, and bone before you get to the meaty bits. I have no idea what you expect I'll be doing while you make the attempt, but let me assure you that I'll be doing it faster and more violently than you can imagine. Four. Unless you immediately tell me why you called and said you had a job only I could do—giving me, by the way, your credit card number—not very smart, Duncan—I will make you forget you ever saw me." Dropping her hand to the tabletop, she leaned forward, her eyes silvering slightly. "Eternity is too short for all this screwing around. Start talking."

Duncan swallowed, blinked, and wet his lips. "Wow."

"Thank you. The job?"

"King-tics."

"What?"

"We don't know if they're alien constructs or if they've risen from one of the hell dimensions . . ."

Oh yeah, way too much Buffy, Vicki acknowledged silently.

". . . but they're infesting the city. Their nest has to be found and taken out."

"Okay. We?"

"My group."

"AD&D?"

"Third edition."

"Right. Nest?"

"They're insectoids. The ones we've seen seem to be sexless workers, therefore they're likely hive-based. That means a queen and a nest."

"You guys seem to have a pretty good grasp of the situation; why not take them out yourselves?"

Duncan snorted. "In spite of what you seem to think, Ms. Nelson, our grip on reality is fairly firm. Three of us are computer programmers, two work retail, and one is a high school math teacher. We know when we're out of our depth. You turned up on an Internet search—you were local and certain speculations made us think you'd believe us."

"About King-tics?"

"Yeah."

"So let's say I do. Let's say, hypothetically, I believe there's a new kind of something infesting the city. Why is that a problem? Toronto's already ass deep in cockroaches and conservatives; what's one more lower life form?"

"King-tics are smarter than either. And they drink blood." Confident that he now had her full attention, Duncan stretched out one leg and tugged his pants up from his ankle.

Vicki stared at the dingy gray sweat sock and contemplated beating someone's head—hers, his, she wasn't sure which—against the table. "Try using hot water and adding a little bleach."

"What?" He glanced down and flushed. "Oh."

A quick adjustment later and Vicki found herself studying two half-healed puncture wounds just below the curve of Duncan's ankle. Slightly inflamed and about an inch apart, they were right over a vein that ran close to the surface. "Big bug."

"Yeah. But they move really, really fast. They use the crowds in the subway stations as cover. Bite. Drink. Scuttle away. Who's going to notice a couple of little pricks when we're surrounded by bigger pricks every day of our lives?"

"Cynical observation?" Vicki asked the expectant silence.

"Uh, yeah."

"Okay." He'd probably been saving it up too. "You didn't feel the bite?"

"No. I'd have never noticed anything except that my shoe was untied and I knelt to do it up and I . . ."

Screamed like a little girl?

". . . saw this bug. It looked at me, Ms. Nelson. I swear it looked at me . . ."

She believed him, actually. She could hear the before and after in his voice.

". . . and then it disappeared. I sort of saw it moving but it was just so fast. We started looking for them after that and well, once you know what you're looking for . . ." He paused then and his gaze skittered off hers but she had to give him credit for trying. "Once you *admit* what you're looking for, it becomes a lot easier to see."

Yeah. Yeah. You know what I am. I got that twenty minutes ago. "Go on."

"I told the group what had happened and we started looking for the bugs. The King-tics. I mean, we spotted them so we figured we should get to name them, right?" When she didn't answer, he sighed, shrugged, and continued. "At first we only saw them at Bloor and Yonge, at the Bloor Station, probably because it's lower. More subterranean. But then, we saw a few on the upper level, you know, the Yonge line. Yesterday, I saw three at Wellsley."

Vicki fought the urge to turn her head. Wellsley Station was a short block south of the coffee shop.

"Thing is," Duncan laughed nervously, "they saw

me too. They were watching me from the shadows. First time I'd ever seen them still. Usually you catch a sort movement out of the corner of one eye but this . . . It was creepy. Anyway, we talked it over and decided to call you."

"So I can . . . ?"

"I told you. Destroy the nest and the queen. One way or another the subway system hooks up to every major building in the downtown core. The whole city could become a giant banquet hall for these things."

Vicki sat back in her chair and thought about giant intelligent bloodsucking bugs in the subway for a moment. When Duncan opened his mouth to . . . well, she didn't know what he was planning to do because she cut him off with a finger raised in silent warning. Giant, intelligent bloodsucking bugs in the subway. Feeding off the ankles of Toronto. Another predator—predators—feeding in her territory, true, but it was somehow hard to get worked up about something called a King-tic.

Giant, intelligent bloodsucking bugs in the subway.

She couldn't believe she was even considering taking the job.

Still, that sort of thing always ended badly in the movies, didn't it?

The Wellsley platform was empty except for a clump of teenagers at the far end discussing the appalling news that 'N Sync would be on the *Star Wars Episode II* DVD. On the off chance that the six simultaneous rants would suddenly stop and silence fall, Vicki pitched her voice too low to be overheard. "That's where you saw them?"

Duncan nodded. "Yeah. Right there. In the corner. In the shadows. Three of them. Staring at me."

"If you're talking like a character in a Dashiell Hammett novel on purpose, you should know I find it really annoying."

"Sorry."

"Just don't do it again." Stepping closer, Vicki examined the gray tiled corner for webs or egg casings or marks against the fine patina of subway station grime and came up empty. Sighing, she turned her attention back to Duncan. "What were you doing while the bugs—the King-tics—were staring at you?"

He shrugged. "I stared at them for a while."

"And then?"

"They left." He pointed up the tunnel toward Bloor.

"Right."

His expectant silence took her to the edge of the platform. A train had gone by just before they'd entered the station. She could hear the next one a station, maybe a station and a half away. Plenty of time. "You wouldn't have a . . . *artist's conception* of these things, would you?"

"Not with me. I could fax it to you when I get home."

"You do that. Go now."

"What are you going to do?"

"What you're paying me to do."

"You're going into the tunnel!"

He sounded so amazed, she turned to look at him. "It's where the bugs are, Duncan. What did you expect me to do?"

"Go into the tunnels," Duncan admitted. "It's just . . ." He shifted his weight from foot to foot and flashed her an admiring smile. ". . . well, you're actually doing it. And it's so dangerous."

"Because of the bugs?"

"No. Because of the subway trains."

"Trust me, trains aren't a problem."

Behind the beard, his jaw dropped. "You turn into mist?"

Vicki sighed. "I step out of the way."

There were bugs in the subway tunnels. There were also rats, mice, fast food wrappers, used condoms, and a pair of men's Y-front underwear, extra large. The bugs were not giants, not bloodsucking, and, although one of the cockroaches gave her what could only be interpreted as a dirty look just before she squashed it flat, not noticeably intelligent. The rats and mice avoided her, but then, so did pretty much all mammals except humans and cats. The fast food wrappers and used condoms were the expected debris of the twenty-first century. Vicki didn't waste time speculating about the underwear because she really, *really* didn't want to know.

At Yonge and Bloor she crossed the station and slipped down to the lower tracks, easily avoiding the security cameras and the weary curiosity of late commuters.

There were maybe—possibly—fewer rats and mice scrabbling out of her way.

Maybe—possibly—sounds that didn't quite add up to the ambient noise she remembered from other trips.

It depressed her just a little that she'd been down in these tunnels often enough to remember the ambient noise.

When the last train of the night went by, she fought the urge to brace herself against the sides of the workman's niche, rise up to window height, and give any passengers a flickering, strobelike look at what haunted the dark places of the city. *Something about being an immortal, undead creature of the night really changes the things you find funny,* she sighed, allowing the rush of wind to hold her in place as the squares of light flashed by.

The maintenance workers traveled in pairs, but it wasn't hard to separate the younger of the two from his companion. A crescent of white teeth in the darkness. A flash of silver eyes. A promise of things forbidden in the light.

Like shooting fish in a barrel. Grabbing a fistful of his overalls, Vicki dragged him into a dark corner, stiffened her arm to keep him there, and locked her gaze with his. "Giant intelligent bloodsucking bugs."

He looked confused. "Okay."

"Seen any?"

"Down here?"

"Anywhere."

Dark brows drew in. "The cockroaches seem to be getting smarter."

"I noticed that too. Anything else?"

Broad shoulders shrugged. "Sometimes I think I'm hearing things, but the other guys say it's just me."

If they're really intelligent and nesting in the tunnels, they wouldn't want the maintenance workers to find them, would they? Even if they did cross over from some television-inspired hell dimension, a couple of TTC-issue flamethrowers would still take them out. They'd wait, hiding quietly, feeding where it wouldn't be noticed until . . .

Until what?

Until there were enough to them to . . . to . . .

The heat under her hand and the thrum of blood so close weren't making it any easier to think. Not that she'd ever thought well on an empty stomach.

Later, when she lifted her mouth from an open vein in the crock of a sweaty elbow, she had the strangest feeling of being watched. Watched in an empty section of tunnel with no feel of another life anywhere near.

Watched and weighed.

Mike Celluci was asleep when Vicki got home an hour or so before dawn. He was lying on his back, one arm under the covers, one flung out over the empty half of the bed. She slipped in beside him and snuggled up against his shoulder, still damp and warm from the shower, knowing this was how she felt the most human—body temperature almost normal, skin flushed. She felt him wake, felt his arm tighten around her.

"So how'd the job work out?"

"Giant intelligent bloodsucking bugs in the subway." She was beginning to enjoy saying it.

"Seriously?"

"Well, so far I'm pretty much taking the word of my employer. I had a look around the tunnels in question and saw sweet FA but he truly believes there's something nasty down there and I think he may be right."

"There's a lot of nasty in the tunnels."

Memory called up the underwear. Vicki winced. "Yeah. I know." After a moment, spent pushing back against the large hand stroking her back, she sighed and murmured, "Any rumors going around Toronto's finest about strange shit in the subway?"

"Sweet talker."

"Just answer the question."

"No one's said anything to me but I'll ask around. You should probably talk to TTC security."

"Tomorrow. Well, technically, later today."

"You . . . hungry?"

Which wasn't really what he was asking her but feeding had gotten so tied up with other things it had become impossible to separate them. They'd tried. It hadn't worked.

"I could eat."

She only took a mouthful or two from him these days. Enough for mutual sensation, not enough to worry about bleeding him dry over time. Every relationship had to make compromises—she never told him she when she got a bite downtown, he didn't die.

Tonight was . . . different.

Sitting up, sheet folding across her lap, she rolled the taste of his blood around in her mouth.

Sharp. A little bitter.

Like something had been . . . added?

"S'matter?" he asked sleepily, rubbing the toes of one foot against the ankle of the other.

"Mike, have you been in a subway station lately?" She crawled to the end of the bed.

"Sure."

"Bloor and Yonge?"

"Yeah."

Two half healed puncture wounds under the outside curve of his left ankle.

Her eyes silvered.

The job had just gotten personal.

*   *   *

The sun set at 6:03 PM.

Vicki blinked at the darkness, back in the world between one instant and the next.

The phone rang at 6:04.

Pulling it out of the adapter, she flipped it open and snapped, "What?"

"Ms. Nelson. I saw another one!"

"Duncan?" The reception inside a plywood box wrapped in a blackout curtain inside Mike Celluci's crawl space wasn't the best.

"This one didn't just stare at me, Ms. Nelson. It started walking toward me. It knew who I was!"

"Maybe it remembers how you taste." The words were out of her mouth before she could consider their effect.

"OHGODOHGODOHGOD . . ."

"Duncan, calm down. Now." A sort of whimper and then ragged breathing.

"St. George station. University line. They're spreading, aren't they?"

"So it seems."

"What should I *do?*"

"Do?" Vicki paused, half folded around, reaching for the folded pile of clean clothes by her feet. "You should stay out of subway stations." She snagged a pair of socks and began pulling them on. "What blood type are you?"

"What?"

Shimmying underwear up over her hips, she repeated the question.

"O—positive . . ."

She cut him off before he could ask why she wanted to know, told him she'd be in touch, and hung up.

Type O blood could be given to anyone because its erythrocytes contained no antigens, making it compatible with any plasma. Knowledge from before the change. After, well, blood was blood was blood; hot and sweet and the type, so not relevant.

A lot of people were type O.

Mike Celluci was type O.

The faxed sketch of the King-tic was lying on the kitchen table under an old bank envelope. On the back of the envelope, Celluci's dark scrawl: "If this isn't a joke, TRY to be careful. Better yet, catch one, use it to convince the city they have a problem, and let them deal with the rest. Call me."

Someone in Duncan's group had talent. Drawn on graph paper, the bug was almost three dimensional. Six legs but grouped around a single, spiderlike body. Feathery antennae, like on a moth, two eyes on short stalks, four darker areas against the front of the body that could be more eyes. It had a *face*, which was just creepy. Notes under the drawing described the color as urban camouflage, black and gray, different on every bug they'd seen. The size . . .

Vicki blinked and looked again.

Giant intelligent bloodsucking bugs.

Still, she hadn't expected them to be so big.

A foot across and another six to eight inches on either side for the legs.

Leaving the sketch on the table, she crossed the kitchen and peered into the cupboard under the sink. Picked up a package of roach motels, put it down again. Grabbed instead for the can of bug spray, guaranteed to work on roaches, earwigs, flies, millipedes, and all other invading insects.

All other?

Probably not, but it never hurt to be prepared.

"Mike? What've you got for me?" Had she still been able to blush, she would have at his response, but since she couldn't, she just grinned. "Stop being smutty and answer the question. Because I'm on the subway and do not need that image in my head."

Feeling the weight of regard, Vicki lifted her chin and caught the eye of the very bleached blond young man sitting directly across the train and let just a little of the Hunger show. He froze, fingernails digging into the red fuzz on the front curve of the seat. When she released him, he ran for the other end of the car.

She really hated eavesdroppers.

"Yeah, I'm listening."

An old woman had collapsed at the Bay Street station and died later at the hospital. Police were investigating because according to witnesses she'd cried out in pain just before she fell. According to the medical report she'd died of anaphylactic shock.

"An allergic reaction to something in her blood? What type? Yeah, yeah, I know you told me what type of reaction, what blood type?"

Type O.

"This isn't the actual size, right?"

"Of course not." Vicki smiled down at the TTC security guard and took comfort in the knowledge that she wasn't, in fact, lying. Not her fault if he assumed the bugs were smaller than drawn.

"I'm afraid I can't help you. I mean, Joe Public hasn't complained about anything like this and none of my people have said anything either." He handed back the sketch, smiling broadly, willing to share the joke. "You've *seen* one of these?"

"Not me. Like I said, I'm working on a case and my client thinks he's seen one of these."

"And you get paid if they're real or not?"

"Something like that."

"Not a bad gig."

"Pays the bills. What's wrong?"

"What? Oh, just an itchy ankle."

"Let me see." Not a request. No room for refusal. She loved the social shortcuts that came with the whole bloodsucking undead thing.

Two holes. Just below the ankle.

"Do you know your blood type?"

"Uh . . . A?"

More people knew their astrological sign than their blood type—useful if they were in an accident and the paramedics needed to read their horoscope.

She moved so that her body blocked the view of anyone who might be looking through into the security office—although most of them were trying to see themselves on the monitors. "Give me your hand."

He shuddered slightly as she wrapped cool fingers around heated skin, shuddered a little harder as her teeth met through the dark satin of his wrist. A long swallow for research purposes, another because it was so good, one more just because. A lick against the wound and a moment waiting to be sure the coagulants in her saliva had worked.

Lowering his hand carefully to the arm of his chair, Vicki smiled down into his eyes.

"Thank you for help, Mr. Allan. Is that someone pissing against the wall in the outside stairwell?"

His attention back on the monitors, she slipped out of the room.

There was nothing in his blood, type A blood, that wasn't supposed to be there.

The old woman, type O, had died from an allergic reaction to a foreign substance in her blood.

Mike, type O, had a foreign substance in his blood.

If Duncan Travis also had a foreign substance in his blood then it would safe to assume the King-tics were specifically marking specific blood types. She should check Duncan for markers, find a B and an AB who'd been bitten and . . .

Screw it. Discovering if they were only marking Os or marking everything but As wouldn't help her find the bugs any faster. The fact that they were marking at all and that she couldn't think of a good reason why, but could think of several bad reasons was enough to propel her into the crowd of commuters and down into the Bloor station.

The fastest way to find something? Go to where it is. *National Geographic* didn't set up all those cameras around water holes because they liked the way the light reflected off the surface.

If the King-tics fed off subway station crowds, then Vicki'd stand in crowded subway stations until she spotted one, no matter how much the press of humanity threatened to overwhelm her. At least at the end of the day, they all smelled like meat rather than the nasal cacophony that poured out of the trains every morning.

Oh, great. Now I'm hungry.

Everyone standing within arm's reach shuffled nervously away.

Oops.

Masking the Hunger, she ran through her list of mental appetite suppressants.

Homer Simpson, Joan Rivers, Richard Simmons, pretty much anyone who'd ever appeared on the Jerry Springer Show . . .

Her mouth flooded with saliva as the rich scent of fresh blood interrupted her litany. A train screamed into the station, the crowd surged forward, and Vicki used the Hunger to cut diagonally across the platform, less aware of the mass of humanity moving around her than she was of the black and gray shadow scuttling across the ceiling. With the attention of any possible witnesses locked on the interior of the subway cars and their chances of actually boarding, she dropped down off the end of the platform and began to run, just barely managing to keep the bug in sight.

Duncan was right. For a big bug, the thing could really motor.

Then it turned sideways and was gone.

Gone?

Rocking to a stop, Vicki flung herself back against the tunnel wall as another train came by, the roar of steel wheels against steel rails covering some much-needed venting. Eleven years on the police force had given her a vocabulary most sailors would envy. She got through about half of it while the train passed.

In the sudden silence that followed the fading echoes of profanity, she heard the faint skittering sound of six fast moving legs. A sound that offered its last skitter directly over her head. All she had to do was look up.

Unlike the King-tic in the drawing, this one had a membranous sac bulging out from the lower curve of its body. Inside the sac, about an ounce of blood.

Vicki's snarl was completely involuntary.

Both eyestalks pointing directly at her, the bug brought one foreleg up and rubbed at its antennae.

Again the feeling of being weighed.

And wanted.

The eyestalks turned and it flattened itself enough to slip through a crack between the wall and the ceiling.

Easy to find handholds in the concrete since the city had trouble finding money to repair the infrastructure people could see. Anything tucked away underground could be left to rot. Pressed as flat as possible against the wall—*What good is saving the world if you lose your ass to a passing subway?*—Vicki tucked her head sideways and peered through the crack at what seemed to be another tunnel identical to the one she was in. In the dim glow of the safety lights, it looked as though the shadows were in constant movement.

King-tics.

Lots and lots of them.

Probably nesting in an old emergency access tunnel, she decided as something poked her in the back of the head.

Turning she came eye to eye to eye with another bug. After she got the girly shriek out of the way, she realized it didn't seem upset to find her there, it just wanted her to move. Backing carefully down two handholds, she watched it slide sideways through the crack, briefly flashing its sac of blood.

Hard not to conclude that they were feeding something.

She slid the rest of the way to the tunnel floor,

waited for a train to pass, and began working her way carefully up the line. If the bugs were using that crack as their primary access, that suggested the main access had been sealed shut. Twenty paces. Twenty-five. And her fingertips caught a difference in the wall.

The TTC had actually gone to the trouble of parging over the false wall, most likely in an attempt to hide it—or more specifically what was behind it—from street people looking for a place to squat. The faint outline of a door suggested they hadn't originally wanted to hide it from themselves. Forcing her fingers through the thin layer of concrete, Vicki hooked them under the nearest edge and pulled, the *crack* hidden in the roar of a passing train.

Under the concern, plywood and a narrow door nailed shut.

The nails parted faster than the concrete had.

Feeling a little like Sigourney Weaver and a lot like she should have her head examined, Vicki pushed into the second tunnel.

It wasn't very big; a blip in the line between Yonge and University swinging around to the north of the Bay Street station, probably closed because it came too close to any number of expensive stores. Although the third rail was no longer live, it seemed everything else had just been sealed up and forgotten. The place reeked of old blood and sulfur.

Well, they certainly smell like they came from a hell dimension.

Closing the door behind her, Vicki waded carefully toward what seemed to be the quiet center in the mass of seething bugs.

The bugs ignored her.

They can't feed from me, so they ignore me. I've done nothing to harm them, so they ignore me. I also feed on blood so they . . . Holy shit.

Duncan Travis and his group had been certain there'd be a queen in the nest. They were just a bit off. There were three queens. Well, three great big scary somethings individually wrapped in pulsing gelatinous masses being fed by the returning blood carrying—no, harvesting—bugs.

You guys haven't missed a cliché, have you?

Sucker bet that the blood being drained down between three frighteningly large pairs of gaping mandibles was type O. The workers could probably feed on any type—since they seemed to be biting across the board—but they needed that specific universal donor thing to create a queen.

Like worker bees feeding a larva royal jelly.

And Mike laughed at me for watching The Magic School Bus.

As she shifted her weight forward, a double row of slightly larger King-tics moved into place between her and the queens. Apparently, their tolerance stopped a couple of meters out. Not a problem; Vicki didn't need to get any closer. Didn't actually want to get any closer. Like recognized like and she knew predators when she saw them. The queens would not be taking delicate bites from the city's ankles, they'd be biting the city off at the ankles and feeding on the bodies as they fell.

A sudden desire to whip out the can of bug spray and see just how well it lived up to its advertising promise was hurriedly squashed. As was Mike's idea of grabbing a bug and presenting it to the proper authorities—whoever the hell they were. Somehow it just didn't seem smart—or survivable—to piss them off while she was standing in midst of hundreds of them. Barely lifting her feet from the floor, she shuffled back toward the door, hurrying just a little when she saw that all three queens had turned their eyestalks toward her.

Odds were good they weren't going to be confined by that gelatinous mass much longer.

So. What to do?

Closing the door carefully behind her, she waited, shoulder blades pressed tight against the wood as another train went by. Options? She supposed she could always let the TTC deal with it. It would be as easy for her to convince the right TTC official to come down to the tunnels for a little look as it would be for her to convince him to expose his throat. Not as much fun, but as easy. Unfortunately, years of experience had taught her that the wheels of bureaucracy ran slowly, even given a shove, and her instincts—new and old—were telling her they didn't have that kind of time to waste.

Still, given that the King-tics were nesting in the subway system, it seemed only right that the TTC deal with it.

Vicki picked up the garbage train at Sherbourne. There were no security cameras in the control booth and coverage on the platform didn't extend to someone entering the train from the tracks. Tucking silently in behind the driver, Vicki tapped him on the shoulder and dropped her masks.

And sighed at the sudden pervasive smell of urine.

"Your hands! Blood all over your hands!"

"It's not blood," she sighed, scrubbing her palms against the outside of her thighs. "It's rust. Now concentrate, I need you to tell me how to start this thing."

"Union rules . . ."

Her upper lip curled.

". . . have no relevance here. Okay. Sure. Push this."

"And to go faster?"

"This. To stop . . ."

"Stopping won't be a problem." She leaned forward, fingers gently gripping his jaw, her eyes silver. "Go join your coworkers on the platform. Be surprised when the train starts to move. Don't do *anything* that might stop it or cause it to be stopped. Forget you ever saw me."

"Saw who?"

Mike was watching the news when Vicki came upstairs the next evening. "Here's something you might be interested in. Seems a garbage train went crashing into an access tunnel and blew up—which they're not wont to do—but unfortunately a very hot fire destroyed all the evidence."

"Did you just say *wont?*"

"Maybe. Why?"

Just wondering." Leaning over the back of his chair, she kissed the top of his head. "Anyone get hurt?"

"No. And, fortunately, the safety protocols activated in time to save the surrounding properties."

"Big words. You quoting?"

"Yes. You crazy?"

She thought about it for a minute but before she could answer, her phone rang. Stepping away from the chair, she flipped it open. "Good evening, Duncan."

"How did you know it was me?"

"Call display."

"Oh. Right. But yesterday . . . ?"

"You called before I was up. It's pretty damned dark inside a coffin."

"You sleep in a coffin!?"

"No, I'm messing with your head again. I expect you've seen the news?"

"It's the only thing that's been on all day. You did that, didn't you? That was you destroying the nest! Did you get them all?"

"Yes."

"Are you sure?"

"They shit sulfur, Duncan. They were pretty flammable."

"But what if some of them were out, you know, hunting?"

"They hunt on crowded subway platforms. No crowds in the wee smalls."

"Oh. Okay. Did you find out where they came from?"

"No. It didn't seem like a good idea to sit down and play twenty questions with them. And besides, they just seemed to be intelligent because they were following pretty specific programming. They were probably no smarter than your average cockroach."

"But giant and bloodsucking?"

"Oh, yeah."

Vicki had no idea what he was thinking about during the long pause that followed; she didn't *want* to know.

"So it's safe for me to go back on the subway?"

"You and three million other people."

"About your bill . . ."

"We'll talk about it tomorrow in the coffee shop—we should be able to get into the area by then." She looked a question at Mike, now standing and watching her. He nodded reluctantly. "Seven thirty. Good night, Duncan."

Mike shook his head as she powered off the phone and holstered it. "You're actually going to charge him?"

"Well, I'd send a bill to the city but I doubt they'd pay it—given that there's no actual evidence I just saved their collective butts. Again." Demons, mummies, King-tics—it was amazing how fast that sort of thing got old. She followed Mike into the kitchen and watched a little jealously as he poured a cup of coffee. She missed coffee.

"Speaking of no actual evidence; how did you get the garbage train to blow?"

Vicki grinned. "Not that I'm admitting anything, detective-sergeant, but *if* I wanted top blow up a garbage train in a specific giant bloodsucking bug-infested place, I'd probably use a little accelerant and a timer, having first switched the rails and cleared the tunnels of all mammalian life forms."

"You closed down the entire system, Vicki."

"Giant bloodsucking bugs, Mike."

"I'm not saying you didn't have a good reason," he sighed, leaning against the counter. "But don't you think your solution was a little extreme?"

"Not really, no."

"What aren't you telling me?"

Moving into his arms, she bit him lightly on the chin. "I'm not telling you I blew up that garbage train."

"Good point."

"I'm not telling you what I really think of people who watch golf."

"Thank you."

She could feel his smile against the top of her head, his heart beating under her cheek, his life in her hands. Nor was she telling him that people like him, with type O blood, had been tagged so they'd be easier to find. Why bother with random biting when it was possible to go straight to the blood needed to create new queens? Even if they'd been harmless parasites, she'd have blown them up for that alone.

Mike Celluci was hers and she didn't share.

"Vicki, you going to tell me what you're snarling about?"

"Just thinking of something that really bugs me . . ."

Sceleratus

"Man, this whole church thing just freaks me right out." Tony came out of the shadows where the streetlights stopped short of Holy Rosary Cathedral and fell into step beside the short, strawberry blond man who'd just come out of the building. "I mean, you're a member of the bloodsucking undead for Christ's sa . . . Ow!" He rubbed the back of his head. "What was that for?"

"I just came from confession. I'm in a mood."

"It's going to pass, right?" In the time it took him to maneuver around three elderly Chinese women, his companion had made it almost all the way to the parking lot and he had to run to catch up. "You know, we've been together what, almost two years, and you haven't been in church since last year around this time and . . ."

"Exactly this time."

"Okay. Is it like an anniversary or something?"

"Exactly like an anniversary." Henry Fitzroy, once Duke of Richmond and Somerset, bastard son of Henry VIII, fished out the keys to his BMW and unlocked the door.

Tony studied Henry's face as he got into his own seat, as he buckled his seat belt, as Henry pulled out onto Richards Street. "You want to tell me about it?" he asked at last.

They'd turned onto Smithe Street before Henry answered. . . .

*   *   *

Even after three weeks of torment, her body burned and broken, she was still beautiful to him. He cut the rope and caught her as she dropped, allowing her weight to take him to his knees. Holding her against his heart, rocking back and forth in a sticky pool, he waited for grief.

She had been dead only a few hours when he'd found her, following a blood scent so thick it left a trail even a mortal could have used. Her wrists had been tightly bound behind her back, a coarse rope threaded through the lashing and used to hoist her into the air. Heavy iron weights hung from burned ankles. The Inquisitors had begun with flogging and added more painful persuasions over time. Time had killed her; pain layered on pain until finally life had fled.

They'd had a year together, a year of nights since he'd followed her home from the Square of San Marco. He'd waited until the servants were asleep and then slipped unseen and unheard into her father's house, into her room. Her heartbeat had drawn him to the bed, and he'd gently pulled the covers back. Her name was Ginevra Treschi. Almost thirty, and three years a widow, she wasn't beautiful but she was so alive—even asleep—that he'd found himself staring. Only to find a few moments later that she was staring back at him.

"I don't want to hurry your decision," she'd said dryly, "but I'm getting chilled and I'd like to know if I should scream."

He'd intended to feed and then convince her that he was a dream but he found he couldn't.

For the first time in a hundred years, for the first time since he had willingly pressed his mouth to the bleeding wound in his immortal lover's breast, Henry Fitzroy allowed someone to see him as he was.

All he was.

Vampire. Prince. Man.

Allowed love.

Ginevra Treschi had brought light back into a life spent hiding from the sun.

Only one gray eye remained beneath a puckered lid and the Inquisitors had burned off what remained of the dark hair—the ebony curls first shorn in the convent that had been no protection from the Hounds of God. In Venice, in the year of our Lord 1637, the Hounds hunted as they pleased among the powerless. First, it had been the Jews, and then the Moors, and then those suspected of Protestantism until finally the Inquisition, backed by the gold flowing into Spain from the New World, began to cast its net where it chose. Ginevra had been an intelligent woman who dared to think for herself. In this time, that was enough.

Dead flesh compacted under his hands as his grip tightened. He wanted to rage and weep and mourn his loss, but he felt nothing. Her light, her love, had been extinguished and darkness had filled its place.

His heart as cold as hers, Henry kissed her forehead and laid the body gently down. When he stood, his hands were covered in her blood.

There would be blood enough to wash it away.

He found the priests in a small study, sitting at ease in a pair of cushioned chairs on either side of a marble hearth, slippered feet stretched out toward the fire, gold rings glittering on pale fingers. Cleaned and fed, they still stank of her death.

. . . confessed to having relations with the devil, was forgiven, and gave her soul up to God. Very satisfactory all around. Shall we return the body to the sisters or to her family?"

The older Dominican shrugged. "I cannot see that it makes any difference, she . . . Who are you?"

Henry lifted his lip off his teeth in a parody of a smile. "I am vengeance," he said, closing and bolting the heavy oak door behind him. When he turned, he saw that the younger priest, secure in the power he wielded, blinded by that security, had moved toward him.

Their eyes met. The priest, who had stood calmly by while countless *heretics* found their way to redemption on paths of pain, visibly paled.

Henry stopped pretending to smile. "And I am the devil Ginevra Treschi had relations with."

He released the Hunger her blood had called.

They died begging for their lives as Ginevra had died.

It wasn't enough.

The Grand Inquisitor had sent five other Dominicans to serve on his Tribunal in Venice. Three died at prayer. One died in bed. One died as he dictated a letter to a novice who would remember nothing but darkness and blood.

The Doge, needing Spain's political and monetary support to retain power, had given the Inquisitors a wing of his palace. Had given them the room where the stone walls were damp and thick and the screams of those the Hounds brought down would not disturb his slumber.

Had killed Ginevra as surely as if he'd used the irons.

With a soft cry, Gracia la Valla sat bolt upright in the Doge's ornate bed clutching the covers in both hands. The canopy was open and a spill of moonlight pattered the room in shadows.

She heard a sound beside her and, thinking she'd woken her lover, murmured, as she reached out for him, "Such a dark dream I had."

Her screams brought the household guard.

He killed the Inquisition's holy torturer quickly, like the animal he was, and left him lying beside the filthy pallet that was his bed.

It still wasn't enough.

*   *   *

In the hour before dawn, Henry carried the body of Ginevra Treschi to the chapel of the Benedictine Sisters who had tried to shelter her. He had washed her in the canal, wrapped her in linen, and laid her in front of their altar, her hands closed around the rosary she'd given him the night they'd parted.

Her lips when he kissed them were cold.

But so were his.

Although he had all but bathed in the blood of her murderers, it was her blood still staining his hands.

He met none of the sisters and, as much as he could feel anything, he was glad of it. Her miraculous return to the cloister would grant her burial in their consecrated ground—but not if death returned with her.

Henry woke the next night in one of the vaults under San Marco, the smell of her blood all around him. It would take still more blood to wash it away. For all their combined power of church and state, the Inquisition did not gather their victims randomly. Someone had borne witness against her.

Giuseppe Lemmo.

Marriage to him had been the alternative to the convent.

He had a large head, and a powdered gray wig, and no time for denial. After Henry had drunk his fill, head and wig and the body they were more or less attached to slid silently into the canal.

As Lemmo sank beneath the filthy water, the sound of two men approaching drove Henry into the shadows. His clothing stank of new death and old, but it was unlikely anyone could smell it over the stink of the city.

"No, no, I say the Dominicans died at the hand of the devil rising from hell to protect one of his own."

Henry fell silently into step behind the pair of merchants, the Hunger barely leashed.

"And I say," the second merchant snorted, "that the Holy Fathers called it on themselves. They spend so much time worrying about the devil in others, well, there's no smoke without fire. They enjoyed their work too much for my taste and you'll notice, if you look close, that most of their *heretics* had a hefty purse split between the Order and the Doge after their deaths."

"And more talk like that will give them *your* purse to split, you fool."

Actually, it had saved them both, but they would never know it.

"Give who my purse? The Hounds of God in Venice have gone to their just reward." He turned his head and spat into the dark waters of the canal. "And I wish Old Nick the joy of them."

His companion hurriedly crossed himself. "Do you think they're the only dogs in the kennel? The Dominicans are powerful; their tribunals stretch all the way back to Spain and up into the northlands. They won't let this go unanswered. I think you will find before very long that Venice will be overrun by the Hounds of God."

"You think? Fool, the One Hundred will be too busy fighting over a new Doge to tell His Holiness that some of his dogs have been put down."

Before they could draw near the lights and crowds around the Grand Canal, Henry slipped into the deeper darkness between two buildings. The Dominican's Tribunals stretched all the way back to Spain. He looked down at Ginevra's blood on his hands.

"Drink, signore?"

Without looking at either the bottle or the man who offered it, Henry shook his head and continued staring out over the moonlit water toward the lights of Sicily. Before him, although he could not tell which lights they were, were the buildings of the Inquisition's largest tribunal outside of Spain. They had their own courthouse, their own prison, their own chapel, their own apartments where half of every heretic's possessions ended up.

It was entirely possible they knew he was coming or that *something* was coming. Rumor could travel by day and night while he could move only in darkness.

Behind him stretched a long line of the dead. He had killed both Dominicans and the secular authorities who sat with them on the tribunals. He had killed the lawyers hired by the Inquisition. He had killed those who denounced their neighbors to the Inquisition and those who lent the Inquisition their support. He had killed those who thought to kill him.

He had never killed so often or been so strong. He could stand on a hill overlooking a village and know how many lives were scattered beneath him. He could stand in shadow outside a shuttered building and count the number of hearts beating within. He could stare into the eyes of the doomed and be almost deafened by the song of blood running through their veins. It was becoming hard to tell where he ended and the Hunger began.

The terrified whispers that followed him named him demon, so, when he fed, he hid the marks that would have shown what he truly was. There were too many who believed the old tales and he was far too vulnerable in the day.

"Too good to drink with me, signore?" Stinking of wine, he staggered along the rail until the motion of the waves threw him into Henry's side. Stumbling back, he raised the jug belligerently. "Too good to . . ."

Henry caught the man's gaze with his and held it. Held it through the realization, held it through the terror, held it as the heart began to race with panic, held it as bowels voided. When he finally released it, he caught the jug that dropped from nerveless fingers and watched the man crawl whimpering away, his mind already refusing to admit what he had seen.

It had been easy to find a ship willing to cross the narrow strait at night. Henry had merely attached himself to a party of students negotiating their return to the university after spending the day in the brothels of Reggio and the exotic arms of mainland whores. Although the sky was clear, the moon full, and the winds from the northwest, the captain of the schooner had accepted their combined coin so quickly he'd probably been looking for an excuse to make the trip. No doubt his hold held some of the steady stream of goods from France, Genoa, and Florence that moved illegally down the western coast to the Spanish-controlled kingdom of Naples and then to Sicily.

The smugglers would use the students as Henry intended, as a diversion over their arrival in Messina.

They passed the outer arm of the sickle-shaped harbor, close enough that the night no longer hid the individual buildings crouched on the skirts of Mount Etna. He could see the spire of the cathedral, the Abbey of Santa Maria della Valle, the monastery of San Giorgio, but nothing that told him where the Dominicans murdered in the name of God.

No matter.

It would be easy enough to find what he was looking for.

They could lock themselves away, but Henry would find them. They could beg or plead or pray, but they would die. And they would keep dying until enough blood had poured over his hands to wash the stain of Ginevra's blood away.

Messina was a port city and had been in continuous use since before the days of the Roman Empire. Beneath its piers and warehouses, beneath broad avenues and narrow streets, beneath the lemon trees and the olive groves, were the ruins of an earlier city. Beneath its necropolis were Roman catacombs.

As the students followed their hired torchbearer from the docks to the university, Henry followed the scent of death through the streets until he came at last to the end of the Via Annunziata to the heavy iron gates that closed off the Piazza del Dominico from the rest of the city. The pair of stakes rising out of the low stone dais in the center of the square had been used within the last three or four days. The stink of burning flesh almost overwhelmed the stink of fear.

Almost.

"Hey! You! What are you doing?"

The guard's sudden roar out of the shadows was intended to intimidate.

"Why the gates?" Henry asked without turning. The Hounds preferred an audience when they burned away heresy.

"You a stranger?"

"I am vengeance," Henry said quietly, touching the iron and rubbing the residue of greasy smoke between two fingers. As the guard reached for him, he turned and closed his hand about the burly wrist, tightening his grip until bones cracked and the man fell to his knees. "Why the gates?" he repeated.

"Friends. Oh, God, please . . ." It wasn't the pain that made him beg but the darkness in the stranger's eyes. "Some of the heretics got friends!"

"Good." He had fed in Reggio, so he snapped the guard's neck and let the body fall back into the shadows. Without the guard, the gates were no barrier.

"You said he was ready to confess." Habit held up out of the filth, The Dominican stared disapprovingly at the body on the rack. "He is unconscious!"

The thin man in the leather apron shrugged. "Wasn't when I sent for you."

"Get him off that thing and back into the cell with the others." Sandals sticking to the floor, he stepped back beside the second monk and shook his head. "I am exhausted and his attorney has gone home. Let God's work take a break until morning, for pity's . . ."

The irons had not been in the fire, but they did what they'd been made to do. Even as the Hunger rose to answer the blood now turning the robe to black and white and red, Henry appreciated the irony of the monk's last word. A man who knew no pity had died with pity on his tongue. The second monk screamed and choked on a crimson flood as curved knives, taken from the table beside the rack, hooked in under his arms and met at his breastbone.

Henry killed the jailer as he'd killed the guard. Only those who gave the orders paid in blood.

Behind doors of solid oak, one large cell held half a dozen prisoners and two of the smaller cells held one prisoner each. Removing the bars, Henry opened the doors and stepped back out of sight. He had learned early that prisoners would rather remain to face the Inquisition than walk by him, but he always watched them leave, some small foolish part of his heart hoping he'd see Ginevra among them, free and alive.

The prisoner from one of the small cells surged out as the door was opened. Crouched low and ready for a fight, he squinted in the torchlight searching for an enemy. When he saw the bodies, he straightened and his generous mouth curved up into a smile. Hair as red-gold as Henry's had begun to gray, but in spite of approaching middle-age, his body was trim and well built. He was well-dressed and clearly used to being obeyed.

On his order, four men and two women shuffled out of the large cell, hands raised to block the light, bits of straw clinging to hair and clothing. On his order, they led the way out of the prison.

He was using them to see if the way was clear, Henry realized. Clever. Ginevra had been clever, too.

Murmured Latin drew his attention back to the bodies of the Dominicans. Kneeling between them, a hand on each brow, the elderly Franciscan who'd emerged from the other cell performed the Last Rites.

"In nominee Patris, et Filii, et Spiritus Sancti. Amen." One hand gripping the edge of the rack, he pulled himself painfully to his feet. "You can come out now. I know what you are."

"You have no idea, monk."

"You think not?" The old man shrugged and bent to release the ratchet that held the body on the rack taut. "You are the death that haunts the Inquisition.

You began in Venice, you finally found your way to us here in Messina."

"If I am death, you should fear me."

"I haven't feared death for some time." He turned and swept the shadows with a rheumy gaze. "Are you afraid to face *me*, then?"

Lips drawn back off his teeth, Henry moved into the light.

The Franciscan frowned. "Come closer."

Snarling, Henry stepped over one of the bodies, the blood scent wrapping around him. Prisoner of the Inquisition or not, the monk would learn fear. He caught the Franciscan's gaze with his but, to his astonishment, couldn't hold it. When he tried to look away, he could not.

After a long moment, the old monk sighed, and released him. "Not evil, although you have done evil. Not anger, nor joy in slaughter. I never knew your kind could feel such pain."

He staggered back, clutching for the Hunger as it fled. "I feel nothing!"

"So you keep telling yourself. What happened in Venice, vampire? Who did the Inquisition kill that you try to wash away the blood with theirs?"

Over the roaring in his head, Henry heard himself say, "Ginevra Treschi."

"You loved her."

It wasn't a question. He answered it anyway. "Yes."

"You should kill me, you know. I have seen you. I know what you are. I know what is myth . . ." He touched two fingers to the wooden cross hanging against his chest. ". . . and I know how to destroy you. When you are helpless in the day, I could drag your body into sunlight; I could hammer a stake through your heart. For your own safety, you should kill me."

He was right.

What was one more death? Henry's fingers, sticky with blood already shed, closed around the old man's skinny neck. He would kill him quickly and return to the work he had come here to do. There were many, many more Dominicans in Messina.

The Franciscan's pulse beat slow and steady.

It beat Henry's hand back to his side. "No. I do not kill the innocent."

"I will not argue original sin with you, vampire, but you're wrong. Parigi Carradori, the man from the cell next to mine, seeks power from the Lord of Hell by sacrificing children in dark rites."

Henry's lip curled. "Neither do I listen to the Inquisition's lies."

"No lie; Carradori admits it freely without persuasion. The demons hold full possession of his mind, and you have sent him out to slaughter the closest thing to innocence in the city."

"That is none of my concern."

"If that is true, then you really should kill me."

"Do not push me, old man!" He reached for the Hunger but for the first time since Ginevra's death it was slow to answer.

"By God's grace, you are being given a chance to save yourself. To find, if you will, redemption. You may, of course, choose to give yourself fully to the darkness you have had wrapped about you for so many months, allowing it, finally, into your heart. Or you may choose to begin making amends."

"Amends?" He stepped back slowly so it wouldn't look so much like a retreat and spat into the drying blood pooled out from the Dominicans' bodies. "You want me to feel sorrow for the deaths of these men?"

"Not yet. To feel sorrow, you must first feel. Begin by stopping Carradori. We will see what the Lord has in mind for you after that." He patted the air between them, an absentminded benediction, then turned and began to free the man on the rack, working the leather straps out of creases in the swollen arms.

Henry watched him for a moment, then turned on one heel and strode out of the room.

He was not going after Carradori. His business was with the Inquisition, with those who had slowly murdered his Ginevra, not with a man who may or may not be dealing with the Dark One.

". . . you have sent him out to slaughter the closest thing to innocence in the city."

He was not responsible for what Carradori chose to do with his freedom. Stepping out into the square, he listened to the sound of Dominican hearts beating all around him. Enough blood to finally *be* enough.

". . . seeks power from the Lord of Hell by sacrificing children in dark rites."

Children died. Some years, more children died than lived. He could not save them all even were he willing to try.

"You may choose to give yourself fully to the darkness. Or you may choose to begin making amends."

"Shut up, old man!"

Torch held high, head cocked to better peer beyond its circle of light, a young monk stepped out of one of the other buildings. "Who is there? Is that you, Brother Pe . . . ?" He felt more than saw a shadow slip past him. When he moved the torch forward, he saw only the entrance to the prison. A bloody handprint glistened on the pale stone.

The prisoners had left the gate open. Most of them had taken the path of least resistance and stumbled down the Via Annunziata, but one had turned left, gone along the wall heading up toward the mountain.

Carradori.

Out away from the stink of terror that filled the prison, Henry could smell the taint of the Dark One in his blood.

The old man hadn't lied about that, at least.

Behind him, a sudden cacophony of male voices suggested his visit had been discovered. It would be dangerous to deal further with the Inquisition tonight. He turned left.

He should have caught up to Carradori in minutes, but he didn't and he found himself standing outside a row of tenements pressed up against the outer wall of the necropolis with no idea of where the man had gone. Lip drawn up off his teeth, he snarled softly and a scrawny dog, thrown out of sleep by the sound, began to howl. In a heartbeat, a dozen more were protesting the appearance of a new predator on their territory.

The noise the monks had made was nothing in comparison.

As voices rained curses down from a dozen windows, Henry ran for the quiet of the necropolis.

The City of the Dead had tenements of its own; the dead had been stacked in this ground since the Greeks controlled the strait. Before Venice, before Ginevra, Henry had spent very little time with the dead—his own grave had not exactly been a restful place. Of late, however, he had grown to appreciate the silence. No heartbeats, no bloodsong, nothing to call the Hunger, to remind him of vengeance not yet complete.

But not tonight.

Tonight he could hear two hearts and feel a life poised on the edge of eternity.

The houses of the dead often became temples for the dark arts.

Warding glyphs had been painted in blood on the outside of the mausoleum. Henry sneered and passed them by. Blood held a specific power over him, as specific as the power he held over it. The dark arts were a part of neither.

The black candles, one at either end of the skinny child laid out on the tomb, shed so little light Henry entered without fear of detection. To his surprise, Carradori looked directly at him with wild eyes.

"And so the agent of my Dark Lord comes to take his place by my side." Stripped to the waist, he had cut more glyphs into his own flesh, new wounds over old scars.

"I am no one's agent," Henry spat, stepping forward.

"You set me free, vampire. You slaughtered those who had imprisoned me."

"You may choose to give yourself fully to the darkness."

"That had nothing to do with you."

Holding a long straight blade over the child, Carradori laughed. "Then why are you here?"

"Or you may choose to begin making amends."

"I was curious."

"Then let me satisfy your curiosity."

He lifted the knife and the language he spoke was neither Latin nor Greek, for Henry's father had seen that he was fluent in both. It had hard consonants that tore at the ears of the listener as much as at the throat of the speaker. The Hunger, pushed back by the Franciscan, rose in answer.

This would be one way to get enough blood.

Then the child turned her head.

Gray eyes stared at Henry past a fall of ebony curls. One small, dirty hand stretched out toward him.

But the knife was already on its way down.

He caught the point on the back of his arm, felt it cut through him toward the child as his fist drove the bones of Carradori's face back into his brain. He was dead before he hit the floor.

The point of the blade had touched the skin over the child's heart but the only blood in the tomb was Henry's.

He dragged the knife free and threw it aside, catching the little girl up in his arms and sliding to his knees. The new wound in his arm was nothing to the old wound in his heart. It felt as though a glass case had been shattered and now the shards were slicing their way out. Rocking back and forth, he buried his face in the child's dark curls and sobbed over and over, "I'm sorry, I'm sorry, I'm sorry."

". . . confessed to having relations with the devil, was forgiven, and gave her soul up to God."

"And I am the devil Ginevra Treschi had relations with."

Loving him had killed her.

*   *   *

When he woke the next evening the old Franciscan was sitting against the wall, the shielded lantern at his feet making him a gray shadow in the darkness.

"I thought you'd bring a mob with stakes and torches."

"Not much of a hiding place, if that's what you thought."

Sitting up, Henry glanced around the alcove and shrugged. He had left the girl at the tenements, one grimy hand buried in the ruff of the scrawny dog he'd wakened and then, with dawn close on his heels, he'd gone into the first layer of catacombs and given himself to the day.

"Why didn't you?"

" 'Vengeance is mine,' sayeth the Lord. And besides . . ." Clutching the lantern, he heaved himself to his feet. ". . . I hate to lose a chance to redeem a soul."

"You know what I am. I have no soul."

"You said you loved this Ginevra Treschi. Love does not exist without a soul."

"My love killed her."

"Perhaps." Setting the lantern on the tomb, he took Henry's left hand in his and turned his palm to the light. The wound began to bleed sluggishly again, the blood running down the pale skin of Henry's forearm to pool in his palm. "Did she choose to love you in return?"

His voice less than a whisper. "Yes."

"Then don't take that choice away from her. She has lost enough else. You have blood on your hands, vampire. But not hers."

He stared at the crimson stains. "Not hers."

"No. And you can see whose blood is needed to wash away the rest." He gently closed Henry's fingers. "Mine . . ."

The smack on the back of the head took him by surprise. He hadn't even seen the old monk move.

"The Blood of the Lamb, vampire. Your death will

not bring my brother Dominicans back to life, but your life will be long enough to atone."

"You are a very strange monk."

"I wasn't always a monk. I knew one of your kind in my youth and perhaps by redeeming you, I redeem myself for the mob and the stakes I brought to him."

Henry could see his own sorrow mirrored in the Franciscan's eyes. He knew better than to attempt to look beyond it.

"Why were you a prisoner of the Inquisition?"

"I'm a Franciscan. The Dominicans don't appreciate our holding of the moral high ground."

"The moral high ground . . ."

"Christ was poor. We are poor. *They* are not. Which does not mean, however, that they need to die."

"I didn't . . ."

"I know." He laid a warm palm against Henry's hair. "How long has it been since your last confession . . . ?"

"The Tribunal's buildings were destroyed in an earthquake in 1783. They were never rebuilt. When I went back to Messina in the 1860s, even I couldn't find the place they'd been."

Tony stared out into the parking garage. They'd been home for half an hour, just sitting in the car while Henry talked. "Did you really kill all those people?"

"Yes."

"But some of them were bad people, abusing their power and . . . that's not the point, is it?"

"No. They died because I felt guilty about what happened to Ginevra, not because the world would have been a better place without them in it, not because I had to kill to survive." His lips pulled back off his teeth. "I have good reasons when I kill people now."

"Speaking as people," Tony said softly, "I'm glad to hear that."

His tone drew Henry's gaze around. "You're not afraid?"

"Because you vamped out three hundred and fifty years ago?" He twisted in the seat and met Henry's eyes. "No. I know you *now*." When Henry looked away, he reached out and laid a hand on his arm. "Hey, I got a past, too. Not like yours, but you can't live without having done things you need to make up for. Things you're sorry you did."

"Is being sorry enough?"

"I haven't been to Mass since I was a kid, but isn't it supposed to be? I mean, if you're *really* sorry? So what kind of penance did he give you?" Tony asked a few moments later when it became obvious Henry wasn't going to elaborate on how sorry he was.

"Today?"

"No, three hundred and fifty years ago. I mean, three Hail Marys aren't gonna cut it after, well . . ."

"He made me promise to remember."

"That's all?" When it became clear Henry wasn't going to answer that either, he slid out of the car and leaned back in the open door. "Come on, TSN's got Australian rugger on tonight. You know you love it."

"You go. I'll be up in a few minutes."

"You okay?"

"Fine."

"I could . . ."

"Tony."

"Okay. I could go upstairs." He straightened, closed the car door, and headed across the parking garage to the elevator. When he reached it, he hit the call button and waited without turning. He didn't need to turn. He knew what he'd see.

Henry.

Still sitting in the car.

Staring at his hands.

Critical Analysis

"You! You're a police officer, aren't you?"

Detective Sergeant Michael Celluci stared down at the pale, long-fingered hand clutching his arm and then up at the tall, unshaven, young man who'd stopped him on the steps of police headquarters and asked the question. "I am."

Pink-rimmed, bloodshot eyes locked onto Celluci's face. "I need your help."

"With what?"

"Someone's going to kill me."

"Uh-huh." The man was sincerely frightened. Celluci'd seen frightened often enough to know it. Sincere . . . well, not so much. Not in his line of work. He nodded toward the doors where condensation beaded the glass barrier between warmth and January in downtown Toronto. "You want to talk about this inside?"

"His name is Raymond Carr and it started with threatening e-mail." Celluci passed Vicki the file folder and headed over to the coffeemaker. "It escalated to someone hacking his system and sticking the threats into his work."

"What's he do?"

"He's a writer. Did you make this when you got up, or is it sludge left over from this morning?" The mug of coffee he'd just poured stalled halfway to his mouth.

"What do you care? You'd drink the sludge anyway. What's he write?"

"Pretty much anything people will pay him for. Of course, people are paying him a lot less when their ad copy comes complete with death threats."

"You'll save, save, save while we beat in your head with a bat?"

"Less wordy. Oh, and he's working on a book."

"Yeah, isn't everyone." She frowned at the top printout. "I assume the word *die* isn't meant to be in here?" A few more pages in. "Or here? Actually, since it's repeated about a dozen times, forget I asked. What did he do and who did he do it to?"

"He doesn't know."

"Well, he clearly pissed off someone with some hacking abilities," she muttered, scanning the rest of the file.

Celluci pulled out a chair and sat down on the other side of the kitchen table. "He says he didn't."

Fingertips against the edge of the table, she leaned back, balancing on two legs of her chair. "So you think it's some kind of a sick joke? Just some bored techno-nerd getting his jollies by screwing with a stranger?"

"That's possible. Point is, Carr's terrified. We wrote him up, but there's not much we can do until we have more to go on than electronic threats."

"Don't you guys have technonerds of your own now?" She beat out a drum roll. "Several someones who can trace an e-mail like this back to the sender?"

"Apparently, we can't do squat without Carr's computer and he won't hand it over. Says his whole life is on that machine."

"Really? I hope he remembers to do backups." She flipped the folder closed and let her chair drop flat. "What does he expect you—where 'you' refers to Toronto's finest, not you personally—to do?"

"Protect him."

"I think I just figured out where this is going."

Cellcui smiled and drained his mug. "Carr's address

is on the outside of the folder. I told him you'd be by this evening."

"Mike, I'm not hired muscle."

"Did I say you were? You have special abilities."

"Special abilities?" Her smile was both threat and invitation.

He cleared his throat. "And," he continued emphatically, ignoring the invitation and disregarding the threat, "you may be an undead creature of the night, but you were a cop, and a good one, for years. Use *those* skills for a change. Find out who's threatening him. Do some detecting. While you're there, see that no one beats his head in with a bat."

Raymond Carr lived on Bloor Street in a third-floor flat over the Korona Restaurant. As Vicki made her way up the steep, narrow stairs, she avoided touching the grimy banister and wondered if he could afford her services. Mike sometimes forgot she wasn't on the public payroll anymore. Or he was indulging in some weird passive-aggressive "let me take care of you" macho thing. She wasn't sure which.

The apartment door had been painted a deep blue sometime in the distant past. It wore a grimy patina of hand-shaped smudges fading down into black scuff marks probably caused by shoving it open with a booted foot.

Hand raised to knock, Vicki paused and frowned. With millions of lives surrounding her—and, more specifically, with the half a dozen lives close at hand behind inadequate walls of ancient plaster and lath—it was difficult to separate out the sounds coming from inside Carr's apartment. Sifting sound, disregarding everything that wasn't life, focusing, she picked out a heartbeat. It was slower than it should be. Struggling.

Not even burning onions on the second floor could mask the smell of blood.

The door had a deadbolt on it and a security chain. Both were screwed into a doorframe that had probably been installed at the turn of the century. The wood gave way with a sound like a dry cough. The mulitiple layers of cheap paint hung on a moment longer, then Vicki was in the apartment and racing down the long hall toward the front room, following her nose.

This door was also locked.

And was unlocked just as quickly.

A young man—blond hair, pale skin, late twenties, approximately six feet tall and a hundred and seventy pounds—lay sprawled on the linoleum, blood spreading out from under his head along the artificial watershed of the uneven floor. He was alone in the room.

Between one heartbeat and the next, Vicki knelt beside him, his head cradled in one hand, a folded towel from the bathroom in the other. Had any assailants still been around, they might have wondered when she'd had time to get back down the hall but had they still been around, she'd have dealt with them first, so the question would have been moot. The room was empty except for the injured man. No one was hiding under the desk. No one lurked in the tiny turn-of-the-century closet.

A couple of mouthfuls of spit on the towel—easy enough to work up under the circumstances, the smell of blood was making her mouth water—and then both spit and towel applied to the wound. As the coagulant in her saliva went to work, she pulled her cell phone from her pocket, flipped it open, and dialed one-handed.

"So you broke down the door?"

"That's right."

"Because you could smell the blood?"

"Yes."

"From out in the hall?"

"That's what I said."

"Just trying to get my facts straight, Ms. Nelson."

Vicki forced her lips back down over her teeth as the earnest young constable went over her statement for the fourth time.

"And then you broke down the inner door as well?"

"Yes."

He gave her what he probably considered an intimidating stare. "You forced the lock right out of the wood. Splintered the wood. So not only do you have a rather unbelievable sense of smell, you're unusually strong."

"I work out." While she appreciated he was just doing his job, enough was enough. Locking her eyes on his, she smiled. "Now go away," she said softly, "and stop bothering me."

"I . . . I think that's all I need to know."

"Good." A more normal tone. A slightly more normal smile.

He backed up two steps, then turned and scuttled down the hall toward the apartment door, nearly bouncing off Mike Celluci.

"Vicki . . ."

"I was cooperating."

"You terrified him."

"So? Back in the day, I used to terrify the uniforms all the time." She sighed as they fell into step heading toward Carr's tiny office. "When did they start hiring children?"

"About the time I started going gray."

They paused to allow the crime scene team to leave, and Vicki reached up to push the curl of hair back off his face. She'd gotten rather sentimental about his scattering of gray hair—after she stopped being furious at it. Raging at the years that took him farther and farther away from her. She would age, but slowly. She'd changed at thirty-four. It would be centuries before she saw forty.

Sunlight and the occasional idiot Van Helsing clone allowing.

She stepped aside so the head of the crime scene unit could have a talk with Celluci and, well beyond normal eavesdropping distance, eavesdropped shamelessly.

"So," she said when they were finally alone in the

apartment. "The door was locked from the inside, the window was painted shut, and they think they've only got one person's prints, although they'll have to get back to you on that. Didn't I once read a Miss Marple book with this plot?"

"You read a book?"

"Funny man."

Celluci shoved his hands in the pockets of his overcoat and scowled at the room. A battered office chair, more duct tape than upholstery, lay on its side against the outside wall. "He could have just tipped over backward and hit his head."

"With the chair over there and this kind of a spatter pattern? Stop playing idiot's advocate, Mike. Looks to me like he pushed away from the desk, spun the chair around . . ." Vicki sketched the arc in the air. ". . . leaped out of it, and was on his feet when he was hit. Whoever it was came in through the door . . ."

"The locked door."

"We don't know for certain that the door was locked when the assailant *arrived*. Came in through the door," she repeated when Mike nodded reluctantly. "Walked very, very quietly around to about here . . ." She indicated a spot by the desk.

"It didn't have to be that quiet. If Carr was writing, he could have been distracted. Lost in his own world."

"Fair enough. But the assailant didn't just sneak in and attack him from behind, or he'd have fallen forward, over the keyboard. He got Carr's attention first. There must have been a fight. Maybe the neighbors heard something."

"Gosh, Vicki." Celluci's voice dripped heavy, obvious sarcasm. "I would never have thought to ask the neighbors if they heard anything. It's a good thing you're here. And frankly, I'm more concerned with how the guy got out, not in." A long stride took him to the other side of the red-brown puddle. He frowned at the window and the layers of paint that had clearly not been cracked. "Last time this was opened, Trudeau was prime minister."

"No one here but Raymond Carr when I broke in. No one passed me on the stairs, and no one came out of the building with a bloody weapon while I was close enough to see the door."

"Would you have seen the weapon under a winter coat?"

She smiled at him. "If it was bloody, I'd have known it was there."

"If. He could have left before you got close."

"Not at the rate Carr was bleeding out. It had to have happened just before I got here or the coroner'd be slabbing him right about now."

He shrugged, accepting her explanation. "Don't these apartments have a back exit into a courtyard?"

"The uniforms checked it. Locked. Three bolts thrown. Impossible to do from outside. And the window in the kitchen has as much paint on it as this one. Plus a layer of grease."

"I hate this kind of shit." Celluci dragged both hands back through his hair, dropping the curl over his forehead again. "I don't suppose our perp turned to mist or smoke, or there's a bat hiding out in a dark corner that we missed?"

"Don't be ridiculous."

"You telling me vampires don't exist?"

"I'm telling you that even if Hollywood didn't have its collective head up its ass, we wouldn't have wasted the blood." Carefully avoiding the splatter trail, she moved to the desk and looked down at the monitor. It was a new model, one of the liquid crystal screens made by a company she didn't recognize. From across the room, it had looked blank. Up close, there was one word, dead center on the screen.

"Mike."

He leaned in for a closer look. "Die."

"It's not an e-mail. They had to have typed it when they were in the room."

"I'll make sure they dust the keyboard when they bring the machine in. What are you doing?"

She frowned at an oval of drying blood nearly invisible on the black plastic of the monitor housing. It was shaped like a thumbprint, but she couldn't see a pattern.

"So you're eyeballing hills and valleys now?" he snorted when she pointed it out to him. "Good work, Vicki, we've got the son of a bitch. Our bad guy had to have left it there when he was typing. Left hand holding the monitor, typing with his right. If you can find another one of these, we might be able to piece together how the fuck he got out of the room."

"If I can find another one?"

"You know, sniff it out."

"Sniff it out?"

He turned to scowl at her. "Would you quit repeating everything I say?"

"I'm not repeating everything," she told him, "just the stupid parts. This room is saturated in blood scent, Mike. And before you ask," she cautioned, "I can't track the bad guy. I'm not a bloodhound."

One dark brow rose.

"Not funny."

"You're right. I'm sorry." Hands shoved deep in his pockets, he looked around the room. "So, what do we have?"

"You have an unsolved assault. And I have to find another client."

"He's not dead."

"You want me to guard him in the hospital?"

"That's up to you."

"I hate hospitals."

Vicki'd disliked hospitals before she changed and she'd started disliking them even more after. Light-sensitive eyes found them far too bright and no amount of disinfectant could keep them from reeking of death. That they also reeked of disinfectant was not a selling point.

Raymond Carr was in a private room at the far end of a quiet corridor, the room the hospital unofficially kept for ongoing criminal cases. Sometimes it held the criminals. Sometimes the cases. With budgets cut and then cut again, the police department hadn't the manpower to guard an unsuccessful writer from an unknown enemy. They'd do their best to turn the unknown to a known, but as long as Carr seemed safe in the hospital, he'd remain unguarded.

Vicki stood in the room's darkest corner and watched the pale man on the bed draw in one short, shallow breath after another. He was sleeping—not entirely peacefully. Long fingers twitched against the covers and his eyeballs bounced behind his lids. Vicki wondered what he was dreaming about.

He'd told the police he couldn't remember what had happened. That one moment he'd been writing and the next he was in the back of an ambulance staring up at a pair of EMTs. It was all still in there, though. Trapped in the dark places.

Vicki did some of her best work in dark places. Unfortunately, Carr was wired—she wouldn't be able to question him without setting off the bells and whistles.

"Who's there?"

Might as well try it the old-fashioned way. The Hunter carefully masked, she stepped out of the shadows. "My name's Vicki Nelson. Detective Sergeant Celluci told you I was coming over tonight."

"What happened to me?"

"You got hit on the head."

His eyes widened and he stared up at her with dawning comprehension. "You're the one he was sending to protect me!"

"Sorry; I got there a little late." And anyone else would have knocked and gone away. "For what it's worth, I kept you from bleeding to death."

"My computer!"

Apparently, it wasn't worth much. "The police have it."

"My book! My God, they have my book!"

"Calm down." A quick glance at the monitors showed a rise in heart rate. "You'll get it back when they finish the investigation."

"It'll never be finished."

She wasn't entirely certain if he meant the investigation or the book. "You must have back-up copies."

"It's on disk." The bandage whispered against the pillowcase as he rocked his head from side to side. "I meant to burn it, but . . ." The rocking stopped. His pupils were so dilated his irises had nearly disappeared. "Why do you want my copy?"

"I don't. I was just reassuring . . ."

"You're trying to steal it!"

"No, I'm not." She let her eyes silver just enough to force him calm.

He panicked instead. The heart-rate monitor screamed as he tried to scramble back through the head of the bed.

Vicki was in the stairwell before the nurses left their station. She waited, the door open a crack, listening as they tranquilized him and strapped him down. He kept yelling that his book was in danger.

"Quite the imagination on him," one nurse muttered to the other as they left the room, her tone suggesting that "quite the imagination" could be translated as "total paranoid nutcase."

As Vicki slipped away, she thought it might be time to find out what else "quite the imagination" might mean.

The yellow crime scene tape remained across the door, but in the still, dark hours of the morning when Vicki returned to Raymond Carr's apartment, the police were long gone. Because of the manner of Vicki's original entrance, the apartment couldn't be secured, so they'd taken the trouble to put a padlock in place—a lot cheaper than keeping a uniform around until the landlord could arrive and make repairs. It was a good lock. It took Vicki about two minutes to pop it.

As well as the computer, the police had cleared

Carr's desktop and taken all the drawers, hoping for a clue amid the debris. While she appreciated their thoroughness, she was a little annoyed by the need to pry a copy of the book out of official channels. Official channels were notoriously narrow.

And speaking of narrow . . . Since she was there, she leaned her laptop case against the wall and stepped into the closet to check the ceiling for trap-doors leading to a closed-off and forgotten attic. Nothing. The cheap linoleum was solidly attached in all four corners, so there was no chance of a trapdoor to the apartment below.

On her hands and knees, peering under the desk at a floor unmarked by secret passageways, she snickered, "Who's the paranoid nutcase now?"

Paranoid nutcase . . .

Carr had thought she was going to steal his book. Had believed it so strongly, the hysterics had protected him from her ability to get into his head.

Vicki twisted and looked up at the bottom of the keyboard slide.

The masking tape that attached the square mailing envelope was almost the same color as the pale wood of the desk. The label on the single disk inside simply said, *Book*.

"The blood on the monitor wasn't a print."

Vicki glanced up from her laptop as Celluci came into the living room and dropped down beside her on the couch. "I'm sorry, Mike."

He grunted a noncommittal response to her sympathy. "What are you reading?"

"Raymond Carr's book. It's weirdly good. He starts off by massacring almost an entire village just so the hero—Harticalder—can go off and kick ass, so the plot's mostly a series of violent encounters strung together on a less-than-believable travelogue, but even doing the most asinine things, the characters are strangely believable. These guys read like real people."

His hand closed around her shoulder, warm even through the fleece of her sweatshirt. "Where did you get that?"

"Calm down, I left the original where it was." She popped the disk out of the side of her computer. "*This* is a copy." Pushing it back into the drive, she set the machine aside and pivoted in place until she faced him. "There's something else."

"What do you mean?"

"I know that look. It's your *I've come to a conclusion* expression."

He sighed and ran his hand back up through his hair. "The lab says there's no weapon, that the floor was the point of impact. One bang."

Vicki snorted. "No one hits their head that hard on a floor. It's a flat surface. Essentially flat," she amended, remembering how the blood had spread.

"And there's no indication of anyone else ever being in that room."

"Except for the blood on the monitor," she pointed out, poking him in the thigh with her bare foot.

"A random splatter. Raymond Carr got tangled up in his chair, fought to get free, and fell. That's why the chair was over by the window. No one pushed him, no one slammed his head down—there isn't another mark on his body."

Carr's skin was so pale that bruises would show almost instantly, blood from crushed capillaries pooling under the surface. "What about the threats?"

"We did a little background check, and it turns out that Raymond Carr is a paranoid schizophrenic. If he was off his medication, the odds are good he was writing the threats to himself."

"And?" Vicki asked pointedly.

"And what?" His hand closed around her ankle before she could poke him again. They both knew he couldn't hold her, but that wasn't the point.

"And you've had all day; is he off his medication?"

"Doesn't seem to have been. But . . . ." He sketched uncertainties in the air with his free hand.

"But even paranoids have enemies."

He smiled then and pulled her close enough to kiss. "I knew you were going to say that."

"What about the blood on the monitor?" she asked when they pulled apart.

Celluci's turn to snort. "You know as well as I do that sometimes not all the pieces fit. You know better than I do that weird happens."

That was an impossible point to argue with, so she didn't bother and later, after he fell asleep, she checked that the bite on his wrist had closed over and slid out of bed to finish the book. Or at least to finish all of the book there was.

The fight scenes continued to be contrived, but the dialogue rang true and as she closed the last file, Vicki had to admit she believed in ol' Harticalder and his people. Almost buried under the preposterous plot, Carr had real talent.

On a whim, she went online and ran a search on the brand of monitor on Carr's desk. Her laptop was almost five years old and, even with the monitor dimmed down as far as it would go, it was still hard on light-sensitive eyes. Odds were good that new ones like Carr's had new features.

According to the official Web site, they did everything but make toast.

It seemed that Quinct, the company, had developed an amazing new technology for manufacturing the liquid crystal screens. They'd produced them for almost a year, claiming the new screens provided a viewing surface a minimum of 60 percent sharper than the competition. And then, they'd gone bankrupt.

A bankruptcy sale explained how Raymond Carr had managed to afford one.

The site gave no reasons for the company's fall, and the best Vicki managed to find elsewhere on the Web was a LiveJournal thread discussing the monitors. Apparently, they weren't just 60 percent sharper—according to the half dozen people in the thread who'd owned them, they made images so clear new details came into focus in the background and even the written word seemed somehow real.

Real. There was that word again.

As she shut down her machine, she decided not to repeat the word to Mike. Although forced to become more open-minded than he'd been, speculation outside the boundaries covered by the crime lab and some good old-fashioned legwork still annoyed him, and an annoyed Mike Celluci was no fun to live with.

Besides, no one knew better than she did that reality came with qualifiers.

But she popped the copy of the book out of her laptop just to be on the safe side.

No one attacked Raymond Carr in the hospital, and the day he was released, the police handed back his computer.

"There was no crime committed," Celluci explained that evening when Vicki commented on the speedy return. "Just a man who slipped off his meds and had an accident."

"You told me it looked like he was taking his meds."

"Let it go, Vicki." Elbows braced on the kitchen table, he rubbed his temples. "I've got two teenagers dead because some asshole in a car thought it would be fun to shoot at strangers. I don't have time to protect Raymond Carr from himself. You think he needs supervision, you do it."

She thought it wouldn't hurt to drop by.

This time the door was unlocked and the blood scent was stronger.

Carr hadn't had time to put a new lock on his office door and his landlord's rudimentary repairs hadn't included replacing the latch mechanism. When Vicki laid her palm against it, it swung open, unresisting.

The only light in the room came from the monitor, but even before the change that allowed her to miss his heartbeat and the song of his blood, she would have known Raymond Carr was dead. The living were never so completely still.

His chair had been tipped back—flung back considering the distance from the desk. He was still in it, his arms outstretched, fingers curled. His feet in old-fashioned, scuffed, leather slippers were in the air, his head rested in a puddle beginning to dry to a brackish brown around the edges. It was difficult to tell for certain without moving the body, but the back of his head looked flat and there were three distinct points of impact.

The police would assume they'd been wrong. That there'd been an assailant the first time. That this mysterious assailant had somehow gotten into and then out of a locked room in a locked apartment and that today—late afternoon by the smell—he or she returned and finished the job. If they'd found no evidence of a second person in the room, they had to have missed something and, blaming themselves for Raymond Carr's death, they'd work like hell to make up for their mistake.

Except . . .

Vicki pulled a latex glove out of her pocket—even the bloodsucking undead left fingerprints—and walked to the desk. There was a single word in the center of the monitor.

Dead.

She moved the cursor down to the next line and typed *Harticalder?*

Then she felt a little foolish when nothing happened.

"Right," she muttered, deleting the name and snapping off the glove. "Vampires exist, werewolves exist, wizards exist, so therefore it's logical that characters can be made so real that they climb out of a new and improved monitors and bash the brains in of the bastard who put them through so much shit. Which is not to say," she added to Raymond Carr, "that you didn't deserve it. You slaughtered the entire village, for Christ's sake!"

Then she frowned as her eyes flared silver for an instant, reflecting the light of the monitor.

When she turned, there was still only one word on the screen.

Dead.

There'd be no marks on Carr's body because no matter how real they seemed, imaginary characters didn't leave marks. Or fingerprints. Or worry about locked doors. Or climb out of monitors and take vengeance on the creator who killed their wives and children to make a plot point.

Vicki pulled the glove back on and reformatted the hard drive. Pulled the plug on the machine, then took a cheap pen from the desk and drove a hole into the corner of the monitor. The part of her that had been a good cop for all those years hated the thought of compromising a crime scene. The rest of her slid the book's backup disk out of its hidden sleeve, snapped it in half, and put the pieces into her pocket.

Half a block away, from the pay phone inside the front door of the Brunswick Hotel, she made an anonymous phone call.

"Obviously, it had to do with the book. This time the hard drive was reformatted—not just erased but refucking formatted—and the copy taken. Carr must have written something that really pissed someone off. I guess it's a good thing you made that illegal . . ." Celluci paused in his pacing to stress the word, ". . . copy, or we'd have nothing."

"Sorry, Mike." Vicki moved a red queen onto a black king and looked up from the laptop. "I copied my notes from the voodoo case onto the disk."

"You what?"

"Well, how would I know you'd need it? You said the lab determined he fell. That it was an accident."

She could hear his teeth grinding. "The evidence at the time . . ."

"Except for the missing book," she interrupted.

"And the destroyed monitor!" he interrupted in turn.

They stared at each other for a long moment.

"You never mentioned a destroyed monitor," Vicki sighed at last. "Fine, except the missing book *and* the destroyed monitor, what evidence do you have this time? Prints? Witnesses? Fibers? Anything?"

"Vicki, no one accidentally slams their own head into the floor three times with force enough to flatten the back of their own skull!"

The volume as much as the content of his protest answered her question; he had nothing. The police had nothing. She set the laptop to one side, stood, and crossed the room to lay a sympathetic hand on Mike's arm. "I'm not saying it was an accident. Maybe he destroyed his own book and then killed himself."

He caught up her hand in his and pulled her around to face him. "No one kills themselves by slamming their own head into the floor three times! Where the hell did you get that idea?"

"I don't know." Raymond Carr had created a village filled with amazingly real characters and then slaughtered almost all of them to make a plot point. Harticalder had ridden away to wreak vengeance on those who'd done the slaughtering. Maybe he'd traveled a little farther than planned. And if not him, well, there'd still been half a dozen other characters left behind to mourn.

"Vicki?"

She shrugged. "I guess I read it in a book."

So This Is Christmas

"So what do you think? The blue or the black?"

Vicki Nelson turned to stare at her companion in some confusion. "The blue or the black what?"

"Scarf." Detective Sergeant Mike Celluci held up the articles in question. "Last time I saw Angela she was doing a sort of goth-lite, so the black might work better, but I like the blue."

"Who is Angela?"

"My sister Marie's oldest girl." he grinned and pulled a virulently fuchsia scarf from the pile. "Maybe I should get her this just to hear her scream."

Vicki rolled her eyes and fought the urge to do a little screaming of her own. She wondered what had possessed her to accompany Mike to a suburban mall on Christmas Eve. At the time, concerned about how little they'd seen each other lately, going with him as he finished his shopping had seemed like the perfect solution. Now, not so much. "Maybe you should do something about the earrings those teenagers have just slipped into their pockets. Over there," she added, when it was clear she had his attention. "Blonde girl in the short red jacket and the dark-haired girl in brown."

"You're sure?"

Her eyes silvered faintly. "I'm sure."

As he walked across the store, she fought down the Hunger that had risen with even such a small display of power. Being stuck in an enclosed space with hundreds of people all sweating inside heavy winter coats as they rushed frantically from one store to another was like sitting a dieter down next to an enormous plate of shortbread cookies. The urge to nibble was nearly overwhelming.

She snarled slightly as someone careened into her, stepped back into the shelter of the scarf display as a harried looking young woman rushed by pushing a stroller piled high with packages, and turned to find Celluci back by her side. "Well?"

"They both think I should get the black scarf." He put the blue scarf back on the pile. Apparently he'd taken them with him.

"And earrings?"

"They put them back."

"Then you left them with store security."

"I gave them a warning and sent them home."

"You what?"

"Oh come on, Vicki, it's Christmas." Angela's gift in hand, he started toward the nearest cash register.

"What the hell does Christmas have to do with it?" she demanded, falling into step by his side. "It's not like they were stealing a fruitcake for their dear old mom. They'd have lifted those earrings if it was Easter or the first of July. Are you going to let them off because the baby Jesus died for their sins? Or because they're wearing red and white for Canada Day? Or . . ."

"I get it." He stopped at the end of a long line and sighed. "This is going to take a while."

"I could move things along." She smiled, her upper lip rising off her teeth.

"No."

"Fine." Hands shoved into her pockets, she turned the smile on the young man crowding into the line behind her. He paled, dropped his penguin-imprinted fleece throw, and raced away. Vicki snorted as she watched him go. Running screaming from the mall seemed like a good idea to her.

*　　*　　*

She liked to watch Mike eat, so the trip to the food court wasn't quite as bad as it could have been. Screaming, tired, overstimulated children—more perceptive than their parents—fell silent around her and not even Mike had objected when she'd leaned toward the two very loud young men at the next table and softly growled, "Shut up."

One of them had whimpered but they hadn't said anything since.

"There're definitely things I love about this time of the year," she said watching Mike lick a bit of ketchup from the corner of his mouth. "Hard to complain about an early sunset and a late sunrise."

He swallowed and grinned. "Here I thought you meant Christmas."

"What this?" One hand waved at the red velvet bows wrapped around every stationary surface and a few that hadn't been stationary until they'd been tied down. "Or maybe," she added scornfully, "you mean the hordes of happy shoppers panicked they won't buy the right piece of name brand garbage, running up their credit cards so far they miss a few payments, lose their house, and end up living with their kids in the back of a van." She paused long enough to duck under a heavily laden tray passing a little too closely. "Next thing you know, Dad's doing five to ten for taking a swing at the cop who ran him in for pissing behind a Dumpster, Mom's turning tricks on Jarvis, and the kids are in juvie. All because of Christmas."

Mike started at her in astonishment. "Who stole your ho ho ho?"

"I'm a realist," she told him. "You do remember that violent crimes increase over the holiday season? A little too much alcohol, a little too much family . . ."

"I have a great family. Which you'd know if you'd come with me tomorrow."

"Mike."

"I love you, I love them. At Christmas you should be with the people you love. I get home from work, you eat, then we spend the evening with them. And don't say you won't go because they'll expect you to eat. Dinner will be long over and I know you're fast enough to fake snacks. You could always fake a food allergy."

"It won't work."

"Why not?" He brushed the graying curl of hair off his forehead and glared at her over the cardboard edge of his coffee cup.

"It's not who I am."

"It's not who you choose to be," he snapped, tossed the empty cup down on his tray and stood. Vicki beat him to the garbage cans. "You're taking too many chances," he grunted, glancing around the food court. "Cut it out. This could be the day some twenty-first century Van Helsing came to the mall to buy his kid Baby's First Vampire Staking kit."

"You're babbling."

The muscle jumping in his jaw suggested he was aware of it. "If you can function here, you can function at my mother's house."

"Is *that* why we're here?" she asked as they headed toward the exit. "To prove I don't lose control in crowds?"

"I talked to Fitzroy. He said you can handle it."

"You called Henry?" Astonishment brought her to a full stop by the fence separating Santa's Workshop from the food court. "You actually called Henry?"

"He thinks you should come with me tomorrow."

And astonishment gave way to pique. "I don't care what he thinks!"

"Come on, Vicki, it's Christmas."

"I know." The warmth in Mike's brown eyes was *not* going to get to her. "And Christmas is a . . ." A screaming child about to be lifted onto Santa's lap cut her off. "Can you believe that," she demanded as Santa settled back and adjusted his beard. "You spend all year trying to street-proof kids and all of a sudden their parents are shoving them onto the lap of some strange old man and paying an arm and a leg for a fuzzy picture that costs about eight cents to produce."

"Who crapped in your stocking?"

The voice came from about waist level. Vicki peered over the fence and into the face of one of Santa's elves—although given his height, the breadth of his shoulders, and the beaded braids in his beard, this one looked more like a dwarf in spite of green tights and red pointy-toed shoes.

"Take a picture," he snarled. "It'll last longer."

"Sorry."

"Yeah, like that sounded sincere." He crossed heavily muscled arms over a barrel chest and glared up at her from under bushy brows. "So what's your problem?"

"With what?"

"With Christmas, for crying out loud. Come on. I haven't got all night."

She glanced up at Mike, who was staring in dopey fascination as a laughing older woman wrestled a pink and frilly little girl back into her snowsuit.

The elf pointedly cleared his throat.

"Look, I have no problem with Christmas. You want to dress up and play Santa's Workshop, that's fine with me. Someone else wants to go into debt until next November, their choice. I just want to be left alone to celebrate Christmas my way."

"Bet you don't."

"Don't what?"

"Celebrate Christmas."

"Maybe I'm Jewish. You ever think of that?"

"Are you?"

"No, but . . ." She waved at hand at Mike, suddenly wanting the elf's too-penetrating gaze pointed somewhere else. "He's working all day."

Dark eyes remained locked on her face. "So the cops with families can have the day off and then I betcha he's spending the evening with about sixty people from nine to ninety who'll be glad to see him. Big Italian-Canadian family. Lot of hugging. You should go with him."

"You should mind your own business."

"Except we're not talking about me," he snorted. "We're talking about you."

"You don't know anything about me." She let the Hunter rise enough to silver her eyes.

To her surprise, the elf met her gaze. "All right, you're not so tough," he muttered after a long moment. "And you need to get moving, lady. The mall's about to close."

Vicki blinked, looked around, and realized that a number of the stores had already pulled down their security grids and the food court was rapidly emptying. Santa had disappeared and his helpers were packing things up.

"I forgot things closed so early on Chrismas Eve," Mike said as he wrapped her hand in his and continued their interrupted walk to the exit. "I hope you didn't still have shopping to do."

A little unsettled, she let him pull her along. "No, I'm good."

"I've always thought so."

His tone of voice made her feel warm, wanted, and unworthy all at once but she recovered enough to snarl at a group of carolers outside the doors. "God Rest Ye Merry Gentlemen" went up an octave and changed key twice.

It wasn't until they got to the car that she thought to wonder how the elf had known Mike was a cop.

Mike was working a twelve-hour shift—six AM to six PM—so Vicki woke him up at five with lips and teeth and kept him distracted for long enough that he had no time to do anything but throw on clothes and race out the door. No time to start in on it being Christmas Day. Time enough to say, "Think about tonight, that's all I'm asking," as he left.

She'd thought about it. She thought it was a bad idea, her mingling with Mike's extended family as if they were a couple like any other.

"And what does your girlfriend do, Michael?"

"Well, Mom, Vicki spends her days unconscious in

a lightproof packing crate in my crawl space and after sunset she works as a private investigator."

"That sounds interesting."

"Have her tell you about the reanimated Egyptian wizard who tried to take over the world sometime. Oh, and did I mention she's a vampire?"

Okay, not likely, but still not a good idea. Besides, with luck she had a couple of hundred Christmases to look forward to. She needed to pace herself.

"A couple of hundred years of Chia pets, dogs in antlers, and 'Rockin' Around the Christmas Tree,' " she muttered, sitting down at her laptop. "I can't wait."

At fifteen minutes to sunrise, she shut down, took her cell phone from the charger, and headed for the crawl space only to find that Mike had hung a wreath on the end of the crate that opened.

"You'd think I could get away from the whole Christmas thing down here," she sighed as she stripped. Sinking into the slab of memory foam, she locked up, slipped under the duvet, and turned off the flashlight.

By sunset, Christmas would be nearly over.

Vampires don't dream.

"All right, if I'm not dreaming, what the hell is going on?" Vicki got out of the enormous wingback chair and peered around the room. There was a window and door and a fireplace, but beyond that, the room seemed a bit undefined—as though only the essentials were in place. There had to be walls, hard to have either a window or a door without them, but they were present more by inference than actuality.

The chair felt real. The green and blue checked dressing gown felt real. The sound of heavy footsteps dragging chains up a flight of stairs, however . . .

She turned as a familiar translucent figure burst through the door.

"In life," he howled, approaching the chair, "I was your informant Tony Foster!"

Because it seemed like the safest reaction, Vicki sat back down. "You're not dead, Tony."

Tony stopped and pulled a script from the pocket of his *Darkest Night* show jacket. "I'm sure that was my line," he muttered, flipping pages. "It's not like I ever wanted to be in front of the cameras, oh, no, I want to direct but what do I get . . . Ah. Here it is. In life I was your informant, Tony Foster. That's what it says." He shoved the script back in his pocket and grinned at her. "Can I go on?"

"Why not?" Eventually, there'd be a punch line and maybe then she'd figure out what was happening.

"I have come from beyond the grave to warn you."

Now they were getting somewhere. "Warn me of what?"

He held up the end of the chain wrapped around his body. About every fifteen centimeters was a classic lunch box. Although it was hard to see them clearly, Vicki recognized *Bewitched, The Brady Bunch,* and *Starsky and Hutch* as well as assorted *Star Wars, Star Treks,* and superheroes. "The chain you bear was as long and heavy as this when I left Toronto and it has grown longer and heavier since."

"I'm dragging lunch boxes?"

"They're metaphors. Each box represents—Hey!" Tony pulled a bit of the chain around to look more closely at the lunch box. "Cool. The old *Batman* television show. Do you know how much one of these things is worth, mint?"

"Do I care?"

"Right. Do you care? That's the problem." He cleared his throat and took up his declamation posture again. "Each box represents a family commitment you blew off."

"Okay." Vicki folded her arms and frowned. "My mother died, was brought back to life, and died again. That's about all the family commitment I've had in the last few years."

"And what about Mike Celluci? I mean, he's not my first choice, but you two are tight."

"How tight Mike and I are is none of your business."

"Friends are my business!"

"I thought you were a TAD on a crappy television show."

Tony threw back his head and howled. Lights flashed. Thunder crashed. Omnious music played. "Why do you not believe in me, O Woman of the Worldly Mind?"

Still frowning, Vicki stared at him. The music stopped. The thunder faded. The ambient light steadied. After a long moment, Tony shrugged, looking sheepish.

"Listen, Vicki . . . ." Adjusting his chain, he sat down on a second chair that had appeared as his butt descended. ". . . sometimes you get family, sometimes you make family; you know what I mean? Like Neil Simon said, no man is an island . . ."

"*Paul* Simon. And that's not what he said."

"Whatever. What I'm getting at is even Dracula had those babes in the basement. Just because you're a member of the bloodsucking undead doesn't mean you should cut yourself off from human intercourse." He paused. Frowned. Started to snicker.

"You're laughing because you said intercouse, aren't you?" When Tony nodded, she rolled her eyes. "What are you, twelve?"

"Sorry."

"Just get on with it."

"Fine." Standing, he drew himself up to his full height and pointed. "You have one chance to escape my fate."

Vicki opened her mouth and closed it again, strongly suspecting that any questions about said fate wouldn't be answered anyway. At least not coherently.

Tony stared at her suspiciously for a moment then continued, "You will be visited by three ghosts . . ."

"You have got to be kidding me."

His shrug set the lunch boxes clanking. "Yeah, surprised me too. I'd have bet you were more the *It's a Wonderful Life* type."

"Get out."

"Expect the first when the bell tolls one!"

Before she could ask *What bell?* or even *What part of get out do you not understand?* he was gone.

Wondering just how high Mike's blood alcohol level had been and how he'd gotten it there before she fed on him this morning, Vicki blinked and found herself in an entirely different scene, lying inside the closed red brocade curtains of a huge four-poster bed. A quick glance under the covers. She was wearing blue flannel pajamas printed with dancing polar bears. Since she didn't own pajamas matching that description, or any pajamas at all for that matter, she was beginning to get a little concerned about just who was supplying the imagery.

A bell, and it sounded like a big one, tolled once.

All things considered, the sudden soft illumination through the red brocade wasn't much of a surprise.

"I can't believe I'm doing this," she muttered, sitting up and pulling the curtain back. On the far side of the room, she could just barely make out a figure in the center of a blazing circle of light. "Turn it down!" she snarled, one hand raised to protect sensitive eyes.

The light dimmed. "Better?"

"Henry?"

Glowing only slightly, Henry Fitzroy, bastard son of Henry VIII, once Duke of Richmond and Somerset, romance writer, ex-lover, and vampire walked toward the bed. He was wearing . . .

"What the hell are you wearing?"

Henry glanced down and smoothed the velvet skirt of his coat. "These are my Garter Robes. I have to say that I'm impressed by the condition they're in given that I haven't worn them in four hundred and seventy years."

"You look like . . ."

He bowed, right leg to the front, ass in the air, and his poofy hat nearly sweeping the floor. "A Tudor prince?"

"Yeah all right, that too." She sighed and dragged a pillow up against the headboard so she could lean back in comfort. "So what's going on? Tony told me I'd be visited by three ghosts."

"I am the first."

"No way."

"I am the Ghost of Christmas Past."

Vicki snorted. "Well, they got the past part right."

"Not my past, your past."

She snorted again. "Then you should be wearing a mullet and leg warmers. Either way, I'm not playing."

"This isn't a game, Vicki."

"And it isn't a dream." Arms folded over the dancing polar bears, she scowled up at him. "Because we don't dream. So what is it?"

"That's not for me to say. I'm here as a guide, nothing more."

"And if I refuse to be guided?"

His eyes darkened and his smile became a scimitar slash across his face.

She felt her own Hunter rise to answer his. Lips drawn back, she threw herself out of the bed, propelled by the territorial imperative that declared vampires hunted alone. How dare Henry show up in her subconscious—or wherever the fuck they were—and challenge? "You think so? Bring it on!"

Henry stepped forward to meet her and, as they made contact, the room and the bed swirled away. When their surroundings came back into focus, they were standing on one side of a familiar room, tucked in between a green vinyl recliner and an artificial Christmas tree. A little girl, about five years old, sat cross-legged on the floor gleefully cheering on the battling plastic robots set up on the coffee table.

"Oh, my God, that's me!"

Henry pulled his cloak from Vicki's loosened grasp. "I told you—Christmas past."

"I loved those robots!" Stepping forward, she knelt at the end of the table. "Now this is what I call a toy with no socially redeeming value."

"Vicki! Uncle Stan's here."

The young Vicki jumped to her feet shrieking, "Grandma!" and raced for the kitchen leaving the red robot lying on its side, fists flailing, plastic feet paddling the air. Unopposed, the blue robot headed for the edge of the table.

"My grandmother always stayed with Uncle Stan's family at Christmastime," Vicki explained. She could almost hear Henry wondering how she'd gotten from her uncle to her grandmother. "If Uncle Stan's here, Grandma's here." She reached for the blue robot only to have it fall through her palm and bounce under the couch.

"This is the past," Henry reminded her. "Shadows of things that were; you can't affect it."

"Which makes me think we're here in order for it to affect me." Still on her knees, she twisted around to face him. "If I'm supposed to get in touch with my inner child, you might as well take me back right now. My inner child is at a boarding school in Uruguay."

"Ah." He nodded as if that made perfect sense. "Well, we can't go back until we've seen everything. There are rules."

"Rules? You tricked me to get me here." Rolling up onto her feet, she took a step toward him.

Henry shrugged. "You're a little predictable."

"And you're a . . ."

A babble of voices cut her off. Her mother led the group into the living room, closely followed by her Aunt Connie holding baby Susie and trying to keep three-year-old Steve from racing straight for the tree. The last time Vicki'd seen her mother, she'd been a rotting reanimated corpse, murdered and brought back to life as part of an insane science experiment. Infinitely preferable to see her young and laughing, even if the home highlight job made her hair look horribly striped.

Young Vicki came next, walking backward, holding her grandmother's hand and listing everything Santa had brought her.

"Oh, my God, I'm wearing a Partridge Family sweatshirt."

"You're very cute."

"I'm five," Vicki snorted. "Even I could manage cute at five."

Last into the room came her dad and her Uncle Stan, conducting a spirited argument about hockey in general and the recent Toronto/Boston game in particular. Her dad, a lifelong Black Hawks fan, was loudly declaring that the Leafs' recent win had been pure luck. Her Uncle Stan, who really didn't care either way but liked to wind her dad up, was declaiming the superior firepower of the Toronto team.

"Weird," she said softly as her father scooped up her cousin Steve just as he was about to climb the tree, "I thought he was taller."

"You were five."

"I haven't been five for a long time, Henry."

Time kindly compressed opening yet more presents and the singing of Christmas carols led by Vicki's no longer decomposing mother. As the sun set, the whole family sat down to a dinner of turkey, stuffing, mashed potatoes, frozen peas, and brown-and-serve buns.

"Good lord," Vicki muttered as the canned cranberry sauce was passed around the table, "could we have been any more middle class?"

"You look happy."

Waving an enormous drumstick, young Vicki was teaching her younger cousin how to make a dam out of potatoes so the gravy didn't touch the vegetables. She did look happy, older Vicki had to admit, but then, it didn't take much at five. "Are we finished here?"

Henry nodded. "Here, yes. Time to move on." He raised a hand and their surroundings wobbled slightly, then came back into focus.

Vicki rolled her eyes. "Wow. They clearly spent a

fortune on the special effects. And in case you didn't notice . . ." She waved a dismissive hand at the table. ". . . we didn't go anywhere."

"We moved two years forward."

"Golly gee. Nothing's changed."

And then she noticed the empty place at the table. "My grandmother . . ."

"Died," Henry said softly.

"She was old. People get old and they die." Even to her own ears, she sounded angry.

"She was surrounded by people who loved her, right to the end. There are worse ways to die."

Vicki remembered the way flesh felt tearing under her teeth, the rush of blood into her mouth, the feel of a life as it fled. "Yeah, well, you should know."

Henry made no response, but then what could he say? *Takes one to know one.* Too trite, however true.

The scene shifted again. This time, although the food hadn't changed, there were only two people sitting at the table.

"Your Uncle Stan just didn't feel right coming this year," Vicki's mother said as she spooned mashed potatoes onto a plate. "Not with your father so recently . . . gone."

Ten-year-old Vicki muttered something that may have been, "Sure," and slapped margarine onto a bun.

"Wow. You lose one, you lose them all." Vicki folded her arms.

"They were the closest family your mother had and they never came back for Christmas after your father . . ."

". . . ran off with the whore half his age. Yeah, tell me something I don't know, Henry, or move on, because if you're the only thing around here I can affect, I'm about to."

His eyes darkened but before Vicki could react, the scene shifted.

There wasn't anything especially Christmas-like about Linda Ronstadt except that "Desperado" was blasting from the speakers at the police Christmas

party. This was the party after the family party—a
staff sergeant from 52 Division sat slumped in a chair
wearing the bottom half of a Santa suit, three couples
shuffled around the dance floor, a group of old-timers
were scaring the piss out of a rookie with exaggerated
stories of Christmas suicides, and everyone had been
drinking. Heavily.

"You're on the dance floor," Henry shouted over
the music, breaking into her search.

"Oh, no . . ."

It was *that* Christmas party.

Grabbing Henry's arm, she leaned toward his ear.
"Let's go."

"Oh, come on, you look cute. Both of you."

Unable to help herself, she followed his gaze to one
of the three dancing couples. Her younger self wore
a navy blue sweater with white snowflakes embroi-
dered onto it over a very tight pair of acid wash jeans
with ankle zippers tucked into a pair of black and
silver ankle boots. Fashion being slightly kinder to
men, Mike wore black jeans, a black dress shirt, and
a red lamé tie.

"Oh, my God."

"At least you weren't in leg warmers. I remember
the eighties," Henry added when she shot him a warning glare. "And trust me, the 1780s were worse."

Both younger Vicki and younger Mike were obviously drunk. He leaned forward and murmured something into her ear. She leaned back, one hand slipped
between their bodies, then she grinned and mouthed,
"Where?"

"Forget it." A hand against his chest kept Henry
from following the couple off the dance floor. "I know
how this ends and we're not watching."

One red-gold eyebrow rose. "Why not? Are you
ashamed?"

"For Christ's sake, Henry, we had sex in a stall in
the women's can. I'm not proud of it." But she
couldn't stop herself from grinning at the memory.

"Okay, I'm not ashamed of it either but we're still not watching."

"We could . . ."

"No."

"Fine." Linda Ronstadt gave way to ABBA. "It seems that after the disappointment of your childhood, you learned how to celebrate Christmas."

She stared at him in disbelief. "Is that why we're here?" When his eyebrow rose again, she started to snicker. "This is the best whoever is in charge of this farce could come up with? I get drunk and done up against some badly spelled graffiti? That's their idea of a merry Christmas?"

"You didn't have a good time?"

"I had a great time." Laughing now, full out. She hadn't laughed like this in . . . actually, she couldn't remember the last time she'd laughed like this. A quick sidestep took her out of the path of the staff sergeant in the Santa suit as he staggered off to empty his bladder, bang on the wall between the cans, and yell at the younger them to keep it the hell down. "I had a great time at least twice," she gasped, forcing the words through the laughter. "I always have a great time with Mike if you must know, but that's not the point."

Henry was looking a little pouty and that was funny too. "Then what is the point?"

"That this is stupid." Wiping her eyes with one hand, she waved the other at the cheesy decorations and the drunk cops. "If you've got nothing better than this, you might as well call it a night! Oh, my God . . ." She'd almost got herself under control but the opening bars of the DJ's latest choice set her off again. ". . . he's going to play 'The Time Warp'!"

Snarling softly, Henry raised a hand, the party faded, and they were back in the bedroom again.

Vicki collapsed on the bed. "Thank you. I don't think I was up to watching that." After a few final snickers, she took a deep breath and sat up to find Henry staring down at her. "You're not finished?"

"Just one more thing." His eyes darkened. "Michael Celluci was the best thing that ever happened to you, as much as it pains me to admit it. He has always accepted you for what you are—opinionated, obnoxiously competitive, and emotionally defensive—and has loved you anyway. He has given you a place in his home and his heart without ever asking that you cease to walk the night. All he asks is that you spend Christmas with his family and yet your fear continually denies him this one thing."

"And it's going to keep denying him." Gripping the comforter with both hands, she kept herself from rising to answer the challenge in his eyes. "That way there's no danger of my skipping the shortbread and snacking on Aunt Louise."

"That's not what you fear."

"Cousin Jeffrey then."

"I have seen four hundred and seventy Christmases, Vicki. I know your fear."

"You know Cousin Jeffrey?"

"Vicki . . ."

She snorted. "You know your fears, Henry. You don't know mine."

"I know . . ."

"No, you don't."

"Our kind . . ."

"Nope."

He was going to lose control any minute, she could see it in the way he'd subtly shifted his weight. His age made the whole one-vampire-to-a-territory imperative—not to mention the one-vampire-to-a-completely-cracked-fantasy—both easier and harder to overcome. "You can be the most irritating person I have ever met," he snarled and vanished.

Vicki pulled her fingers out of the holes in the comforter and the mattress beneath and raised them over her head. "I win."

Although it didn't, unfortunately, appear that she could go home yet.

Three spirits, Tony had said.

"Next," she sighed.

Right on cue, lights blazed under the door in the wall to the left of the bed. She could hear music. Pink. "Get the Party Started."

"I wonder what happens if I just sit here?" she asked no one in particular, folding her arms and shifting her weight more definitively onto the bed.

The music got louder, the world blurred, and Vicki found herself standing in the open doorway. Across the room, sitting in a familiar tacky Santa's Workshop, wearing a familiar tacky red velvet suit, nearly buried under piles of brightly wrapped packages, was Detective Sergeant Michael Celluci.

Vicki sighed. "The Ghost of Christmas Presents, I presume?"

"That's Ghost of Christmas Present," Mike told her, tugging down the ratty beard, "as in not past or future."

"Then you might want to shuffle your playlist, because this song . . ." She paused just long enough to allow the music to rise to the foreground. ". . . is very 2001."

"The music is not important." Tossing the beard over a sixty inch flat screen TV, Mike beckoned her forward. "Come in and know me better!"

"If I knew you any better, we'd be breaking a few laws." But since she didn't seem to have a choice in the matter, she walked toward him. Away from the door, she could see that besides the workshop and the presents there were also tables laid out with roast turkey and torteire and mashed potatoes and roast squash with a maple sugar glaze and bear claws and a steaming carafe of coffee and, yes, the party-size box of assorted Tim Bits. It all looked great but her appreciation was aesthetic only—these days she had no visceral reaction to food she had loved for over thirty-four years. She remembered enjoying them but the desire was gone. *Mostly gone,* she amended silently with a last look at the coffee.

"Just what exactly is a room full of food I can't eat

suppose to be teaching me?" she asked as she turned toward the workshop.

Mike stood and closed the remaining distance between them. When he was close enough that Vicki could feel the warmth coming off his body, he unbuttoned Santa's jacket and slipped it off his shoulders, standing before her in a tight white tank and the bottom of the costume. She could hear his heart beating, the blood moving through his veins. His scent threatened to overwhelm her.

Ah, yes. *There* was desire.

"The food is for me," he said, holding out one bare, muscular arm. "I need to keep up my strength."

Vicki stared at the inside of his wrist, mesmerized by the pulse throbbing under the soft, pale skin. Between one heartbeat and the next her teeth could be in his flesh, his blood running warm and salty down her throat . . .

"Vicki?"

"No, thanks, I'm not hungry." As she spoke, she realized it was true. Taking a deep breath, more for emotional grounding than physical necessity, she lifted her head and met his eyes.

He smiled. "You know that I am always here for you."

"Yeah. I know."

Given the theme of Henry's segment, she expected Mike to ask why she wasn't then there for him in turn, but all he said was, "Come on, there're some things you need to see."

"Families celebrating . . ." The scene changed. ". . . Christmas?" The last word was a near growl as Vicki adjusted to being suddenly perched on a snowbank in a pair of pajamas. "You know that's really fucking annoying! Where are we?"

"Don't you recognize this place?" Mike asked, buttoning the Santa jacket.

They were standing on the edge of a farmyard looking in at a redbrick house and a long low barn. It looked familiar but . . .

Just then the door to the house slammed open and a very large black dog charged outside followed by a pair of white, half-grown puppies.

"It's the Heerkens farm." Vicki grinned as she watched the black dog allow himself to be caught and tumbled in the snow. "The big willow tree's gone but they . . ." She waved a hand at the two pups barking like crazy as they leaped around their companion. ". . . are unmistakable."

The door opened again, a little less violently this time, and a very pregnant young woman with silver-blond hair leaned out into the yard. "Come on you three, back inside! Breakfast is ready!" When no one started toward the house, she shook her head and growled, "Shadow!"

Black ears went up.

"Shadow?" Vicki felt her jaw drop.

"It's been a few years since you've been by," Mike pointed out. He sounded amused but Vicki decided she'd let that go for now. The last time she'd seen Shadow, he'd been a half-grown pup, not this danger-ous looking animal whose head probably came higher than her hip. "The mother-to-be?"

"Rose. The little ones are hers, too."

"Impossible." Rose had been a teenager the last time Vicki'd seen her, all teasing and tossed hair.

Two steps forward took Vicki inside the farmhouse kitchen—an impossible distance covered but then, nothing much about this night had been particularly possible. The shabby kitchen was comfortingly famil-iar, the same oversized furniture, the same drifts of dog hair, the same piles of clothing tossed haphazardly about. The man sitting at the end of the table but-tering a huge pile of toast was obviously Stuart Heerkins-Wells, Rose's uncle and the old dominant male. A new scar ran from his throat along the top of his shoulder—new in that Vicki hadn't seen it be-fore, but actually about six or seven years old.

The outside door slammed back against the kitchen wall, and as Shadow herded the two younger animals in from outside, he changed to become a not-very-tall but heavily muscled dark-haired young man. Daniel. The fact that he was naked was less disconcerting than the undeniable fact he was no longer the cheerful ten-year-old she'd known. The pups charged across the room to leap up and down around Rose's legs, becoming, as they leaped, boys around six or eight years old with their mother's white-blond hair.

"Hey!" Rose expertly smacked a reaching hand away from the large pan of sausages on the stove. "Why don't you two do something useful and go get your father. He's in the living room."

"After breakfast can we take the toboggan Santa gave us out to the hill?"

"Only if your father goes with you."

"But, Mom . . . !"

"Or your Uncle Daniel."

From the whoops of glee and the clatter of eight sets of toenails against the worn linoleum as the two pups raced around Daniel before heading into the living room, they considered their uncle a soft touch. Or at least more likely to agree to a Christmas Day spent out in the snow than their father. It was as impossible not to smile as they passed as it had been not to smile at a much younger Shadow.

As Rose slapped Daniel's hand away from the sausages in exactly the same way she'd discouraged her son, a full choral rendition of "Joy to the World" exploded out of the living room. "Oh, no, if they start singing I'll never get them to eat!"

"I'll go." Stuart pushed the plate of toast into the center of the table and stood, smiling fondly at his niece. "Get my lazy son to help you with that pan. You need to start being careful about heavy lifting or we're going to end up with a Christmas baby." He kissed the top of her head as he passed.

"I have done this before, you know," she muttered as Daniel took the pan and started transferring the sausages to a platter. "Why don't I . . ."

"Answer the phone," Daniel suggested with a grin

as the old black plastic phone still hanging on the wall by the ratty sofa started to ring.

She rolled her eyes but she went to answer it anyway. "Good morning and Merry Christmas! Peter? Where are you? Of course I expected you to call, but it's early." With one hand cupping the curve of her belly, she leaned against the wall and smiled as she listened to her twin.

Shoving a basket of oranges to one side, Daniel set the sausages on the table, then bent and took a pan of home fries from the oven where they'd been keeping warm. As he worked, he hummed a baseline to the multipart harmonies pouring out of the living room.

Vicki felt a hand close over her shoulder.

"Although they live separately from a society that would fear and destroy them, although their lives are often violent and the space they need grows less with every passing year, still they celebrate Christmas."

Vicki frowned as the music changed. "They're singing 'Don't Cry for me Argentina.'"

"So werewolves are fans of Andrew Lloyd Webber, that's not the point." Celluci's fingers tightened. "The point is . . ."

She turned inside his grip and looked up at him. "The point is that they manage to celebrate Christmas, so why can't I? Right?" when he nodded, she smiled. "Subtlety has never been your strong point and whoever is arranging this . . ." She patted him gently on the Santa suit. ". . . is playing to your strengths. So let's go."

"Go?"

"Unless this is it?"

Shaking his head, he took her hand. "You're taking this better then I expected."

"I'm bowing to the inevitable." His fingers were warm around hers and she took a moment to enjoy it before nudging him with her free hand and saying, "Well?"

The kitchen, Daniel, the sausages disappeared.

Another kitchen reappeared around them.

"You know, I'm not really a big kitchen person anymore," Vicki sighed, looking around and recognizing Mike's parents' huge Mississauga kitchen. "Actually, I never was. You might have more success it you took me someplace I enjoyed."

"Like the roof of police headquarters?"

"That is not what I meant by *took*," Vicki muttered. "And your mother is sitting right over there."

"She can't hear us. We are but shadows." His voice faded as his mother's rose. A little overly dramatic as far as Vicki was concerned but it did make for a faster segue. Just because she was the next thing to immortal didn't mean she wanted to hang around indefinitely.

"He says he'll come without her, but if she makes him choose. . . ." Mrs. Celluci shook her head, curls tumbling much as her son's did.

Another woman, who looked so much like Mike she had to be his sister, set her mug on the counter and patted their mother on the arm. "He loves us. He'll always come."

"He loves her and if she says stay . . . Another Christmas, Marie, and we may not see him here. . ."

Vicki stared up at Mike in disbelief. "Oh, give me a break; you're also playing the part of Tiny Tim?"

His cheeks flushed.

"She used to come here with him sometimes, when they were both in the police, I don't know why she stopped . . ."

Marie shrugged philosophically. "People change."

That was an understatement.

"But to separate a man from his family . . . What kind of a change does that?"

With any luck, she'd never know.

"She is the kind of woman who wants everything her way."

"Selfish," agreed Marie.

"I am not," Vicki snapped. "You don't understand."

"They can't hear you," Mike reminded her quietly.

"She wants him to live with her wrapped in a cocoon. Like a bug."

"Like a spider," Mike's sister declared with relish. "Wrapping him in her web."

Mrs. Celluci rolled her eyes. "She doesn't want to eat him, Marie. She just wants to keep him with only her. I wonder . . ." A long swallow of coffee. "I wonder what she is afraid of."

"Okay." Vicki's eyes silvered as she turned away from the conversation. "That's enough pop psychology for one day. Wrap it up, Santa."

"There's more you should hear."

"Wrap it up now!"

"Or?"

Her answer was a low, warning growl.

Mike's gaze flicked over to the two women leaning on the counter. "We're shadows here, remember? You can't hurt them."

Vicki wrapped her fingers around his throat, resting them gently against the heated skin, feeling his life pulse past. "You're flesh and blood."

"Yes."

The sorrow in his response stopped the Hunter cold. Unable to look away, Vicki watched as he faded within her grip, growing fainter and fainter until she held only the memory of his warmth. Her heart pounded faster than it had since the night Mike had cradled her in his arms while Henry pressed a bleeding wrist to her lips. She swallowed with a mouth gone dry.

Then she frowned, pivoted on one heel, and grabbed a double handful of black fabric draped over the figure that had appeared suddenly behind her. "Fuck that," she snarled. "It stops right here." A vicious yank dragged the fabric clear of whoever gave it shape. Vicki tossed it aside, expected to see the elf from the mall, and saw instead . . .

Nothing.

The fabric she'd tossed aside stood beside her now, a hint of features under the drape.

"Well, nice to see the Nazgul are getting work. Missed the casting call for Dementors, did you?" She kept her tone flip, but power recognized power. Whatever had plunged her into this insane tour of reworked Victorian cliché was under that fabric. Vampires didn't dream, but that hadn't stopped it. It had plundered her memories, exposed her feelings, and . . .

Shown her things she hadn't known which, if true, proved it was operating outside of her psyche. Whatever it was, it wasn't all in her head. Something had gone to a lot of trouble to get her to celebrate Christmas.

So what? She really hated being manipulated.

"All right." Her lips drew up off her teeth. "Now you show me that no one cares when I die."

Under the fabric, power shifted so that it seemed to be pointing into the fog.

Fog? "Interesting weather patterns." Vicki took a step forward and the fog cleared. She blinked as lightning flashed. "That's um . . ." Another look. "That's a mob with torches and stakes attacking Cinderella's castle."

When she turned to face the fabric again, she sensed it was waiting expectantly.

"I get staked at Disney World?"

The fabric had no eyes to roll no arms to fold but Vicki still had the unmistakable feeling that time was running out.

"Okay. Fine." She folded her arms, since it seemed someone had to. "Torches and stakes are historic ways of dealing with a vampire. Historically, vampires kept to themselves, creating fear and distrust in the general population. If I don't learn from history, I'm doomed to repeat it." To sum up, she added sound effects to a mimed rim-shot.

Another power shift and the fabric pointed into a new section of fog.

Under the circumstances, the misty outline of gravestones wasn't unexpected.

"If there was enough to bury, I guess that kills the vampires turn to dust theory," she muttered, walking forward. "I'm not afraid of dying," she added in a slightly louder voice, "so I doubt we're going to have any major breakthrough here."

But it wasn't her name on the stone. The grave hadn't been filled in. The coffin hadn't been closed.

She stared down at Mike, watched silently as he slowly rotted, ignoring the pain from the half moon cuts her fingernails gouged into her palms. When bone finally turned to dust, her eyes flashed silver and with bloody hands she ripped the fabric into so many pieces they fell into the open grave like black snow.

The sun set.

Vicki fumbled her cell phone up from the blankets beside her, flipped it open and blinked at the display. Four forty-eight PM, December 25. In the faint blue light, she could see four semicircular cuts on each palm, the deepest still seeping blood.

Vampires didn't dream.

Nothing she could do would keep Michael Celluci from dying. If she left now, if she dressed and threw everything she had in her van and drove until sunrise and made sure he never found her and if she stopped seeing age overtake him, he'd still die.

And rot.

People died. But before they died, they should get a chance to spend time with people they loved.

"You didn't tell me anything I didn't already know," she snarled at the darkness.

The darkness felt smug.

"Bite me."

As it happened, it wasn't about Christmas at all.

She was wrapping the last 500 gram package of organic free-trade Mexican coffee when Mike got home from work. He stared at the presents on the table, at the ceramic candy canes dangling from Vicki's ears, and shook his head.

"What the hell is going on here?"

"I could hardly go to your parents' on Christmas Day without presents."

"You're going to my parents'?"

"We're going to your parents'."

"Yeah, that's sweet. I repeat, what the hell is going on?"

She sighed and stuck a bow down over the mess she'd made of one end of the package. Considering what she'd paid for the wrapping paper, it was crap. "I want to be with you, you want to be with your family—you're the detective, connect the dots."

His smile almost wiped out the memory of teeth in a crumbling skull. "Where did you get all this stuff?"

"Toronto's a big, multicultural city, Mike. Not everyone celebrates Christmas. You'd be amazed at what's open."

"I thought you'd stopped celebrating Christmas?"

She snorted. "Not likely."

"And the vampire thing?"

"Isn't going away. But neither is the human thing." She stood and pulled him toward her. "Just keep me away from your cousin Jeffrey."

"I don't have a cousin named Jeffrey."

Mouth pressed to the warm column of his throat, she felt his confusion and smiled. "Good."

Writing "Stone Cold"

In April of 2007, just before the episode first aired on Lifetime Television in the U.S., I posted to LiveJournal about the experience of writing "Stone Cold" for *Blood Ties,* the television show based on the Blood books. This is that post—tidied a tad, but just a tad, for publication.

As y'all know—and if you don't you're hanging around in the wrong LJ—some years ago I wrote a series of five vampire books called, in order of their appearance: *Blood Price, Blood Trail, Blood Lines, Blood Pact, Blood Debt.* There was never a series title although around the DAW office they were occasionally referred to as "the blood noun books." (Later, there were short stories but as they don't figure into this particular story, we'll ignore them for now.) The books featured a kick-ass heroine and witty repartee—my minimal requirements for personal enjoyment—as well as an attractive, tall, somewhat put-upon police detective and the bastard son of Henry VIII, a romance writer and a vampire. Together, the three of them kept busy rescuing the world from demons, mummies, zombies, and ghosts. Once, they rescued a pack of werewolves from the world.

Jump ahead a bit to where the fine and perceptive people at Kaleidoscope Entertainment read the books and said, "Damn, those books'll make good television!" I'm paraphrasing for effect, of course. Although they may have said that, who knows. Long story short, they optioned the series.

Now as well as being both fine people and perceptive people, they were also incredibly persistent people and they worked their collective butts off to actually bring the series, now called *Blood Ties*, to television. I'd like to emphasize here that this is so incredibly complicated and difficult and downright annoying (there's a fair bit of muttering and returning to ground zero involved) that it almost never happens. Be impressed. Be very impressed.

In order to adapt the books to a brand new medium, they hired Peter Mohan as the show runner. In brief, the show runner is just what the title suggests—the person who runs the show. They're also, almost all the time, a writer. *The* writer. Usually—as in this case—also the series creator. This makes series television writer driven which is pretty damned cool. Besides having years of experience in genre television, Peter had already read the books and loved them. Things were good to go and there was no reason whatsoever that I, as the original author, needed to be further involved.

Round about here, I realized either I'd done something remarkable in my last life in order to rack up massive amounts of good karma or I was borrowing karma points from my next few lives.

Although, for monetary reasons, the show would actually be shot in Vancouver (it was cheaper) for some months before the move, the writing room was in Toronto and Peter asked me if I'd come into the city a few times and assist the writers in staying true to the characters in the books. That happened. It was fun. Then Peter asked if I might like to take a crack at writing an episode. . . .

I was, to understate the matter slightly, thrilled. Actually, hysterically excited would also be understating the matter slightly. I'd put Peter up for sainthood at this point. Would I like to write an episode? Dude, I have an almost pristine degree in Radio and Television Arts!

And what follows is the true and more or less accurate story—given my somewhat crappy memory—of how I wrote "Stone Cold" for *Blood Ties*. It gets a bit stream of consciousness in places and occasionally careens around the timeline, so make some popcorn and get comfy; this is going to take a while.

E-mails began flying back and forth and we all (where *all* includes myself, Peter, and the other three staff writers) agreed that Medusa would be my monster-of-the-week (it's way too complicated for freelancers to do myth-arc episodes, particularly freelancers who are writing their very first episode some not inconsiderable distance away from the action) and I returned to the city and the writing room just before they left for Vancouver to break the story.

Now, here's the first difference between the writing I usually do and writing for television. At this point in my career, some twenty-odd years and twenty-three books in, when I set out to write a book, I send the concept of what I want to do to my agent and he presents it to my editor and she tells me when they need me to have it finished. Okay, there's some other stuff about money in there but that's pretty much it. I mention what I'd like to do, there's some small amount of discussion, then I do it. For about a year. All by myself. Television, on the other hand, is collaborative. Roughly translated, this means you may get to go to the toilet by yourself but that's about it. And no one's making any promises about the toilet.

So, I'm in the writing room with Peter and Shelley and Dennis and Mark and we're about to break an idea down into a teaser and four acts. And I say something along the lines of, well, what if there're these guys and they're unloading statues in a warehouse and one of the statues has bleeding eyes. And instead of someone saying, "Go for it, this is when we need it done," the four other people in the room take the idea and start throwing it about. Ever been to a concert and seen a beachball go bouncing over the heads of the crowd? Like that.

Ideas are flying thick and fast and all of them are either good or interesting or both but none of them are being explored. Or not in any way I recognize. Oh wait: the bouncing and the flying thick and fast—that's the way they explore the ideas! Oh! (Little lights go off in my brain.) So I throw a few ideas in too. This is fun! It doesn't seem to be actually accomplishing anything, but it's fun.

Except—and I'm still not entirely certain how this happened—at the end of the day, we have all the points of the episode up on the white board. Beats are being hit, acts are ending with a bang, the most basic outline of the story is complete, and Peter, who is, as you'll remember, the man in charge because this show is *his* baby, not mine, has essentially agreed to what's been created. I say essentially because he was actually on the phone with casting for part of it and we kind of snuck act four in under the radar. As far as I recall, my main contribution here was to say, "Why don't we use his mother again since we're already paying her?" And Shelley said, "Man, the producers are going to love you."

I took copious amounts of notes. Which I still have and planned on quoting from but I can't find the damned things although while searching I did find my old line dancing notes and I'd been looking for them ever since downloading "Boot Scoot Boogie" so . . . um . . . never mind.

And so buzzing with the kind of energy that comes from being bathed in somewhat manic creativity for eight or nine hours, I went home. On the train, while I could still make sense of my handwriting and somewhat eclectic shorthand, I wrote up the beat sheet as we delineated it in the room.

It's important to remember here that I'm writing the beat sheet for a potential episode nine at the same time as episodes three through eight are being broken.

Not only do I not know what's happened in the episodes directly before mine—at this point, no one does. And that doesn't really matter because it's going to change anyway.

For the sake of bandwidth (ETA: remember, this was first posted online) I'm going to use the teaser as an example of how the script changes throughout the writing process. The teaser is the bit that happens before the opening credits. It usually introduces the plot and establishes where the main characters (or some of them) are emotionally and how it will impact with the theme of the episode. Ish. Unless someone comes up with a really kick-ass idea that works better.

This is the teaser we broke that day in the writing room.

TEASER

In what is clearly the loading dock of a shipping company, a crew loads a large crate onto a forklift. As the forklift backs up a little too soon and a little too quickly, the crate wobbles and falls. When it lands it breaks open.

The crew hurries to check the contents and discovers the statue inside was cushioned with Bubble Wrap and thus protected. But there's a dark smear on the on the inside of the plastic . . .

One of the men carefully unwraps the statue's head and slowly crosses himself. The statue's eyes are bleeding.

You'll notice, there's bugger all about the main characters here. Clearly, we're a little skint on content. Needless to say, there were copious notes returned to me.

By now, the writing team had moved out to Vancouver and were beginning to put together the other episodes. Specifically, the episode directly before mine where, so as not to give too much away to those who haven't seen "Heart of Fire," Mike and Henry have a small disagreement.

These were the notes that came back top of the first page of the beatsheet. Just to give you some idea of the number of changes, when I saved the file, I named it MedusaBeatSavaged. Although, the teaser had only this added:

Color beat with Vicki and Henry. Something that's kind of fun about their characters: she's a detective, he's a vampire! THEN CUT TO:

There were larger changes throughout and I added this note to the top of page one just to give me some idea of where the hell I was going with the emotional arcs:

WHERE MIKE AND VICKI ARE AT: MIKE IS SAYING "I DON'T KNOW WHAT YOU'RE GOING THROUGH WITH HENRY AND I DON'T HAVE TO LIKE IT, BUT I DON'T WANT TO LOSE YOU FROM MY LIFE. TELL ME HOW WE CAN MAKE THIS BETTER."

VICKI ISN'T SURE WHAT TO DO, SHE'S STILL PISSED ABOUT HOW MIKE ENDANGERED HENRY AND DIDN'T TRUST HER.

THEN LATER WHEN MIKE IS TURNED INTO A STATUE SHE REALIZES SHE CAN'T LOSE HIM EITHER, THAT WOULD BE TOO PAINFUL FOR HER.

So I beat things into the new shape, sent a sketchy outline in and in a few days get a message from Shelley Eriksen one of the writers that said . . .

* * *

∞ OK, so you're about to find out why it's tough to be an "outside writer."

Your outline was great. Hit all the beats, moved well. Nothing wrong, lots right, with what you did.

So we're looking it over in the room, and somebody says, You know, what if . . . ?

and then somebody leaps on that, and says, Oh Yeah, and what if this . . . ?

Cue, two days later. We've completely reworked the outline. And that's what we're sending you.

Just to reassure you—it's still a Medusa show. What's changed in a big way (aside from the setting) is that Vicki figures out that it's a Medusa very quickly—and a lot of the story is about Vicki tryingto convince Mike of what's going on.

At the top of the outline there's a few notes about where Mike's at, and much of what's going on for Vicki is not being willing to let Mike go, and learning how to be willing to move forward.

You can blow this one out to more of a formal outline. Peter's available if you have any questions.

Don't worry. You're doing great.

They've just changed the whole thing and I'm doing great? Weird business, television. At some point in here, Dmitri was a cyclops. He wore sunglasses. That didn't actually last long. There was also some discussion of Medusa using the snake venom to control people. That lasted a little longer than the sunglasses. But not much.

So I incorporate all the new bits, write up a more formal outline, and this is the new teaser: WARNING:

FROM THIS POINT ON THERE ARE SPOILERS FOR "STONE COLD." Okay, small ones, but they're there. You've been warned. Stop reading now if you don't want even the teaser spoiled.

TEASER

FADE IN

1. INT: ELENA'S HOUSE—FOYER—NIGHT
We're in the foyer of what is obviously an expensive house, dimly lit by the sort of lights you leave on for security. The front door opens and in the much brighter light spilling in from outside, Elena Kanapolous, a very attractive woman in her thirties, currently wrapped around Brendan Ledford, a very attractive and well-muscled young man in his late teens—early twenties tops. The age difference doesn't seem to be bothering either of them as they stumble into the house playing tonsil hockey at the Stanley Cup level.

After closing the door, Elena shoves Brendan against the wall and manages to strip his shirt off him without removing the lip-lock. When he wonders if maybe they shouldn't go upstairs, she tells him she doesn't want to wait that long.

Her hands move down out of the shot.

IN TIGHT on Brendan, his head goes back and he moans. Among other things, he moans, "Elena . . . " At the sound of some fairly enthusiastic hissing, his eyes snap open.

And he turns to stone.

2. EXT: VICKI'S TOWNHOUSE—NIGHT
Vicki is carefully on the path of light to the front door when a man-sized shadow detaches

itself from the darkness beside the path and . . .

. . . Vicki slams her fist into the shadow's stomach and as it folds forward into the light, we see it's Mike Celluci who gasps out, "What the hell was that for?"

Vicki, backing cautiously out of reach, tells him it's what he gets for sneaking up on her. She's not buying his protests that he wasn't sneaking.

"Look, I just came by to apologize . . . again."

While Mike is clearly sorry, Vicki's not buying his apology either. "Somehow, I'm sorry just isn't enough weighed against what you did."

"What do you want me to do, Vicki, beg? Go down on my knees?"

She looks like she's thinking about that for a moment (like 90 percent of the women and at least 10 percent of the men watching) but says no, turns and walks away.

He stands on the path watching her, looking angry and defeated both.

When she has her door open, she turns and repeats, "Sorry isn't enough." Before going inside and closing the door.

Mike sighs and wonders what the hell is.

The first scene with Brendan and Elena will remain essentially unchanged although later it'll be thematically expanded. The Vicki and Mike scene though will eventually be changed to better reflect episode eight. (It had a brief existence as a scene between Vicki and Henry and a guy running an insurance scam but that didn't last long enough for me to even keep a copy.) Episode eight, at this point, is also in the process of being written by a freelancer and "roomed" by the staff writers.

A few days after sending this version off, I get an e-mail from Peter Mohan—the showrunner, remember?—and it said:

∞ Sorry it took a while to get back to you. Read the outline and loved it. You actually made some sense out of the stuff we threw at you . . . And added fabulous character touches and humor.

  We'll get back to you in the next day or so with specific notes, although I'm tempted to send it to the net as-is.

Well, dude, don't I just totally rock! Um . . . apparently not quite yet although Peter did end up sending this version to network. And then it came back attached to this e-mail.

∞ Hi Tanya,

  Here is a revised outline, the network notes on the outline, my notes on the outline and a further commentary on my notes once I took it back to the room.

  If you have any thoughts or concerns, please call or e-mail us at any time throughout the drafting process.

  Otherwise, have fun writing the draft!

  Talk to you soon,

So now I have Peter's notes and his commentary on his notes. And network's notes. And Shelley's translation of network's notes particularly as they pertained to Peter's notes. And thank God for Shelly's notes, that's all I have to say right here—mostly because I can too be diplomatic when I have to be.

I'd like to point out right now that it would have been about 112 percent easier at this point for them to write the damned thing themselves but they hung in there and kept talking me though it.

They now know more of what's going on in episode eight and, in the teaser, at least, the changes have to reflect that. The bits with the lines, those are Peter's changes and/or additions.

FADE IN

EXT. VICKI'S HOUSE—NIGHT
Vicki is carefully on the path of light to the front door when a man-sized shadow detaches itself from the darkness beside the path and . . .

. . . Vicki slams her fist into the shadow's stomach and as it folds forward into the light, we see it's Mike Celluci who gasps out, "What the hell was that for?"

Vicki, backing cautiously out of reach, tells him it's what he gets for sneaking up on her. She's not buying his protests that he wasn't sneaking.

He wonders how long she's going to have a problem with him for having sold out Henry.

For her, it's not just Henry who got sold out. He didn't trust her and her judgment. He sold her out too.

He feels like he's going crazy. There's nothing in the rule book about how you deal with a situation like this. Sharing your girlfriend with a freaking vampire. Who does he think is the girlfriend? And who's sharing?

* * *

Forget being in a relationship. If he even wants to know her from now on, he has to get his head past his prejudice against Henry. Hey, it's hard. Is it his fault his parents let him stay up late that time and watch *Dracula*? And doesn't the fact that he gave his own blood to save Henry count for anything?

She suggests he talk to her the next time he decides to sell someone out.

As she heads into her house and closes the door, he stands on the path watching, looking frustrated.

INT. ELENA'S HOUSE FOYER—NIGHT
We're in the foyer of what is obviously an expensive house, dimly lit by the sort of lights you leave on for security. The front door opens and in the much brighter light spilling in from outside, Elena Kanapolous, a very attractive woman in her thirties, currently wrapped around Brendan Ledford, a very attractive and well muscled young man in his late teens, early twenties tops. The age difference doesn't seem to be bothering either of them as they stumble into the house playing tonsil hockey at the Stanley Cup level.

After closing the door, Elena shoves Brendan against the wall and manages to strip his shirt off him without removing the lip-lock. When he wonders if maybe they shouldn't go upstairs, she tells him she doesn't want to wait that long.

Her hands move down out of the shot.

IN TIGHT on Brendan, his head goes back and he moans. Among other things, he moans,

"Elena . . . " At the sound of some fairly enthusiastic hissing, his eyes snap open.

We see Elena from the back, she's naked and her head is now a mass of writhing SNAKES!

As the terrified Brendan's eyes lock on her, he screams and . . . TURNS TO STONE.

So, I learn a new program—although for the most part Movie Magic Screenwriter is fairly fail-safe and kind of fun—and I write the first draft. And the teaser now looks like this:

TEASER

FADE IN

EXT. VICKI'S TOWNHOUSE NIGHT
VICKI NELSON is carefully walking the path of light to the front door when a man-sized shadow detaches itself from the darkness beside the path and . . .

. . . Vicki slams her fist into the shadow's stomach and as it folds forward into the light, we see it's MIKE CELLUCI.

> MIKE
> (gasping)
> What the hell was that for?

Vicki backs cautiously out of reach as he straightens, clutching his stomach.

> VICKI
> It's what you get for sneaking up on
> me. And stop being such a girl, I didn't
> hit you that hard.

*   *   *

MIKE
(definitely ignoring the second
comment)
I wasn't sneaking.

VICKI
You were standing quietly in the
dark, waiting . . .
(considers)
Fine. Not sneaking. Stalking.

She goes to push by him but he stands in her
way.

MIKE
We have to settle this.

VICKI
Settle what?

MIKE
This. This *problem* between you and
me. I admit I made a mistake . . .

VICKI
Mistake? Are you seriously calling
what you did a mistake? You sold
Henry out, Mike.

MIKE
And then I worked my butt off to
save him!

VICKI
Not good enough.

She goes to push by him again but again he
stands in her way. This time, however, he
backs off, both hands raised. She passes him,
then turns.

*   *   *
VICKI CONT'D
You didn't just sell out Henry, Mike.
What you did, when you showed
you didn't trust me, showed you
didn't trust my judgment—you
sold me out too.

MIKE
You're overreacting.

VICKI
I'm . . .

Mike cuts her off hurriedly as he realizes that
might not have been the smartest thing to say.

MIKE
(interrupting)
Come on, Vicki, give me a break. I'm
making this up as I go along.
There's nothing in the rule book
about sharing with a freaking
vampire!

VICKI
Sharing? Sharing what? Sharing
me? Like I'm some kind of . . .
object to be passed back and forth?

MIKE
That's not what I meant.
(He runs his hand back through
his hair)
We used to be able to talk, you and
me. Remember? Back before
Henry freakin' Fitzroy and all this
monster of the week crap he's
gotten us mixed up in.

*   *   *

                              VICKI
                             This . . .
                (she waves a hand between them)
                    This isn't Henry's fault.

                              MIKE
                        How do you figure?

                              VICKI
                      How do I figure what?

                              MIKE
                     You're denying Fitzroy's a
                            vampire?

                              VICKI
                No, I'm suggesting you're an ass.
                   If you want anything to do with
                  me from now on, you've got to get
                    past this thing you have with
                             Henry.

This time when she starts walking, she keeps
moving toward the house.

                              MIKE
                  Doesn't giving my own blood to save
                      him count for something?

Vicki pauses on the step.

                              VICKI
                         (without turning)
                         It's not enough.

                              MIKE
                  What do you want me to do, Vicki?
                   Beg? Go down on my knees?
                          *   *   *

She doesn't answer, goes into the house and closes the door. Mike stands on the path, watching, looking frustrated.

INT. ELENA'S HOUSE, FRONT HALL—NIGHT
We're in the foyer of what is obviously an expensive house, dimly lit by the sort of lights you leave on for security. The front door opens and in the much brighter light spilling in from outside, Elena Kanapolous, a very attractive woman in her thirties, currently wrapped around Brendan Ledford, a very attractive and well muscled young man in his late teens, early twenties tops. The age difference doesn't seem to be bothering either of them as they stumble into the house playing tonsil hockey at the Stanley Cup level.

After closing the door, Elena shoves Brendan against the wall and manages to strip his shirt off him without removing the lip-lock.

> BRENDAN
> (attempting to gain control of the
> situation)
> We should go upstairs.

> ELENA
> I don't want to wait that long.

Elena's hands move down out of the shot.

ANGLE ON Brendan's face. His expression very clearly says, Go me! He's smugly proud of making a conquest. Then his head snaps back and he moans.

PAN DOWN as *something* slithers away from his arm leaving two small holes trickling blood.

*   *   *

ANGLE ON Brendan's face. His eyes are closed
and he's definitely in the throes of something.

                    BRENDAN
                    Elena . . .

At the sound of some fairly enthusiastic hissing, his eyes snap open.

Elena rises into the shot. We see her from the
back. She's naked and her head is now a mass
of writhing snakes.

    As the terrified Brendan's eyes lock on her,
he screams and . . . TURNS TO STONE.

    Okay, I have to admit that I love the line "At the
sound of some fairly enthusiastic hissing, his eyes snap
open." Hee. The whole fairly enthusiastic hissing thing
just makes me laugh. (ETA: In the actual screened episode, those were some sufficiently enthusiastic snakes!)
    So, I've written the first draft and I send it off to
Peter and Shelley and Dennis and Mark and I wait
while they do their own work for a while and then I
get back some detailed notes. Some of them are general craft things about formatting and the like and
then they get meaty. . . . Still staying with the teaser
we have:

∞ Hitting Mike is a big thing. She's tough enough
   that it would really hurt.
∞ Vicki's voice way too angry. Mike almost died at
   the end of 108 and made a huge sacrifice. He
   saved Henry's life. Watch her anger throughout
   the whole show. Think House.
∞ Mike too pussified. We're finding him apologizing
   way too much in many of the shows.
∞ At the end of 108, an important switch occurred.
   Vicki and Henry were locked in the room. He

asked her to kill him. She didn't. She realized that she was willing to give up her life for him. And he realized he was too dangerous for her to be with. So now, although she's always said the relationship with Henry was just a partnership, she tells Mike (when pressed) that she's confused. When she goes back to Henry, expecting him to want the relationship on, he's pulling back. Mike's position, after she tells him, she's confused is that he's royally pissed (not a wimp for once). He's almost died for her and her friend. She's kept him cut off because of her anger over her vision, her indecision over Henry and he feels like he's been stuck in relationship limbo. He doesn't want to be part of the world of Vamps and demons and she's dragged him into the deep end. If this is what she wants, fine. He's out. (Parse this out as needed throughout the episode, but give a good strong shot at the beginning where we set the story flying). By the end of the episode, he's dragged back in by the Medusa thing and has to admit that once you're in, you're in. The big movement for everyone in this show is that they all have to decide if they're part of the "team" by the end of the episode. He does come to a point where he realizes these things do exist and people do have to be protected from them and he has to participate. He will, however, look for his own emotional interests more rather than waiting for her.

∞ Trim scene overall. We've been trying to be no longer than three pages and one page should be the Elena scene.

The House comment actually led to an extended exchange of e-mails between Peter and me about House being cranky and Vicki being cranky and how alike they are in their crankiness. Ish. We also all do a little talking about Elena's motivation—mythically and all.

Meanwhile, I rewrite the episode. Although there are some other e-mails exchanged along the way:

Me to Peter: Since you took out both references, can I assume that Vicki kicking anyone in the nuts is verboten?

Peter's answer: Have her mash those bad boys. With prejudice. If she played with them, kissed or dealt with them in any loving way, they'd be inaccessible to us. Kicking or mashing them however would be network friendly. Thank God for the unwritten Canadian TV code.

Somewhere in here, I naively mention to Peter that I could get a better handle on where the characters were emotionally if I could see episodes 3 to 8. Unfortunately, they exist in much the same condition as my episode. Which is to say, they won't be particularly useful.

And the teaser for the second draft looks like this:

TEASER

FADE IN

EXT. VICKI'S TOWNHOUSE—NIGHT
VICKI NELSON is carefully walking the path of light to her front door when a shadow emerges from the darkness beside the path. She flicks out her ASP as the shadow moves into the light and we see it's MIKE CELLUCI.

                    MIKE
          And here I thought you'd be glad to
                    see me.

As Vicki puts the ASP away, Mike moves close. Vicki stops him with a hand on his chest, only her fingertips actually touching him. Dropping her arm, she looks into his face.

                    VICKI
          What do you want, Mike?

MIKE
(with an edge)
Oh you know, the usual: peace on
earth, decent hockey tickets, to
find out where you and I stand.

VICKI
You and I?

MIKE
Yeah, cute couple, worked well
together. Remember them?

Vicki starts to speak, stops, it's clearly killing
her to say this, to be this emotionally honest.

VICKI
Things have gotten complicated.

Mike raises an eyebrow, waiting.

VICKI CONT'D
And I'm . . . confused.

MIKE
Confused? I almost died for you and
your *friend*—that strikes me as
pretty damned definitive.

He's looming over her, using his height.

VICKI
(hackles rising)
Look, you're angry and . . .

MIKE
(sarcastically)
Am I?
(thinks about it)

Yeah, you know, I think I am. I
think I've finally had enough. If
you want to live your life with
Henry Freakin' Fitzroy and the
extended *Twilight Zone* episode that
goes with him then maybe it's
time for me to just walk away.

VICKI
Oh, that's mature. It doesn't matter
who I "choose . . ."

She sketches an incredibly sarcastic set of air
quotes around the word choose.

VICKI CONT'D
. . . you walking away won't change
the fact that there are things—
strange and sometimes horrible
things—really out there, really
going bump in the night.

MIKE
It will if you walk away with me.

Vicki stares at him for a long moment, all the
fight going out of her stance. This is a point of
no return and that realization shows on her
face. Finally, she shakes her head, a minimal
movement easy to miss if Mike (and the camera) weren't watching her so closely.

Mike's expression doesn't change but when he
speaks his voice is rough.

MIKE CONT'D
All right then.

He turns on one heel and walks away.

* * *

VICKI'S RP POV: IT LOOKS LIKE THE DARK-
NESS SWALLOWS MIKE UP.

INT. ELENA'S HOUSE, FOYER—NIGHT
We're in the foyer of an expensive house, dimly
lit. The front door opens and in the brighter
light spilling in from outside, we see ELENA KA-
NAPOLOUS, a beautiful woman in her thirties,
currently wrapped around BRENDAN LED-
FORD, an equally beautiful young man in his
late teens or early twenties. The age difference
doesn't seem to bother either of them as they
stumble into the house, lips locked.

Elena closes the door, shoves Brendan against
the wall and strips his shirt off him.

                    BRENDAN
                    (gasping)
            We should go upstairs.

                    ELENA
        My house, Brendan, my rules.

                    BRENDAN
        Fine. Whatever. Oh, God . . . Elena,
        you're just. . . . You're too . . .

He takes a deep breath and manages a moment's coherency.

                BRENDAN CONT'D
        I can't believe how beautiful you
                    are.

                    ELENA
        Because you're too clever to believe
            in the lies beauty tells?

* * *

BRENDAN
(confused)
Wha . . .

Elena slides down his body, out of the shot.

ANGLE ON Brendan as he reacts. His head
slams back against the wall and his eyes close.

ELENA V.O.
(creepily)
Pretty, pretty young things who
think being pretty is all they
need.

At the sound of some fairly enthusiastic hissing, Brendan's eyes open. Elena rises into the
shot. We see her from the back. She's naked
and her head is a mass of writhing snakes.

As the terrified Brendan's eyes lock on her, he
screams and . . . TURNS TO STONE.

FADE OUT

And that's the second draft. Which is accepted. And
I'm paid. Woot! I'm a television writer.

Everyone from my new media agent to the execu-
tive producers is saying what a good script it is. But I
don't hear anything from Peter . . . who is hip deep in
the pilot and more than a little busy and why haven't I
heard from him, damn it! He must have liked it, he
agreed to use it.

That was early September. Later in the month, I
head to Toronto to watch them do some second unit
work on the pilot and I wrote all about that earlier
so there's no point in recapping the whole thing now
but what's relevant is the part where Peter and Dylan
and I are sitting around for a bit after supper (which

happened at midnight) and either Peter or I mention I've written episode nine. And Dylan makes a comment about how in his experience I'll be lucky if they actually use three lines.

I laugh and say, "All things considered, I think they might keep six."

And Peter laughs, nervously.

Half of me thinks Dylan is kidding and half of me . . . well, Dylan's wife is a screenwriter and he's done some writing too and what the hell do I know about it? So Dylan says three, I counter with six, Peter laughs a little more, and we all say good night.

Jump ahead to November and my trip to Vancouver to watch them film the episode (which was really remarkably wonderful of Kaleidoscope for a number of reasons and I'm really remarkably grateful and, honestly, you can never thank people too much for being amazing).

One of the first things I do when I get to the studio is take a look at the script. I know it's been rewritten and this is where being a freelancer as opposed to a staff writer kind of sucks. If you're on staff, you're in the room while the changes are being suggested and you get to make them. If you're half a continent away, not so much.

The teaser on the blue edition dated November 16 is pretty much what you'll see on Sunday night. It's a bit different from what I wrote but in its essentials the same—Vicki and Mike (now jogging) talk about Henry and Elena turns Brendan to stone. Although it's shifted around a bit, there's a bunch of my dialogue still there. There are some larger changes in later scenes however. . . .

Changes weren't only made to reflect the earlier episodes and the overall arc of the show (past and present) but also to take into consideration the budget (early drafts always require more money than what's available—regardless of how much money is available) and the locations (the club we used had two stories so that was worked into the script) and network concerns (no one's clothing was removed) and the time available (the art department nearly killed themselves finishing the number of statues you see in the episode—literally, those things are fiberglass and were still gassing off while we were shooting) and the abilities of the cast (Christina with a sword—oh, yeah!). Mostly the budget though.

. . . but I'm seeing lines I wrote. I should have bet with Dylan. I'd so win.

Then I pick up the pink pages from November 17. There are changes on twenty-six pages. Of a fifty-five page script. Now most of these are small, single line changes but my line count is dropping. Then I pick up the green pages from November 20 and there are changes on twenty-one pages although since we're now a fifty-four page script I suppose statistically . . . Actually, no. It's starting to look like a good thing I didn't make that bet with Dylan.

They actually ended up going one more rewrite to yellow but I don't have paper of that, just the locked Writer's Guild PDF which can't be cut and pasted and, frankly, ~~I don't love y'all enough to retype~~ this is long enough already. (ETA: The shooting script has been included in this volume so you can now check the final changes if that's what floats your boat.)

Now, Peter and the other writers are watching my reaction to this with some . . . concern. At this point, with the killer workload they're under, the last thing they need is the creator of the source material running around having an artistic hissy fit. They know that I usually have a lot more control over my writing than this and they've all heard the stories of book writers being complete pissheads about changes once they get on set. Not to mention, it's not unusual for rookie script writers (and occasionally experienced script writers who should bloody well know better) to freak about how little of their original dialogue remains by the time the script goes in front of the camera.

Taking their concerns in order:

As the creator of the source material, I'd been fully

aware from the beginning that the show was not my baby. It was, to stretch the metaphor pretty much as far as it'll go, my grandbaby and everyone knows that if grandma wants to remain in contact with the grandbaby, grandma doesn't make comments on how said baby is being raised as long as baby is happy and healthy. Anything Peter and his writers have changed for the show doesn't impact on the books. They're the same as they ever were. So, no reason for a hissy fit.

The contract for the script was outline, first draft, and second draft. Which I delivered, had approved, and was paid for. I doubt very much there's ever been a script written for an hour long TV drama that made it to the screen on second draft. Peter's script of the pilot went one more rewrite than mine (he went to salmon) and he's in charge of the whole thing! There have been scripts, although not so far on *Blood Ties,* that have been rewritten so often they've gone to double colors. (There's a fairly famous *X-Files* story about this that, I think, referred to John Shiban who's now with *Supernatural.*)

So, I counted my lines, bounced back upstairs, announced I still had six lines of my original dialogue in the script so I won! Woot. And everyone in the department breathed a sigh of relief.

I made sure to point this out to Dylan who was gracious in defeat. Later, when we were shooting on location and I heard another line I'd written (although it had been moved from the scene I'd originally put it in), I told him I was now up to seven lines. I rule! In spite of the fact it was four in the morning after a very long workday which wasn't actually over yet, he seemed pleased for me. Dylan has lovely manners.

At one point, while I watching them shoot one of the scenes in Henry's apartment, I loved one of the lines so much I ran back upstairs to find out which of them had written it. (It was Shelley.)

And what did I think when I saw the finished cut of the episode?

Of course there were lines of mine I wished they'd

kept in. Of course I wished that mine would be the script that went right from second draft to the screen. Of course I wished we'd had a big enough budget for my original vision. Everyone who writes for television wishes that. They'd also like a little recognition for their craft from the world at large but they're pretty sure they're not going to get that either so they suck it up and keep writing.

I'm still both happy and proud to be the credited writer for "Stone Cold." It's not bad for a first attempt. And those seven lines kick ass.

To sum up:

Writing for print is a solitary endeavor.

Writing for television is writing by committee and you'd better be able to play well with others if you're going to attempt it.

Creatively, egotistically, they are apples and oranges. And I'm sure there's a fruit salad comment in there but you'll have to make it yourself.

As I understand it, outline, first and second draft, and an availability for polishing if requested are the requirements for script credit by the Writer's Guild of Canada. If a script moves far enough away from the second draft that a show runner wants to credit a second writer or another writer altogether, well, I expect that's the sort of thing that'll go to arbitration.

I wrote the outline, first, and second draft of episode nine of *Blood Ties,* "Stone Cold," without having seen anything to do with episodes three though eight—because they were also being written at the time. (Although by the second draft, Peter had some idea of where eight was going and was able to have me make some small adjustments.)

Essentially, I wrote the story.

There were four rewrites after that by the staff writers changing the way the story was told.

Peter changed a line of dialogue while they were shooting to better reflect the emotional space of the character at that moment. (Not one of mine.)(I win again.)

New lines of dialogue are occasionally looped in during editing although I don't know if that happened in this instance.

As my third year sociology professor said, "Change is constant."

Would I do it again?

Do you even have to ask?

In a heartbeat.

"Stone Cold" Screenplay

TEASER

EXT. JOGGING TRAIL—DAY
VICKI NELSON enjoys an early morning jog along a barely-there trail.
She sees someone up ahead of her, jogging toward her. She's not used to seeing someone on this path, but what the hey . . .
It's MIKE.
   He slows as they approach one another, and then reverses direction and starts running with her.

> MIKE
> How far you going?

> VICKI
> Twenty K.

Mike nods. OK, he's down with that.
Uncomfortable silence . . . stretching out like the trail in front of them. . . .

> MIKE
> How's Henry?

> VICKI
> He's fine.

MIKE
Good. That's good.

VICKI
After he snacked on the mad monk
who nearly killed him, he was just
like a kid again. Four hundred and
eighty years young. A spring lamb.

Mike stops jogging. Vicki follows suit.

MIKE
We're not past this, are we?

VICKI
We're fine.

MIKE
Yeah, sure.

VICKI
Henry nearly died.

MIKE
There was a lot of that going around
that night.

VICKI
I know. But it doesn't make it any
easier.

Mike nods. Unconsciously touches his neck,
where Fitzroy sucked his blood.

VICKI
Does it hurt?

MIKE
I'm heading back.

                    VICKI
                    Mike.

                    MIKE
              Just not feeling it today.

Mike starts jogging in the opposite direction.

                    VICKI
                 We'll be fine.
                (he keeps going)
                    Mike!

EXT. ELENA'S HOUSE—NIGHT
An anonymous but monied downtown house. Dark.
A light goes on in the foyer. And then it goes
out again.
INT. ELENA'S HOUSE—LIVING ROOM—NIGHT
A young man, BRENDAN, twenties, model-
handsome, fumbles for the light switch again.

                    BRENDAN
                I want to see you.

ELENA KANAPOLOUS, thirties or forties, beautiful, mass of wild dark hair, takes his hand
away from the light switch.

                    ELENA
         Shhh. Close your eyes. Concentrate
              on your other senses.
                (he complies)
              Tell me what you feel.

                    BRENDAN
         Your skin. It's soft. Like silk.

                    ELENA
           Good. What do you smell?

*   *   *

Brendan bites her neck, breathes in deeply.

> BRENDAN
> You're like—you smell like the
> ocean. Like you're . . . forever.

> ELENA
> You're very perceptive, Brendan.

> BRENDAN
> (gasps)
> God, Elena—oh God.

Clearly she's touched him somewhere special,
and offscreen. He opens his eyes, and spots a
mirror on one wall. He kisses her, pulling
them along the wall so that they're opposite
the mirror. He turns her around, so that she's
in front of him, and they're both facing the
mirror.

> BRENDAN
> What's wrong with me saying
> you're beautiful? You are. Ever
> since I saw you, you remember?
> And now we're finally . . .

He kisses her neck.

> ELENA
> So my beauty moves you, does it?

> BRENDAN
> Yes.

WATCHING THE MIRROR, Elena takes Brendan's right hand, places his hand on her cheek,
smooth and alabaster—like a mask.

*   *   *

ELENA
Would you do anything for my
beauty?

Still holding his hand to her face, she twists to
face him—

BRENDAN
What do you want me to do? I'll do
it, Elena, I swear . . .

She slips down, out of sight of the mirror. Brendan sighs in anticipation—and then a quizzical
look crosses his face. In his right hand, he's
holding a mask, one that looks like an ancient
Greek statue's face.

ELENA (O.S.)
Tell me Brendan—how do you like
me now?

From the mirror, we see the back of Elena's
head as she rises up, and her head is a mass of
hissing snakes—and as Brendan, terrified,
looks at Elena—
He turns to stone.
END TEASER

ACT

EXT. VICKI'S OFFICE—DAY
To establish.
INT. VICKI'S OFFICE—DAY
Vicki watches as TERRI FULLTON, forty-two, a
no-nonsense woman, hands over a photo of a
young man we recognize as Brendan. It's a
modeling shot.

TERRI
He's not the kind of kid who misses

a booking. Then he's not answering
his phone? Something's up.

VICKI
Early twenties . . . you're sure he's
not sleeping it off somewhere?

TERRI
Brendan's a responsible kid. Very
dedicated to his career.

VICKI
I assume you've talked to his
family.

TERRI
(shakes her head)
His mother's dead. The father left
when Brendan was a pre-
schooler.

Vicki takes a close look at the picture of Brendan, one that shows the youth and vulnerability
of the boy.

VICKI
So you're all he's got in the world?

TERRI
I'm twenty years older than him—
I've got more sense than that.
I'm genuinely worried about him.

VICKI
And . . .

Terri acts like there's no "and," but realizes
Vicki's not buying it.

                         TERRI
              I loaned him six grand before he
                       disappeared.

                         TERRI
               I was supposed to get it back this
                  week—or I was before he
                       disappeared.

                         VICKI
                         Drugs?

                         TERRI
              No. He likes clubbing, late nights,
                 girls—but he's careful.
                         (beat)
              That detective said you could help.

                         VICKI
                    That detective?

        Coreen enters with tea on a tray:

                        COREEN
              Detective Mike Celluci. He referred
                      Ms. Fullton.

                         VICKI
                   Oh, that detective.

                         TERRI
               I know it's supposed to be forty-
               eight hours until he's considered
                 a missing person. But all the
                  literature tells you the first
               twenty-four hours are what counts.
                 It makes no damned sense.

                         VICKI
              No damned sense is our specialty.

*   *   *

INT. VICKI'S OFFICE—RECEPTION—DAY
Vicki flips through Brendan's "book," essentially a photo résumé. It shows a boy in his teens becoming a young man. The pictures are winsome, striking, hokey, hot.

> COREEN
> You realize Mike sending you this case is like other guys sending flowers.

> VICKI
> Flowers are nice, but you can keep a card.

> COREEN
> He can't do anything right by you, can he?

> VICKI
> (taken aback)
> What?

> COREEN
> I know he made a mistake, and it nearly killed Henry, and you. But I thought the whole finding-Henry, feeding-Henry thing sort of redeemed him.

> VICKI
> When did you turn into my mother?

> COREEN
> Cut him a break.

> VICKI
> I tried. He turned me down.

                          COREEN
                    What was on offer?

                          VICKI
                    (slighty embarrassed)
                    Qualified mistrust.

Coreen rolls her eyes.

INT. HENRY'S APARTMENT—NIGHT
HENRY looks at a canvas. It's a painting of a
woman, her face half-turned, obscured, but somehow you know she's beautiful—and menacing.

                          VICKI
                       (carefully)
                 Let me get this straight. You do this
                       every year?

Vicki stands beside Henry, looking at the painting.

                          HENRY
                       Every year.

                          VICKI
                   It's kind of obsessive.

                          HENRY
                So is lighting candles. And I don't
                       eat—cake.

                          VICKI
                  So that's her. Christina.

                          HENRY
                   This year's version.

                          VICKI
                What are you thinking about, when
                       you paint her?

HENRY
Of everything she gave me. Eternal
youth. Strength. Power.

He turns to face Vicki, finally.

HENRY
And everything she took away.
(correcting himself)
Everything I let her take away.

VICKI
You were seventeen years old. She
knew what she was doing. You
didn't.

HENRY
Maybe. She was beautiful. And I
loved her.

VICKI
Then she was lucky.

HENRY
Are you feeling lucky?

She smiles, turns away to hide it. Henry leans
toward her, almost imperceptibly. Vicki takes a
step back, and he gets it. Leans away.

VICKI
So are you coming to this nightclub
with me or not?

HENRY
The last time we played sleuth I
didn't feel so good.

VICKI
There's a missing kid who might

need our help. Last reputed
sighting at a nightclub full of
young hotties.

> HENRY
> When you put it that way . . .

As he strides away, Vicki takes one last look at
the painting of Christina. Then, a thought—

> VICKI
> Hey—what happened to the other
> four hundred and eighty
> canvases?

EXT. HADES NIGHTCLUB—FRONT DOOR—
NIGHT
Vicki and Henry approach the door, and the im-
posing and THUGLIKE bouncer, DIMITRI, thirties. He steps aside to let Vicki in.

> VICKI
> They never card me anymore. It's
> tragic.

> DIMITRI
> What's tragic is caring about that.

> VICKI
> Wow, a bouncer and a philosopher.

Dimitri blocks Henry's entrance with an arm.

> DIMITRI
> You, I'll card.

Vicki looks up, Give me strength.

> HENRY
> I'm an old soul.

> DIMITRI
> That counts, buddy, but not for
> much.

Henry digs out his ID.

INT. HADES NIGHTCLUB—DOWNSTAIRS BAR—
NIGHT
Vicki, bar-side, shows Brendan's picture to AN-
GELA, a waitress who's waiting for her drink
order to be filled.

> ANGELA
> Model?

> VICKI
> You know him.

> ANGELA
> Educated guess. It's model central
> here.

> VICKI
> Yeah, they calculated my body
> mass index before they let me
> in. So?

> ANGELA
> Brian, Brendan, something like
> that, right?
> (Vicki nods)
> He looked to be crushing on the boss
> lady. Hanging around her
> whenever she was in the club.

> VICKI
> She return his attentions?

ANGELA
She gets a lot of attention. I don't
know what she returns to who.

The BARTENDER puts the last drink on her
tray. She hefts it, ready to move out into the
crowd.

VICKI
Where can I find her?

ANGELA
Private booth. Look for the
medieval curtain. 'Scuse me.

INT. HADES NIGHTCLUB—BLUE HALL—NIGHT
Henry shows Brendan's picture to a hot girl,
MISERY, twenties.

MISERY
Oh sure, Brendan. He brought his
own backlight.

HENRY
Sounds obnoxious.

MISERY
Are you kidding? You need a lot of
self-love in a place like this.

HENRY
So this the kind of place where he'd
make friends? Or enemies?

MISERY
Enemies? C'mon. Everybody loves
everybody. But define friend.

HENRY
Someone who might know his

    birthday . . . his sock size . . . the
    thread count on his bedsheets.

                MISERY
      Two hundred. He's kinda cheap.

                HENRY
      Sounds like heartbreak.

                MISERY
    It was a nice night in. Coulda done
      without the broadcast on Fox
          City though.

                HENRY
      What's Fox City?

                MISERY
      That'll cost you.

She teasingly presses up against him—as he
leans in:

                HENRY
    I happen to carry that legal tender.

Vicki bursts out of the crowd.

                VICKI
      You busy?

                HENRY
      Not anymore.

Misery pouts, then looks to Vicki. Dismissive:

                MISERY
    Whatever happened to beauty
        before age?

VICKI
Age stomped beauty's ass.

Vicki grabs Henry's arm and they move into
the crowd.

INT. HADES NIGHTCLUB—PRIVATE BOOTH—
NIGHT
A private booth surrounded by a chain-link curtain. Vicki and Henry, sitting on the banquette,
watch as Elena ushers out two seemingly-
smitten male CLUBGOERS. She closes the curtain after them.

VICKI
Must be hard getting work done
here.

Henry proffers a picture of Brendan to Elena.
She takes a look.

ELENA
I've learned to tune out the
distractions.
(beat)
He's quite beautiful.

VICKI
No shortage of that here.

ELENA
We cater to the young here. And
youth is beauty.

HENRY
It's one kind.

Elena smiles. Compliment duly noted.

VICKI
Brendan was here Tuesday night.
He didn't show up for a booking
the next morning.

ELENA
Maybe he met someone.

VICKI
He doesn't miss bookings.

ELENA
(shrugs)
Things happen.

HENRY
So you haven't seen him.

ELENA
Sorry. I meet a lot of people. Most
of them
(a look to Henry)
start to look the same after a while.

VICKI
Any trouble here with drugs?

ELENA
I run a clean club.

VICKI
But as you noted, things happen.
You mix booze with hormones . . .

HENRY
Boys will be boys.

ELENA
(with an edge)
Yes, they will.

                    *   *   *

Vicki picks up that edge.

> VICKI
> Brendan act up with a girl here?
> With you?

> ELENA
> As I told you, I don't remember
> him. As for acting up, my
> security staff is well-trained.

> VICKI
> What about people acting up with
> him? Someone who wanted
> something from a beautiful young
> man?

> ELENA
> Sexual predators?

> VICKI
> Yes.

> ELENA
> If you could tell me how to spot
> them, I'd stop them. But they
> hide in plain sight, don't they?
> (beat)
> My club is safe, Ms. Nelson. Ask
> around. No one has ever been
> harmed here. Is there anything
> else?

> HENRY
> I think we're done. You're sure you
> can't tell us anything about
> Brendan?

ELENA
I wish I could. But feel free to
question the staff.

With Brendan's photo in her hand, Elena leans
over her desk to offer it to Henry. In so doing,
both Henry and Vicki get a nice cleavage shot—
and a view of a distinctive tattoo of interlocked
Greek letters on the curve of her breast. Henry's still looking as:

HENRY
Thank you.

ELENA
You're welcome.

She smiles at him. Sure of herself.

INT/EXT. HADES NIGHTCLUB—FRONT DOOR/
BLUE HALL—NIGHT
Vicki and Henry walk away from the club. Dimi-
tri watches them go.

HENRY
She's hiding something.

VICKI
Too bad it wasn't her tattoo.

HENRY
When did you become a prude?

VICKI
Five minutes ago.

HENRY
Funny, that's when the case got
interesting for me.

VICKI
What makes you think she's
hiding something?

HENRY
Her heart beat faster when she said
she hadn't met him.

VICKI
You're the best lie detector a girl
could have.

HENRY
What do you think?

VICKI
When you said boys will be boys,
she got a little edgy. And she
used the term sexual predator, not
me.

HENRY
So?

VICKI
Shows you where her mind's at.
It's interesting.
(beat)
Where was your mind at, with
that girl?

HENRY
On the job, of course.

VICKI
You find anything?

HENRY
Possibly. "Fox City."

Off Vicki's look . . .

                    END OF
                    ACT

INT. VICKI'S OFFICE—DAY
Coreen has a Web site up on her computer—
"Fox City." The homepage features blurry pic-
tures of body parts. Prominent text that says,
"Post 'em" and "Boast 'em."

                    COREEN
        It's frat boys and wanna-bes,
            posting pictures of their
                  conquests.

Vicki watches as Coreen enters a member
name, "Space Invader," and a password.

                    VICKI
            Space Invader.

                    COREEN
                (innocently)
        My favorite video game.

                    VICKI
        Brendan posted to this?

                    COREEN
        He's M.C. Model citizen. We can
            search by poster.

She clicks a button, and we get to all of M.C's
postings. Happy grinning girls for the most
part, flashing 8 PM nudity.

                    VICKI
        Good God. Do the girls know?

> COREEN
> Check out the comments.

She clicks on the "comments" hot tab.

> COREEN
> (reading)
> The ever-popular "Whoa, I look
> hot." Here's "I'd do me." And my
> favorite, "I need that shot for my
> college application."

> VICKI
> Whatever happened to the winsome
> awkwardness of teenagers?
> Their endearing shyness?

> COREEN
> Different Web site.

Coreen continues scrolling down the site.

> VICKI
> Stop.

Coreen stops on a slightly blurry image of a
cleavage shot, featuring a tattoo that looks familiar to Vicki. The initials "M.C." underneath.

> COREEN
> Bitchin' ink.

> VICKI
> You got that right.

INT. HADES NIGHTCLUB/BLUE HALL/DOWN-
STAIRS BAR—DAY
Mike enters the nightclub—stripped of the
lights, the music, the dancers, it seems somehow sad.

Mike spots a woman behind the bar, diligently scrubbing the bartop. It's Elena, but the dangerous glamour is MIA—she's just this lovely Greek girl doing a domestic shimmy.

>MIKE
>Hi.
>(flips his badge)
>Detective Mike Celluci. I'm looking for a kid who may have gone missing—Brendan Ledford.

Elena pushes her hair back out of her eyes as she looks at Mike's badge.

>MIKE
>The manager around?

>ELENA
>You think the manager actually knows something about what goes on around here?

>MIKE
>Sounds like my chief.

They exchange a smile.

>MIKE
>So you know him? Apparently he hung out there.

>ELENA
>He must be popular. There were people looking for him last night too.

>MIKE
>Woman with glasses?

ELENA
And a young man. Yes.

MIKE
Vicki Nelson. She's a private eye.
But it became a police matter a
few hours ago. So you're what, the
bartender?

ELENA
Why, you want a drink?

MIKE
Not right now.

ELENA
Does that mean later?

MIKE
(grinning)
You work here, right? Do you
remember seeing him?

ELENA
I'm afraid I'm the owner. So I'm
rather useless.

MIKE
Doubt that, somehow.

ELENA
(rescrutinizes picture)
I wish I could help you. But he
doesn't look familiar.

MIKE
Guess a lot of people pass through.

ELENA
(smiling)
Even those you wish would stay a
little longer.

He can't help it—smiles back.

EXT. ELENA'S HOUSE—NIGHT
Vicki and Henry walk toward the dark house.

HENRY
So the picture of the tattoo proves
she knows him.

VICKI
Thereby proving she's a liar.

HENRY
Can't hide that note of glee, can
you?

VICKI
Don't deny me my small
pleasures, Henry.

They stop at the door.

HENRY
So if we're about to lean on her to
get more information—I call
Brisco.

Vicki leans on the bell.

VICKI
We're counting on her not being
here. And we're PIs, not cops.

HENRY
Columbo then.

> VICKI
> Also a cop.

> HENRY
> Cannon.

> VICKI
> You wanta be Cannon? Fat?
> Balding?

> HENRY
> Good point.

> VICKI
> (satisfied)
> It appears that no one is home.
> Could you check?

With elegant exaggeration, Henry cups his hand over his ear and leans toward the door. Vicki watches, then:

> VICKI
> We good to go?

He mimes a heart beating against his chest.

> HENRY
> Buh-bump, buh-bump, buh-
> bump . . .

> VICKI
> What's her problem, she should be
> at work, a nightclub on a Friday
> night—

> HENRY
> If it's her, something's wrong. The
> heartbeat's too slow.

VICKI
Then we proceed with Plan A.

Vicki goes into her purse to get out lockpicks—
and when she looks up, Henry has already scuttled up the wall and is entering the second-floor
window.

VICKI
Show-off.

INT. ELENA'S HOUSE—LIVING ROOM—NIGHT
Vicki and Henry enter the large dark room. Lots
of foliage here—but Henry is following the
heartbeats.

HENRY
There.

WE CAN SEE a figure in the dark. A young man.

VICKI
Brendan Ledford?

He doesn't move. Vicki walks toward him,
Henry just behind.

HENRY
(urgent)
Vicki.

Vicki realizes—Brendan is a statue. His eyes
are blank, like a classical Greek statue, but his
face is half-averted, scared, repulsed.

VICKI
It's just a statue.

Henry again mimes that heart beating against
his chest.

                    HENRY
          He's alive.

At that moment, a light FLASHES ON from the
hallway. They're about to be caught.

                    HENRY
                    C'mon.

                    VICKI
                    Wait.

She looks at the statue.

EXT/INT. ELENA'S HOUSE—FRONT DOOR—
NIGHT
Elena leans against the doorframe, flirty . . .

                    ELENA
          Thanks for the lift home.

And now we see Mike, on the doorstep.

                    MIKE
               My pleasure.

                    ELENA
          Is it true that policemen aren't
          supposed to drink on duty?

                    MIKE
          It's true that they're not supposed
                    to.

                    ELENA
          And what kind of policeman are
                    you?

                    MIKE
          Off duty, actually.

ELENA
That sounds promising.

MIKE
So are we going to stand here all
night, or . . . ?

There's a strange sound from the back of the
house—

MIKE
Someone here?

ELENA
(tense)
Shouldn't be.

Mike steps into the house.

ELENA
Don't—

MIKE
—Wait here.

Mike moves forward. Elena follows behind
immediately.

EXT. ELENA'S HOUSE—BACKYARD—NIGHT
Henry stands with the statue at the open gate
at the end of the property. He sees the light go
on inside the house.

HENRY
C'mon, Vicki.

A car's headlights sweep the alley behind the
property, and Henry's Jag pulls up, Vicki in the
driver's seat.

                         HENRY
                  Can you see anything?

                         VICKI
                      Not much.

                         HENRY
                 Pull forward a couple feet—and
                      move over.

                         VICKI
                 Get him in the back, we'll argue
                   about who's driving later.

The car pulls forward, as Henry starts to pick
up the statue.

INT. ELENA'S HOUSE—KITCHEN—NIGHT
Mike enters the kitchen, eyes quickly checking
the room—
Elena enters behind him, and she looks in the
living room—no statue.
As Mike checks the back door—

                         ELENA
                 I think it was just a noise—

                         MIKE
                     Let's be sure.

Mike pulls the door open and steps outside.

EXT. ELENA'S HOUSE—ALLEY BEHIND HOUSE—
NIGHT
The statue secured, Henry passes the open gate
and sees Mike. In the dark, the vampire has the
advantage, and hasn't been spotted yet.

                         HENRY
                      Floor it.

Henry leaps in as Vicki puts pedal to metal.

> HENRY
>> To the right!

The car veers to the right.

EXT. ELENA'S HOUSE—BACKYARD—NIGHT
Mike and Elena hear the engine. Mike races out into the yard, as Elena waits behind. She sees immediately that the statue is missing.

EXT. ELENA'S HOUSE—ALLEY BEHIND HOUSE—NIGHT
Mike races into the alley, just in time to see—Nothing.

INT. VICKI'S OFFICE—RECEPTION—NIGHT
Coreen, Vicki, and Henry inspect the statue.

> COREEN
> This is the actual Brendan Ledford?
> In the actual not-flesh?

> HENRY
> It is.

> COREEN
> Why is he half-naked?

> VICKI
> He's half-dressed.

> COREEN
> (to Henry)
> I see half-full, she sees half-empty.

> VICKI
> So how'd she do this? Is she a
> witch?

COREEN
It might be a spell. But in the turns-
to-stone department, I'd bet on a
basilisk or a Gorgon.

VICKI
(Greek to her)
One's an herb, the other's a cheese.

COREEN
Basilisk, half chicken, half lizard,
one look and you're stoned.

HENRY
The Gorgons were sisters. Greek
myth.

COREEN
Also practiced at turning people
into stone.

VICKI
(recalling)
There's one called Medusa?

COREEN
You've been reading!

VICKI
I read.

COREEN
Firearms manuals.

HENRY
If it's a Gorgon we're looking for,
all Elena has in her arsenal is
being Greek. No snakes, no ugly.

COREEN
But not a lot of basilisk sightings in
town lately. Ever, actually.

HENRY
Nonetheless, I will keep an eye out
for chicken-lizards.

VICKI
Why would you do that?

HENRY
Because we were face-to-face with
the woman and weren't turned
to stone.

VICKI
You're trying to tell me to keep an
open mind.

HENRY
I know there's no point in doing
that. Speaking of which, Mike
was at the house.

VICKI
What?

HENRY
Michael Celluci, of your
acquaintance, was at the home of
Elena Kanapolous, suspected
Gorgon, as we were leaving.
(acts it out)
I—saw—him.

VICKI
(thinking quickly)
It's been forty-eight hours since
Brendan went missing. It's a

        missing persons case—Homicide
        handles them. He caught the case
                is all.

               COREEN
        So shouldn't he have been at the
              nightclub?

               HENRY
        Probably quieter to question her at
               home.

               VICKI
        Regardless. It's not a conflict. We
        work with Mike all the time.
        (off statue, to Coreen)
        In the meantime, find out if we can
        break this spell or whatever it is.
        There's a twenty-two-year-old boy
        still alive in here . . . and we're
        the only ones who can help him.

Vicki looks at the statue—the mute expression
of terror carved in stone.
             END OF
             ACT

EXT. POLICE STATION—DAY
To establish.

           VICKI (O.S.)
        Brendan Ledford was at Hades the
        night he disappeared, and Elena
        Kanapolous lied about knowing
              him.

INT. POLICE STATION—DETECTIVE AREA—
DAY
Mike listens to Vicki presenting her case.

VICKI

Brendan posts phone pictures of his
conquests to a Web site, Fox City.
Elena's on it.

MIKE

You're sure it's him, posting her?

VICKI

She has a distinctive tattoo.

MIKE

Is her face in the photo?

VICKI

It's her, Mike. She lied about
knowing him—and you and I both
know that lies never stand alone.

MIKE

So a phone-camera picture of a
tattoo—would it stand up in
court?

VICKI

You're defending her.

MIKE

I'm asking Police one-oh-one type
questions here, Vick. You've got
a cell-phone picture that could have
been posted by anyone, point
one. Am I right?

VICKI

We could confirm that it was
Brendan—

MIKE
—Any witnesses who saw them
together? Any priors on Elena?

MIKE
How about motive? Elena get pissed
because he didn't tip a waitress?

VICKI
What did you find out?

MIKE
I ran her, her address, her
company. No priors, no
complaints, nothing.

VICKI
Doesn't mean there isn't something
to find.

MIKE
Doesn't sound like you found it.

VICKI
She knows Brendan, saw him,
before he disappeared. She's got
this weird thing about sexual
assaults . . .

MIKE
Weird.

VICKI
Thinks it only happens to women.

MIKE
Lot of people think that. Doesn't
make her guilty.

VICKI
You've decided she's innocent.

MIKE
I'm following the facts. What are
you doing? You should have
informed your client that this is a
police matter now.

VICKI
I sent her my bill.

MIKE
Then why are you still following it?

VICKI
Brendan needs my help.

MIKE
Because the police aren't help
enough.

VICKI
Not if they won't listen.

Mike draws a long breath.

MIKE
Enough already, Vicki. How I
operate as a cop, how I operate
in my life . . . you don't have a say
in that anymore. So let's end it
here. No harm, no foul.

Vicki takes a breath, not wanting to blow this.

VICKI
Come back to my office. There's
something I want to show you,
about the case. Some evidence.

MIKE
I don't think I can.
(checks watch)
There was a break-in at Elena's last
night. I've got some paperwork
to do.

VICKI
Homicide cop doing a robbery
report? Anything missing?

MIKE
No.

VICKI
Nothing?

MIKE
Why?

VICKI
Nothing.

MIKE
(beat)
If you say so.

And he leaves. Just like that. Vicki watches him
walking away from her—and feels the loss.

EXT. HADES NIGHTCLUB—DAY
Vicki waits outside the door, which is finally opened
by Dimitri—who easily blocks the entrance.

VICKI
Your boss here?

DIMITRI
No.

VICKI
Oh c'mon, I thought we had a real
connection, you and me.

Silence.

VICKI
Fine, Aristotle. Give her a message
for me. Ask her—Does your
house feel empty now?

Vicki smiles, walks away.
Dmitri steps outside to watch her go—REVEAL-
ING Elena, standing a few steps behind him.

DIMITRI
Did you hear her?

ELENA
(a beat)
Dmitri—I need your help.

His look tells her she could ask him for
anything.

OMITTED

INT. VICKI'S OFFICE—OUTSIDE HALLWAY—
NIGHT
Vicki on the phone with Henry:

HENRY (V.O.)
Was issuing a challenge wise?

VICKI
Now she knows we're on to her. It
makes most criminals nervous.

HENRY (V.O.)
She didn't seem like the nervous
type.

Vicki sees a flashlight moving inside her office—

VICKI
Somebody's here.

HENRY (V.O.)
Vicki, wait—I'm nearly there—

Vicki disconnects, grabs her asp, inserts the
door key.

INT. VICKI'S OFFICE—RECEPTION—NIGHT
Vicki enters, asp out, and furious—
A shadowy, large figure raises something—a
sledgehammer—to take a swing at the statue.
Vicki doesn't hesitate. She steps in, swinging
the asp, connecting solidly with the shadowy
figure (Dimitri)—

VICKI
Back off!

Vicki DUCKS as the Figure swings at her with
the sledgehammer.
Vicki jabs with her asp, connecting solidly—
The Figure steps back again—Vicki's gaining
the upper hand.
He takes two steps back, throws the sledgehammer at her head—
She ducks again, and realizes in the same moment what's about to happen—
The sledgehammer sails over her head and con-
nects solidly with the statue—

VICKI
No!

And the statue breaks into pieces—
The Figure pushes Vicki, hard, and runs out
the door—
Vicki lands on the floor, the shattered face of
Brendan beside her.

INT. VICKI'S OFFICE—RECEPTION—NIGHT
Henry charges through the door, and stops.
The room is lit up. Vicki has piled some of the
statue pieces into a box, but at the moment she
sits on the floor, holding the two shattered
pieces of Brendan's face.

VICKI
I was fine, you know, I was cleaning
up . . . and then I started
wondering . . . what if I put the
pieces back together? I can do
that, can't I?

Henry gently takes the two pieces away from
her.

INT. VICKI'S OFFICE—NIGHT
Vicki pours herself a glass of booze.

VICKI
This'll be a fun call. "Hey, we found
your client. His shattered pieces
are sitting here in a box for you."

HENRY
Vicki . . .

VICKI
I'll tell her Brendan left town. End

of story. All she cares about is
her money anyhow.

HENRY
How about you figure that out
tomorrow? Right now you could
use some sleep.

VICKI
Yeah, that's a sweet solution. Sleep
half your life away.
(regrets it instantly)
I'm sorry.

Henry shrugs, it's OK.

VICKI
What is it about the young,
anyhow? Their insane attraction
to the bad boys, the bad girls.

HENRY
I'm sure Brendan thought there
was something more.

VICKI
Her looks.

HENRY
Beauty isn't everything.

VICKI
Doesn't hurt.

HENRY
But when it goes, and it does . . .
you need to have a deeper
connection.

                    VICKI
        You think Brendan felt that with
                  Elena?

                    HENRY
        Sometimes it only goes one way.
        But you don't find out until it's
                  too late.

                    VICKI
        Your story, with Christina?

                    HENRY
                    Yes.

And maybe not just Christina. They both know
that.

                    VICKI
        Mike's "looking into" the break-in
        at Elena's. That's not what he
            does for a living.

                    HENRY
        You think he's interested?

                    VICKI
            You saw her.

                    HENRY
        Mike's not that person.

                    VICKI
        None of us are that person
        anymore. Not since we started
          seeing into your world.

Hard to argue with that.

             *   *   *

INT. HADES NIGHTCLUB—DOWNSTAIRS BAR—
NIGHT
CLOSE ON Mike, talking to Angela, the waitress
from Act One.
Other bar staff mill about, preparing for the
club's opening.
WE PULL BACK to find Elena watching.
Mike nods, takes a note. He moves away, says
something to another STAFFER as he walks
toward Elena.

                         ELENA
                        Helpful?

                          MIKE
            Couple people think they saw him
             Tuesday night, but they're not
               sure. "One night blurs into
              another," that sort of thing.

                         ELENA
                       I'm sorry.

                          MIKE
                          Nah.
                         (beat)
            Apparently Brendan was crushing
                        on you.

                         ELENA
                    You're kidding.

                          MIKE
            Yeah, your waitress there said you
              get a little too much of that kind
                    of action to notice.

                         ELENA
            I wish I'd noticed. At least then I

could have helped out. What are
you going to do now?

          MIKE
More interviews. Credit card
     checks. Stuff.

          ELENA
Stuff you can't talk about.

          MIKE
Not with a civilian.

          ELENA
I'm a civilian?

          MIKE
Rather be a suspect?

          ELENA
Depends. Are you going to
   interrogate me?

          MIKE
I might have to.

          ELENA
Then be suspicious.

They're close by this point, real close—
And suddenly Dimitri appears, flushed and
excited—
Until he sees how close Elena and Mike are.
Elena clocks that, and takes a step back.

          ELENA
Detective Celluci—did you get a
   chance to question Dimitri?

MIKE
We spoke earlier.

DIMITRI
About that boy, yeah. I mostly
remember the ones who make
trouble.

ELENA
Apparently he had a crush on me.

DIMITRI
Go figure.

Mike picks up on the edge in Dimitri's voice.
This guy jealous?

DIMITRI
I gotta go set up the front.

MIKE
I'll help you.

DIMITRI
I don't need help.

Elena's a little concerned.

ELENA
I thought we were going out.

MIKE
Just take a minute.

Mike walks toward the entrance. Dimitri flashes
a quick look at Elena, then follows.

EXT. HADES NIGHTCLUB—FRONT DOOR—
NIGHT
Mike has already started questioning Dimitri,

who is setting up the foliage, hauling out the
rolled red carpet . . .

> DIMITRI
> I admire her. We've worked
> together for a while.

> MIKE
> Must hurt you to see all these guys
> chasing after her.

> DIMITRI
> As long as she doesn't get hurt, it's
> none of your business.

> MIKE
> So if she does, it is?

> DIMITRI
> That's not what I mean.

> MIKE
> Lot of good-looking guys too. Tough
> competition for you.

> DIMITRI
> Looks aren't everything.

> MIKE
> You say that, but she's a beautiful
> woman.

> DIMITRI
> Why don't you ask me about the
> kid. Aren't you supposed to be
> looking for him?

> MIKE
> That's what I'm doing.

DIMITRI
I haven't seen him. I don't know
anything. And Elena—can
handle herself.

Dimitri kicks the carpet, and it unrolls down
the sidewalk.
END OF
ACT

INT. VICKI'S OFFICE—RECEPTION—NIGHT
Vicki looks at the box of broken statuary.

VICKI
Henry . . . were there statues at
her nightclub?

HENRY
Not that I noticed.

VICKI
You didn't hear anything?

HENRY
Lot of bodies. Lot of heartbeats.
(beat)
But there was that section we never
went into.

VICKI
The VIP section. I'm worried that
Brendan might not be the only
one.

HENRY
We can go to the club and find out.

Vicki pulls out a small digital camera.

VICKI
If there are, get pictures. We'll find
some way to ID them.

HENRY
You're not coming?

VICKI
I don't think I'd be welcome.
(beat)
And there's something else I need
to do.

EXT. HADES NIGHTCLUB—ENTRANCE—NIGHT
Dimitri stands at the entrance, as Coreen sa-
shays up to the door.

DIMITRI
ID.

COREEN
A compliment. Thanks.

Coreen sees Henry walk towards the door.

DIMITRI
Miss, your ID.

COREEN
(flirtatious)
If you want my name and number,
go ahead and ask for it, ya big
lug.

Coreen watches as Henry vamp-speeds behind
Dimitri.

DIMITRI
Three strikes and you're out.

COREEN
Here you go.

She hands him her ID. He waves her in.

EXT. JOGGING TRAIL—NIGHT
Vicki's spade bites into the soil, again and
again. A flashlight on a rock nearby illuminates
the scene. Beside the rock is the box of broken
statuary.

INT. HADES NIGHTCLUB—BLUE HALL—NIGHT
Henry sweet-talks their way into the VIP section. He and Coreen see statues along a wall.

EXT. JOGGING TRAIL—NIGHT
Vicki has finished digging. She carefully places
each piece of the statue into the hole she's dug.

INT. HADES NIGHTCLUB—VIP ROOM—NIGHT
Henry gets close to a statue, a YOUNG MAN
whose blank white eyes still somehow express
shock. He touches the statue gently. Coreen
looks at him questioningly, wondering if the
statue is alive. Henry taps his chest twice—he's
alive. Coreen takes a picture.

EXT. JOGGING TRAIL—NIGHT
Vicki shovels dirt into the "grave."

INT. HADES NIGHTCLUB—VIP ROOM—NIGHT
Henry boosts up Coreen to take a picture of a
YOUNG MAN. As he boosts her, he sees Dimitri
coming inside, and a WAITER pointing directly
at him and Coreen.
Coreen takes the picture, and Henry grabs her
arm and whisks her away.
Dimitri arrives where they were, but they're
not to be found.

EXT. JOGGING TRAIL—NIGHT
Vicki sits on the rock where the flashlight was,
contemplating the grave. When she gets up, her
face is set and determined. She leans over and
touches the loose earth for a beat—and then
moves off resolutely.

INT. ELENA'S HOUSE—LIVING ROOM—NIGHT
There's an empty bottle of wine and two near-
empty glasses on the coffee table.
Mike and Elena sit on the couch, and they're
cozy, and it's on the cusp of getting cozier.

ELENA
I wish we'd met some other way.

MIKE
Why's that?

ELENA
Because you're so honorable.
You're investigating this missing
kid, and maybe I'm part of the
picture, so you can't . . .

MIKE
Can't have a glass of wine? Too
late.

ELENA
That's not what I was thinking.

She leans in—and they kiss. And then Mike
pulls back.

ELENA
You're not attracted to me?

                    MIKE
        Sure. But I'm outta practice on the
                dating thing.

She leans in . . .

                    ELENA
            Then let's practice.

He gets an eyeful of the tattoo. Whoa, Nelly. He
kisses her lightly, then pushes her back gently.

                    ELENA
        Is it the woman with the glasses?
            The private detective?

                    MIKE
            Vicki? No.

                    ELENA
        When I said she'd been in the club,
            you reacted strangely.

                    MIKE
        She used to be a cop, we used to be
            partners. Nothing more than
                    that.

                    ELENA
            You don't seem sure.

                    MIKE
            I'm sure.
                (beat)
        Maybe we should call it a night.

Elena regards him like an alien species.

                    ELENA
        You don't think I'm beautiful?

MIKE
Elena. I like you. But a woman who
isn't happy with her looks, you
can't change her mind. If you need
me to tell you what you should
already know . . .

She takes his hand.

ELENA
I don't.

MIKE
Good. 'Cause I'd like to see you
again.

She places his hand against her face. Over his
shoulder, there's another mirror, and she can
see herself in the mirror, just as she was with
Brendan.

ELENA
You will.

INT. VICKI'S OFFICE—RECEPTION—DAY
CLOSE ON Coreen's computer screen. On one
side of the screen, a picture of one of the
statues.
On the other side, a bar that says "Processing."

VICKI
Where'd you get this software?

COREEN
It would be better if you pretended
it wasn't here.

VICKI
Does that say FBI?

There's a *ding* from the software.

> COREEN
> We have a match!

ONSCREEN, the statue's face has matched with that of missing teen RYAN HENDERSON, eighteen.

> VICKI
> Ryan Henderson. How did she get
> her hooks in you?

Vicki hits the print command on Coreen's keyboard.

> COREEN
> I haven't found any way to change
> the statues back; it's nowhere in
> the mythology.

> VICKI
> Don't all the spells wear off when
> the witch dies?

Coreen hits a couple buttons on her keyboard, and the database starts looking for a match on a different statue.

> COREEN
> Spells and witches, Vicki. Different
> strokes. But I investigated the
> Medusa myth a little deeper. It's
> actually a horrible story.

> VICKI
> Obviously.

> COREEN
> No, for her.

Coreen pushes a book over to Vicki, it shows a drawing of a beautiful young Greek maiden.

COREEN
Medusa is this beautiful young
woman who Poseidon covets. He
follows her to the temple of Athena
one day and rapes her—very
standard operating procedure in
the day. Then Athena gets mad
about the desecration of her temple,
blames Medusa, and turns her
into this hideous creature—the
snakes, the stone gaze, all that.
She gets punished for being raped.

VICKI
So what, her nightclub is her
temple? And anyone who is
attracted to her beauty gets
punished?

COREEN
Considering what happened to her
the first time . . .

Another *ding* from the computer. Another
match.

VICKI
When I was a cop, I met people
who'd been through horrific
abuse, violence. The ones who turn
it around against other people
and cry "victim" at the same
time . . . It's a choice. Not a
good one.

Vicki looks at the match on Coreen's screen.

VICKI
She doesn't get to work out her
issues by turning kids into stone.

COREEN
You going to tell Mike about this?

VICKI
Mike doesn't want to know.

COREEN
Maybe he should. If he's getting
busy with the bad lady.

Vicki gives her a look.

INT. POLICE STATION—DAY
Mike at his desk, looking at the Fox City site.
He scrolls down and finds the picture with the
tattoo.
Picks up the phone.

MIKE
(on phone)
Hey Coreen, Vicki there? . . . OK—
you got a minute?

INT. VICKI'S OFFICE—RECEPTION—DAY
Coreen pulls pages off the printer as Mike looks
at the Gorgon/Medusa literature. He holds up a
picture of Medusa.

MIKE
So you think Elena is . . .

COREEN
Turning guys into stone as she
relives her sexual trauma and
seeks revenge? Yep. And there's
more.

MIKE
I'm still processing the first part.

Coreen hands him a printout from Fox City.

COREEN
A couple of the statue-dudes used to
post on Fox City. Their last
postings are within a week of their
disappearances.

MIKE
All that proves is that they
disappeared.

COREEN
But it's the type of coincidence you
guys love to build a case out of.

Mike returns to the Medusa literature. Trying
to reconcile the picture of the Gorgon with the
beautiful woman he met.

EXT. HADES NIGHTCLUB—DAY
Elena walks toward the front door of the club—
then slows as she sees Vicki leaning against the
front door, waiting for her. Vicki holds up a
photo of the Ryan Henderson statue—and then
holds up the matching photo.

VICKI
Ryan Henderson. You remember him?

ELENA
Excuse me.

She waits for Vicki to move. Long wait coming.
Vicki holds up another statue face, another
matching kid.

VICKI
How about him?

Another pair.

VICKI
Or him?

ELENA
Now I understand why Mike thinks
you're crazy.

Vicki holds up the two pictures of Brendan—
stone and living.

VICKI
OK, Brendan Ledford. Surely you
remember him. A day ago he was
still alive, somehow, and now he's
dead.

ELENA
That's very sad. Struck down in his
youth and beauty like that.

VICKI
Like all of them. Like you.

Elena looks a trifle surprised.

VICKI
I guess you got a raw deal back
then, but it doesn't excuse you
now, Medusa.

ELENA
(amused)
You think you know something
about me?

VICKI
And Mike doesn't just think I'm
crazy. He knows I am.

ELENA
That's what bothers you the most,
isn't it? You pretend it's about
these young men, but if he wasn't
sniffing around, would you be?

VICKI
That's the thing with anyone who's
worked homicide. We can't stop
speaking for the dead.

ELENA
Maybe you'd like to join them.

Eyeball to eyeball.

VICKI
Go ahead. Turn me to stone.

ELENA
You think I won't?

VICKI
I'm standing here asking.

Elena is tempted . . . but this venue is too
public.

ELENA
You can't prove anything, and you
can't do anything. So why don't
you go home.

VICKI
Tel you what. I am gonna go home,
maybe freshen up a little. And

            then I'll come back for you. And I'll
            finish the job some hack Greek
            hero couldn't.

One more last venomous gaze—and then Vicki
walks away.

INT. HENRY'S APARTMENT—NIGHT
Henry looks at the recent portrait of Christina
that he's finished. In the windows, the lights of
the city spread out to the horizon. His world.

                    HENRY
            The mythical Medusa was slain.
            She's been dead for centuries.

WE REVEAL Vicki is in the apartment. Trying
her best to wait patiently.

                    VICKI
            And when Perseus killed her, some
            of her spilled blood had the
            ability to raise the dead, so why
            couldn't she self-resurrect?

                    HENRY
            You are reading.

                    VICKI
            I'm reading, and I'm wondering
            why you're stalling on this.

                    HENRY
            Motivation counts, Ms. Nelson. Do
            you know why you're doing this?

                    VICKI
            That twenty-two-year-old kid didn't
            deserve to be killed because he

fell in love with a pretty face. You
should understand that.

HENRY
And Mike?

VICKI
Mike might be in danger. And I'm
not OK with that.

Henry doesn't really care about Mike. But . . .

HENRY
If I do this . . . it's for you.

Vicki nods. Good enough by her.

Henry strides to the door. As Vicki follows, she
stops by the sword mounted on the wall.

VICKI
Henry . . . one more thing.

Henry turns and looks—at Vicki looking at the
sword. Her intention is clear.
END OF
ACT

OMITTED: 49

INT. HENRY'S APARTMENT—NIGHT
Vicki has taken down the sword. She looks at
its blade, feels the weight of the thing.

HENRY
I could carry it.

VICKI
That would make it easy, wouldn't
it. Letting you do my dirty work.

(resolute)
I'm doing it.

HENRY
It's not like killing a windigo, or a
demon. She's human in many
respects.

VICKI
Just what she's showing us.

HENRY
She's not going to be easy to kill.

VICKI
I know.

HENRY
Then maybe this isn't your job.

Vicki looks out the window at the city below.

VICKI
The third year I was on the force
this guy, barely more than a kid
really, he had a bead on my
partner, was about to pull the
trigger and I tapped him . . .
(beat)
He died pretty much instantly and
I've thought about it almost
every day since it happened.

A beat.

HENRY
I don't have that problem.

VICKI
I don't believe you.

HENRY
At times, I think you forget what
I am.

VICKI
I know that sometimes . . . I'd like
to.

After a beat, Henry tries to take the sword.
Vicki keeps a firm grip.

HENRY
I won't be haunted by this.

VICKI
Then let me be. Because I think you
forget who you could be.

INT. HADES NIGHTCLUB—VIP ROOM—NIGHT
It's a closed night at the club, and Elena is
alone. She stares around at all the statues, "ac-
cusing" her. Dimitri approaches.

DIMITRI
I'm worried. That woman, and the
cop—

ELENA
—Break the statues, Dimitri. All of
them. And get them out of here.

DIMITRI
What's wrong with the statues?

ELENA
They're bloodstains. And I'm the
knife.

DIMITRI
That's not true.

She looks at him, his ugly but caring face. And she wants to hurt him, for caring.

ELENA
You think you know me because
you've seen me change.

DIMITRI
I do know you. And I'm not afraid—

ELENA
—Every statue is a person, Dimitri.
Some beautiful, shallow person
who wanted to hurt me. And
they're still alive in there.

DIMITRI
The statue I broke . . . ?

ELENA
When I asked you to break it, I was
asking you to kill him. So . . . do
you still know me?

Her eyes flash at him, challenging him to love her still.
A beat.

DIMITRI
You want me to smash them all?

Elena stares at Dimitri, finally understanding how devoted he is. Before she can answer, footsteps approach. Mike.

MIKE
Hey. Quiet here tonight.

DIMITRI
We're closed.

ELENA
It's nice to see you.

MIKE
Goes double for me. Can we sit and
talk, you think?

ELENA
Dimitri, I'm starving. Can you pick
up something for me down the
street?

Dimitri, not liking it, slowly walks away. Mike
begins walking them toward a banquette.

MIKE
There's something I'm wondering,
and I hope you won't take
offense.

ELENA
I'm thirty.

MIKE
(smiles)
Last night . . . there was something
in the way things were between
us . . . the way you talked about
your looks . . .

Elena can see herself in a mirror. She touches
her face.

ELENA
Yes . . .

MIKE
I hope you don't think I'm out of
line here . . . but it made me
wonder if something happened to

you in the past. If somebody
hurt you.

Elena is suddenly guarded.

                    MIKE
          Because if that's what happened, I
          think I can help. I want to help.

To Elena's surprise, her eyes well up with tears.

INT. HADES NIGHTCLUB—NIGHT
Vicki and Henry enter the club quietly. Henry
gestures upstairs—he can hear Mike and Elena.

INT. HADES NIGHTCLUB—VIP ROOM—NIGHT
Mike watches Elena intently as she speaks.

                    ELENA
          He told me he loved me. He didn't
          even know me. Just what he saw.
          When I tried to leave, he grabbed
          me. And he forced me, he raped
                    me.

Mike takes her hand.

                    MIKE
              I'm sorry.

She looks at his hand on hers, can feel his
sympathy.

                    ELENA
          He told people afterward that he did
          it. And they said I deserved it,
          because I was vain. They said it was
                  my fault.

MIKE
You were innocent, but people
blamed you.

ELENA
Like I'd wanted to be violated.
(beat)
They destroyed me. Made me
hideous.

MIKE
You're not.

ELENA
I am. I've done things . . .

She can't go on.

MIKE
There was this lowlife in Parkdale,
attacking women, cutting them.
We figured out who it was, but for
a lot of reasons, we couldn't get
him on it.
(beat)
I knew where he lived. I went out
one night on my own, followed
him to his local. We had a couple
drinks, me and this creep,
laughing together. And then he
went out in the alley for a whiz.
I met him back there.

ELENA
What happened?

MIKE
You know how it is—you can't let
people like that run around,

think they own everything they
look at. So you take care of it.
(beat)
The guy who raped you. The people
who blamed you . . . They still
around?

ELENA
They're always around.

MIKE
You find a way? To take care of
them? Cause I could help you, if
you didn't.

ELENA
I found a way.

MIKE
Good for you.

Mike nods like she's done a good thing, but his
eyes flick over to the statue nearest them—and
Elena sees that.

ELENA
What are you looking at?

MIKE
I'm here for you.

ELENA
You think you know. You think you
understand.

And he realizes she's seen past him.
ANGLE ON :
Vicki coming up the stairs, spotting Mike and
Elena.
ANGLE ON :

Mike and Elena both stand up slowly.
Mike puts his hand on his pistol under his jacket, as Elena puts her hands to her face, preparing to move the mask—

> ELENA
> You're all the same.

> MIKE
> Take it easy—

Elana whips off the mask, and the snakes hiss, and she glares at Mike—

> VICKI
> Mike!

And he turns to stone.
Elena turns around to face Vicki—
Henry rushes ahead, blocking Vicki, and he's in full vamp mode, about to attack Elena—
And Henry launches himself at her—
And Elena glares at Henry, and he turns to stone—
Then Elena looks up as Vicki comes toward her, sword raised—

> ELENA
> That won't help you!

Elena stares at Vicki—
And Vicki holds up the sword in front of her eyes. Elena's gaze bounces off the reflective surface of the sword.
And then Vicki swings the sword and cuts Elena's head off.
The head flies through the air, and it has been turned to stone—
ANGLE ON :
Mike, turning back to flesh.

Henry, restored to himself.
Around the nightclub, the other statues return
to flesh. Young men all, they are dazed and
confused.
Those who try to take a step quickly crumple.
Henry is quickly at Vicki's side.

> HENRY
> You had to do it.

> VICKI
> Doesn't make it any easier.

They look over at the Medusa's head—and
see that it has turned, not just to stone, but
to her original form, as a beautiful woman.
Mike approaches them.

> VICKI
> You all right?

Mike nods.
MOS AS:
Dimitri comes up the stairs. He drops the plas-
tic bag, the takeout, that he was carrying, and
rushes toward Elena.
Vicki looks at the sword. The blood on the blade.
Dimitri kneels beside Elena's stone head. Tenta-
tively touches her brow.
Vicki looks up and catches Mike's gaze. Both of
them look over at Henry.
Something tacit in their gazes—they're all on
the same page.

INT. HENRY'S APARTMENT—NIGHT
Henry rolls up the painting of Christina.

INT. POLICE STATION—DETECTIVES' OFFICE—
NIGHT
Mike looks at the "active cases" board for a

beat . . . then leans forward and erases "Ledford."

EXT. JOGGING TRAIL—DAY
Vicki sits on the rock beside the area where she buried Brendan's statue. She seems serene, contemplative—and looks up when she hears someone approaching.

> MIKE
> Am I intruding?

She shakes her head no. He stops at the graveside, looks down at it.

> VICKI
> I like it here. It's quiet.

> MIKE
> Yeah.

CAMERA WIDENS TO FIND
Another patch of ground where the earth seems to have been disturbed.

> MIKE
> Henry does good work. You can't
> even tell . . .

> VICKI
> If anybody ever finds her, Mike . . .

> MIKE
> How else were we gonna take care
> of the body? We sure as hell
> couldn't explain it.

True enough.

                          VICKI
              When his manager hired me, she
              was worried about the six grand
              she'd loaned Brendan. I found it.

                          MIKE
                          Yeah?

                          VICKI
                Brendan bought two tickets to
              Greece. His name and Elena's. He
              really thought they had something.

                          MIKE
              People fall in love with the wrong
                      person all the time.

                          VICKI
                      Yeah. I know.

There's another rock nearby. Mike takes a seat.
And they both look out at the view, in a com-
panionable silence.
OUT.

Tanya Huff

Tony Foster—familiar to Tanya Huff fans from her *Blood* series—has relocated to Vancouver with Henry Fitzroy, vampire son of Henry VIII. Tony landed a job as a production assistant at CB Productions, ironically working on a syndicated TV series, "Darkest Night," about a vampire detective. Tony was pretty content with his new life—until wizards, demons, and haunted houses became more than just episodes on his TV series...

"An exciting, creepy adventure"—*Booklist*

SMOKE AND SHADOWS
0-7564-0263-8 $6.99

SMOKE AND MIRRORS
0-7564-0348-0 $7.99

SMOKE AND ASHES
0-7564-0415-4 $7.99

DAW 46